The Noonday Sword

'I suppose in middle life one may come to a point when all the comforts, the creeds, the things which have made a handrail for you to walk by, seem to fall away and you stand on an edge, with nothing to prevent you from dropping into space . . .'

Thus Simon Calder sums up his disenchantment. We first meet him on the 26th September, 1938, at the peak of the Munich crisis. The high tension of this time is parallelled in Simon's own life: relationships with wife, son and mistress are all suddenly menaced and undermined. While the nations edge towards war, he seems to be on the slide to disaster. Then, at the end of two days of violent events, an unknown young woman arrives at his house, bringing a large question, stirring the echo of things far back.

We follow him into those dark and hazardous years, 'Fourteen-Eighteen'—the sword which lay across the noonday of his life. 1914; here are the beginnings: a Sussex village, his father, mother and elder brother; the old Norman church; the Rector and his son, David. Here is the young Simon, believing all things; devoted to David himself, in whose friendship he finds the root of all happiness. And here as the story moves into war, to the Somme in '16 and the Ypres Salient in '17, we watch Simon's rapid maturity turn sour; we see him on these wastelands of slaughter, losing faith and hope; and in a final desperate and abortive attack, when his company is destroyed, finding himself in a world where man seems abandoned by God.

From this place of disillusion, we return to the time of Munich, to the strange girl, and the question mark. The exciting climax of this story, played against the mounting tension of events in Europe, reveals a chance of hope. As the shadow of a second war falls over the world, a measure of peace returns to Simon, even though he and his family may have to face all the old hazards again.

The Noonday Sword

By
DIANA RAYMOND

CASSELL · LONDON

CASSELL & COMPANY LTD
35 Red Lion Square, London WC1
Melbourne, Sydney, Toronto
Johannesburg, Cape Town, Auckland

Printed in Great Britain
by Cox & Wyman, Ltd., London, Fakenham and Reading
F.565

To my Father

LIEUT. WILLIAM THOMAS YOUNG

Royal Garrison Artillery

Killed

Third Battle of Ypres, 1917

Part I

Wheels on the road most like, or thunder

*'What sound awakened me, I wonder,
For now 'tis dumb.'
'Wheels on the road most like, or thunder:
Lie down; 'twas not the drum.'*

A. E. HOUSMAN

1

September, 1938

'Nightmares?'

'Pretty often,' I said, wishing this had never started.

The doctor pushed himself at an angle from his desk. 'Anything worrying you?'

'Oh no,' I said. 'A man of forty-five with a family, all the bills to pay and a world war practically on his doorstep hasn't anything to worry about, has he?'

I could see McEwan remembering that I had a reputation for being difficult. He was a young man, not much over thirty, yet he wore all the time a deep, middle-aged frown as if he feared people might not take him seriously. He said, his accent sharpened, 'I meant anything specific. Pairhaps some family trouble.'

'Families mean trouble, don't they?'

He sighed. For a moment I considered the prospect of talking at length about Griselda and Jeremy, and even bringing in Kate, but the impulse quickly died. It would lead nowhere, and be merely embarrassing in recollection. McEwan would present a few worthy platitudes about give-and-take in family life which would have as much relevance to the murky tumult at the back of my mind as the quotations on a calendar.

'What kind of nightmares?' he asked.

'Mostly about my son.'

He looked surprised. 'A fine-looking boy.'

I turned my head away, because in the dreams Jeremy wasn't fine-looking any more. When I turned back, I saw McEwan's eyes on me.

He said, 'I'm not a psychiatrist—'

'No, thank God. I have the least possible enthusiasm for lying flat on my back and putting my sub-conscious in the hands of someone quite possibly of less intelligence than myself.'

'As I was saying, I'm no' a psychiatrist. As far as your physical condition's concairned, everything's fine. A slight trace of degeneration at the back of the neck, but nothing unusual for a man of middle-age.' He pulled his note-pad towards him. 'These ought to deal with the headaches. As for the rest—' he sat back, put down his pen, swung his chair so that he was turned towards the window. Grey autumn weather showed behind the London planes: the house opposite was empty, as if its occupants had already fled the city. It stood in moist shadow, flying its flag: 'FOR SALE. Apply Warwick, Greystock and Brown.' Who'll buy? With the threat so close, who'll buy? 'These are times of great anxiety. We are none of us immune.'

I got to my feet, anxious now to escape. 'No indeed.'

'War is a tairible thing.'

'So I've heard.'

'I was merely making a general obsairvation.'

I limped across the room. He made a gesture to my leg. 'You say that causes you no trouble?'

I grinned at him. 'None, except that I try to avoid stripping down to my underpants in mixed company.'

McEwan had a way of letting this kind of remark go past him and land on the wall. 'I should try to get away, if I were you.'

4

'Couldn't possibly; I've handed my name in to a chap in the War Office: Officers' Emergency Reserve. Top age limit fifty-five, so I dare say I stand a chance. Someone might pull my name out of a hat and pitch me off to Salisbury Plain; the War House works in a mysterious way, as you may know.'

He let this go past him too. 'A long week-end, perhaps.'

'My wife would want to come with me.'

His look said, 'Well, why not?' but he didn't. 'You could tell her that I've advised you a short rest in the Cotswolds on your own.'

'She'd imagine I'd got a blonde in Chipping Camden.'

Here again he played no shot. 'Come and see me in a few weeks' time if there's no improvement.'

I shook hands with him. Once I was on the steps I knew how glad I was to escape. The consulting-room, now behind me, had the lineaments of a trap. Mention of the nightmares had slipped out; for a moment the impersonal intimacy of the room, a floating aftermath—amongst the brown leather, the screened couch and the nondescript walls—of other people's confessions, had loosened my tongue.

'Nothing unusual for a man of middle-age.' The vaguely depressing words lingered in my mind as I walked on. At forty-five I found my hair greying heavily, my eyes needing help, my teeth for the first time causing trouble. These small outrunners of mortality did not greatly worry me: they were still new enough to have interest, even a beguiling quality of change. For what could give greater balm to the soul than to be at forty-five another person, delivered of all one's regrets, of guilt, of the pattern one's steps had made in the dust?

But the change, of course, existed only in the region of my skin. The shaving-mirror which gave daily proof of gradual decay contained somewhere in its depths all the same memories. These I could not escape; and these accounted for the nightmares, the formless sense of hurry

5

which nudged and crowded my day, the fear that kept me company; for the third and fourth drink which I knew it would be better to leave alone; for my reputed truculence in argument. (I could hear Griselda's voice: 'Simon, you will be friendly to them, won't you? You'll be *nice* at dinner, won't you; I do so want it to go well.') Nice: what a word. Poor Griselda, who would till her dying day want everyone to be nice.

Perhaps it was this thought of Griselda which sent me to the telephone-booth. The booth was in a side-street off Buckingham Palace Road, comfortably secure, but I looked once or twice up and down before I went into it. I dialled the Whitehall number, asked for the extension, and waited. The street was almost empty; a newspaper blew along the gutter. I could just make out the word 'Sudeten' in the headlines. The switchboard girl said, 'Trying to connect you'; I began to rattle my fingers on the coin box.

'Hullo?' The voice at the other end was breathless.

'Hullo, Kate.'

'Simon?'

'Yes, of course.'

'Sorry; have you been there long? I was summoned to the Chief.'

'Not very. I thought I might come and see you this evening, before dinner.'

'Oh—Simon—this evening I can't. I have to take Midge to the theatre.'

Midge was a young woman, a cousin or something, who was alone in London doing her first job, and for whom Kate felt responsible. Take any kind of woman, I thought, and you will find her sometime, when you are anxious to see her, doing some tiresome or boring thing because she thinks she ought to.

'Tomorrow then,' I said.

'Yes. Yes.' She still sounded breathless. She didn't say she was looking forward to it, or that she was pleased, or

6

that it would be lovely, or any of the things she usually said. Perhaps there was someone else in the room.

'About half past six,' I said.

'Yes.'

'Good-bye, darling.'

'Good-bye.'

Yes, there must have been someone in the room, I thought as I walked away from the booth. I limped on towards Victoria Street. In the damp unadventurous sky and the rain-polished street there was a feeling of hurry, of unrest; the plain ponderous buildings seemed to mock their own solidity with images of destruction. ('The German Air Fleet will not spare civilians. Its noses are pointed towards England.') *Hitler Speaks Tonight* said the placards; others read *Fitting of Gas Masks*. Amongst the umbrellas and shopping bags which people carried I saw the small brown cardboard box; some looked as if they were ashamed of it and some carried it like a talisman. Behind the accustomed movement of a London evening, behind the lag and start of the traffic, monstrous things lurked; some rough beast, its hour come round at last, slouched towards Europe to be born.

I joined the crowd buying from the newsboy, and went into a pub. Deprived of Kate, I was in no hurry to go home. Griselda was going out: like Kate, she was taking someone to the theatre: I couldn't remember who. Perhaps it would be the same theatre: such things happened.

I bought a whisky and opened my paper. Hitler would speak at eight o'clock in the Berlin Sports Palace; Mussolini said there was still hope of peace, and the leader said that the situation recalled ominously the last week of July 1914. I looked for some moments at a muffled picture of a French reservist on duty on a bridge over the Marne. The echoes sounded, as they had been sounding all these past weeks.

I turned the pages of the paper, half listening to an argument across the bar-counter: a man in a macintosh had

7

clear views about the Czechs; they were making a bloody
nuisance of themselves, and it was no part of our job to dig
them out and get shot up by the Germans for our pains.
The barman on the other hand didn't care for being bul-
lied; no one shouted at *him* from any bloody Sports Palace,
particularly a nasty little twerp with his arm stuck up like
that all the time as if he wanted to leave the room; best to
stand firm and have a crack at the Huns; wouldn't do them
any harm and we'd win; we always did in the end. A small
sad gentleman in a grubby pullover shook his head; it
wasn't, he said, possible to talk like that about winning: the
next war would mean the end of civilization; London'd be
nothing but a heap of rubble and we'd all be living in
caves. He took a long sad drink of beer.

I bought another whisky. I was beginning to wish I were
seeing Kate: Kate wasn't a solution to anything; she
couldn't, in the nature of things, put my world straight, but
she was a bandage over the eyes; she stopped, for the time
we were together, the questions that flew against my mind
like hailstones against a pane of glass. The evening stretched
ahead of me; time to be filled in while the harsh voice savaged the air and war came closer. All ears, the newspaper
said, would be glued to the wireless set. Not mine.

A film, perhaps? I looked down the list in the paper; it
seemed to be a choice between Snow White and Hedy
Lamarr. I had half a mind to settle for Hedy Lamarr, when
I remembered that Mrs. Drayfield, who lived in, cooked,
cleaned and on demand waited at table for us, would have
been detailed to prepare a meal for me. If I didn't turn up
she would be upset, and Mrs. Drayfield being upset was
like a pall over the house. Once I suggested pulling down
the blinds, but Griselda wasn't amused: she would look
desperate on these occasions and move in Mrs. Drayfield's
wake, making supplicating sounds of friendship and apology, pausing only to give me a glance of exasperated dis-
like. All this would have been worth risking for Kate, but

not for Hedy Lamarr. I emptied my glass; drank another quickly; then left.

§

It was nearly half past seven when I came to the house. In Bryon Street near Vincent Square, it lay in a district which Griselda called Westminster and I Pimlico.

All the lights were on. Puzzled, I stood on the pavement, aware of the whisky I'd drunk, blinking at the strangeness of the lights. A flick of apprehension touched me: something was wrong, and at the back of my mind I was beginning to know what it was. I went warily, digging for my key. As I put it in the lock, the door was pulled open from inside, and Griselda faced me in the hall.

The light was behind her, and when the light is behind her Griselda looks less than forty-two, which is her age. The wide green eyes, beautifully spaced, and the bobbed fair hair belong to someone much younger, and I can see her suddenly, Griselda Sanderson, wandering through the Sussex lanes in that sunlit and threatened time when I most clearly remember her.

She said, 'Simon, where *have* you been?'

The door shut behind me. From the hall where I stood I could see the dining-room, the table laid for guests, the candles, the flowers, the best mats, the wine warming on the sideboard. It was all coming further and further into focus. I said, 'I thought you were going to the theatre.'

'That's *tomorrow* night. Tonight's the dinner for the Wilcotts: you *couldn't* have forgotten.'

No, I couldn't have: but I had.

'You promised to be home early.'

I closed my eyes for a moment. There was nothing to be gained from lying. I could only offer private thanks that I had not spent the evening with Kate or—what would in some ways have been worse—with Hedy Lamarr. Should

9

I mention McEwan? I thought not; the interview seemed best forgotten. I said, 'I'm dreadfully sorry, darling.' Pity about the whisky; I must be breathing it all over the hall.

'But you know how important this is. I've been talking about it for days—only this morning—'

'Now, please. I've said I'm sorry. I'll change and wash—how long have I got?'

'You don't understand. Jeremy isn't here.'

'Jeremy isn't here: why isn't he here?'

'How should I know? I've been nearly frantic, waiting for you both.'

'Well, I suppose he'll turn up—'

'Wearing those awful clothes he went away for the week-end in?'

I gave a sigh and began to climb the stairs.

'The whole point is that Jeremy should make a good impression on Harold Wilcott.'

She stood looking up at me. I tried to subdue a feeling of exasperation; it arose maybe from my own guilt, yet I couldn't help thinking that this was no time to have the Wilcotts to dinner; and the sort of dinner, what's more—smoked salmon and duck and two kinds of wine—that was above our station.

'We must simply press on,' I said, going up to the bedroom. 'Perhaps the Wilcotts'll forget too; let's look on the bright side.'

'And what about all the food and everything?'

'You and I can dine *en prince* and drink to the end of the world which seems to be imminent.'

'No, please don't talk like that—'

'Well, it is; read this.' I tossed down the evening paper, but she made no attempt to catch it, merely glancing at it as it fell, 'Anyway, Geoffrey's coming; *he* won't forget.'

'Oh God; not Geoffrey?'

'Simon—please—'

'I have Geoffrey all day in the office: I don't want him at night as well.' (And why to goodness, if he was coming to dinner, couldn't he have reminded me about it? Perhaps he had, and I'd not been listening.) Griselda was looking more and more desperate, and now I began to feel sorry for her. From the kitchen Mrs. Drayfield was calling '*Ma*dam! *Ma*dam!' in the genteel pipe that made my flesh crawl.

Griselda said, 'In a minute; I'm coming in a minute. Simon, you're quite unreasonable about Geoffrey. He's one of the best and kindest people we know: he always talks of you with the greatest affection—'

'Do we have to have hymns of praise to Geoffrey just now?'

'But you'll be nice to him?'

'I'll kiss him on both cheeks: what a perfectly horrible idea.'

'*Ma*dam!'

'Oh—coming.'

Griselda flew to the kitchen, and I went to our room. It smelt strongly of Griselda's scent; her dressing-table was scattered with jars and tubes and sticks of paint: as she grew older there were more of these and she used them more lavishly.

I pulled off tie and shirt. My head still buzzed with the whisky, and the thought of Geoffrey was still getting under my skin. I might have been angry about Jeremy too, but I had learned that if one of us was angry with our son the other entered immediately upon a state of friendship. For most of the time Griselda treated him with what seemed to me maddening lenience, but every now and again he over-stepped the mark, and I became his refuge in time of trouble. Some comfort in this because the nightmares still haunted me, and I would be glad to meet him on friendly ground.

But Geoffrey was something else. (I pulled a clean shirt from the drawer, put in the gold and onyx cuff links: they carried echoes from far back, from my coming of age. Long past.) Geoffrey King was Griselda's cousin, my senior partner in the Calder–King Group of magazines; he was a man of endless patience; a High Churchman who ducked and crossed himself all over the place and called his priests 'Father' and talked about Mass. He was never late or rude: I had known him for most of my life and in all that time I had not learned to like him.

I found it hard to explain exactly why. Sometimes it seemed to me that he played the part of a hostile mother-in-law and had long sympathetic talks with Griselda about what a terrible time she must have being married to me. 'He always talks of you with the greatest affection,' she'd said, but of course it is perfectly possible to do this and tear a person apart at the same time.

There was, I reflected, choosing a tie, something of the old woman about Geoffrey. Ten years ago, to everyone's surprise, after staying a bachelor till forty, he had become engaged to a young woman called Helen who did social work in the East End. She was dark, perhaps thirty, the first touch of the spinster on her, but with a friendly smile and excellent legs. Geoffrey had seemed fond of her, and everyone said—until you could have screamed—how suitable it was.

And then, in a surprising flurry, Geoffrey had his ring back, wedding presents returned whence they had come with, as it were, their tails between their legs, and there was a notice in *The Times*. Geoffrey gave no explanation, went about preoccupied but controlled, and a few months later the young woman married a curate. Geoffrey spoke of her only in the kindest terms, and everyone said he was splendid. Quite possibly this was true, and my antagonism sprang from jealousy. Certainly he lived outside my understanding: he had never married, and it was impossible to imagine his having an affair, so I could only suppose he didn't sleep with anyone. This, while in its way impressive, gave me no fellow-feeling at all.

I searched for socks in the chest of drawers, and the photograph caught my eye. Myself with Jeremy, nine years ago in Cornwall: Jeremy, ten years old, a nice little boy with fair hair and sandals, laughing into the sun; myself in open shirt and canvas trousers looking down at him with pleasure in the brilliant light. I could see that my own face was nine years younger; the hair dark, without grey, a nostalgic smoothness about the cheeks; you would have said automatically, 'A young man.' Not good-looking: 'My face begins well but quickly drops behind,' I had said once to Griselda, and this was manifestly so in the photograph, where the eyes and nose were quite good and the rest nowhere. Jeremy looked like any rather pretty little boy on holiday, and the whole thing might have had the falsity of an advertisement for different sizes of underwear, except for the knowledge that this was a true moment of affection, shadowed by change.

Meanwhile, Jeremy who was supposed to make a good impression on Harold Wilcott in the hope of being offered a job still wasn't back from his week-end.

And diminishing all this, the thunder from Eastern Europe; the abyss that came closer.

Poor Griselda.

§

I decided, when the dinner was half-way through, that if one had to entertain people with whom one had little in common, a meal was the best way to do it: food diluted their impact.

Harold Wilcott, the head of a large advertising agency, was loud with bonhomie; his wife, forty-ish and red-haired, was flirtatious to the extent of imagining risqué compliments where none had been intended: colour swarmed over her face and she showed her pretty teeth at the most prosaic remarks, meant to do no more than keep the conversation going. Both of them, I was sure, were good to their children, kind to animals, and with compassion for the aged. Nevertheless they had said some bone-headed things about the Czechs, and sooner or later I was going to lose my temper. Meanwhile I got on with my duck.

Griselda kept looking at me as if I were an alarm clock set soon to go off. Without cause, I thought; I'd made affable remarks to the Wilcotts and greeted Geoffrey as if I were pleased to see him. What more could she want?

I glanced over the table. Griselda insisted that we ate by candlelight: this, she said, made the women look more beautiful and the meal more exotic. True, perhaps, but it made it more difficult to see one's duck, and it made it more difficult to see Geoffrey: in the amber unscientific light of our dining-room his silver hair and glasses were about all I could clearly define. These were of a piece with the image I kept of him: precise, controlled, somehow antiseptic. Just now he was trained attentively on Mrs. Wilcott, yet aware of my eyes on him; his glance flickered for a moment sideways, while Mrs. Wilcott went on blushing and throwing her head back.

There was still no sign of Jeremy: his empty place remained, a mute suggestion of a different world, of events running counter to a small dinner party in Bryon Street. Griselda had told the Wilcotts some story about a telephone call late this afternoon from Brighton where Jeremy apparently nursed a sick friend. What happened when he arrived back with some totally different explanation, I had no idea.

'Quite possibly,' Harold Wilcott was saying, 'the speech is over by now.'

Geoffrey gave a stern look at his watch, as if he were timing it. 'No, I shouldn't think so. The man usually has a lot to say. Or rather he has one thing to say, but he repeats himself.'

14

'I find it very hard to understand,' Wilcott went on, 'how any Englishman in his right mind can talk of going to war. If there's anything we can do—anything at *all*—we must do it to ensure peace.' He took another mouthful of duck, went on talking before he'd quite finished it. 'I've no time for the Nazis, of course I haven't: some of my best friends are Jews. But war is another thing. *We* know that at our age, don't we? Are we prepared to have that over again? For *any* reason? No, of course not: not if we're sane men. What a splendid duck.'

I chased a dusky piece of vegetable round my plate. The candle flames occasionally swung, a little smoke went up and the wax crept downward. For a moment I saw not the elegant green candles of Griselda's dinner-table, but the coarse swollen things stuck in jars or in the lids of tobacco tins, their flames shaken not by the shiver of passing traffic but by the slamming of the guns, the noise that battered iron fists against the sky.

'Safety at all costs,' I said, spearing the vegetable at last. 'Is that it?'

'You can't talk in those terms. Schoolboy ideas of standing by one's friends—'

'Nothing schoolboy about it. The facts are simple enough. Bit by bit, Hitler's swallowing Europe. Austria in March. Czechoslovakia now. Next—'

'He only wants the German parts of Czechoslovakia—'

'German fiddlesticks. Take a look at the map. He wants the nerves and guts of the country; the mountain defences; the munition factories; give him those and you've handed the Czechs over, blind and bound. To a man who—'

'But granted we're on the *side* of the Czechs; that doesn't mean we have to go to war for them.'

'And of all the blinkered remarks I've ever heard—'

Griselda made a little plunge towards the vegetable dish. 'Please, Mrs. Wilcott, won't you have some more?'

Startled, Mrs. Wilcott said she was dieting; and Wilcott

gave a stern shake of his head, as though being offered the prospect of war itself. 'Blinkered. What absolute nonsense: you're the one, if I may say so without offence, who's blinkered. Prepared to send another generation to the slaughter as our generation was slaughtered, *kill* thousands upon thousands because of some remote quarrel—'

'Remote be damned,' I said, and Griselda made some sort of muddle with her spoon. 'People aren't remote because they're far off—'

'Sentiment,' snapped Wilcott. 'Some men have to suffer, endure injustice. As things are, it's the turn of the Czechs. A pity, and no one's pleased about it. But to say you're prepared to go to war for their sake is sentimentality run mad.'

'I'm damned if it is.' My hands were trembling; I clasped them together. 'There are principles, God help us, aren't there? Things more important than one's own safety?' I tried to smother the protest in my mind; after all, if only good men could make a stand for the right we'd be in a poor way, wouldn't we? 'I bowed my head over Schuschnigg and Austria; I don't want to do it again over Benes, and any man who tells me I must—'

'Look here, Simon.' This was Geoffrey; he was turned towards me, with a sudden gleam of eyeglasses in the candle-light. 'All of what you say does you credit, but it's based on a quite false assumption—'

'Like hell it is.'

'No, no; let me finish. The Germans have a case, you know: and we're partly responsible for it. The men at Versailles twenty years ago planted some dangerous seeds. Now they're beginning to come above ground. That's not to say that we haven't great sympathy for a small nation under pressure—'

'Sympathy!'

'Under pressure and forced to make sacrifices for the sake of world peace. We've shown that sympathy through the tireless efforts of Lord Runciman and Sir Nevile Henderson—'

'One wouldn't want them to be tired, of course—'

'But just because we've done our best as counsellors, we don't have to plunge our whole nation—indeed the whole world—into a bloody conflict whose outcome no man can see.'

This sounded like the last line in a leader-writer's column, but then Geoffrey so often did. 'All you're doing is making out a good case for cowardice—'

'Darling, Mrs. Wilcott's glass is empty.'

I grabbed the wine bottle and filled all the glasses, including my own. Some of the wine splashed on the table. Griselda was sitting up straight, doomed and anxious; Mrs. Wilcott, not seeing any chance in all this for a flirtation, just sat there looking like someone waiting decoratively on a platform for a train that hasn't come in.

'And another thing,' said Geoffrey, after taking a reverent sip from his glass. 'You have to realize that it gives one a feeling of superiority, a spurious sense of altruism, to be prepared to sacrifice your own country for the sake of another. . . . No, let me finish, there's a good boy. It may not sound so splendid to speak up for your own people, but it's a good deal better sense.'

'Hear, hear,' said Wilcott. 'I must say, when I listen to any man talking glibly of another war I can only suppose that he's managed to shut his mind to what happened twenty years ago—'

'Yes, indeed,' said Geoffrey. 'After all, Simon, you can't deny that what you're proposing to do is to send men like David to their death over again.'

The curious thing was then the way we were all silent, and the way Griselda's eyes fled up to mine. There was suddenly a frozen band round my head, the kind of headache that had sent me earlier in the day to McEwan. I was wordless, impotent, meeting the place of conflict, the dark tangled place where reason was defeated and the hauntings took over. I went on looking at Griselda, and she said, as if in answer, 'Simon, would you please ring for Mrs. Drayfield; I think everyone's finished.'

I pressed the bell so hard it rang in the kitchen like an alarm.

'That's true, isn't it?' Geoffrey pursued, and without waiting for an answer, 'Of course it is. If you'll give the whole thing a moment's clear thought, you'll see that one has to put common sense before quixotry—'

'Common sense! If it's common sense to throw a small nation to the wolves to save our own skins, then God deliver us from it. As for sending men to their death, several thousand have gone already: or don't we count them, being foreigners?'

Into the loaded silence which followed this, Mrs. Drayfield arrived with the pudding. Griselda said something to Mrs Wilcott about cheese from Harrods, giving meanwhile directions in mime to Mrs Drayfield as to where to put the cream. Geoffrey looked calm and resolute, as if he were waiting for a swell on the sea to subside. And then the long curtains, crimson with grey birds on them, Griselda's choice, swung in the sudden draught from the hall, and my son Jeremy stood in the doorway.

It must have been plain to a half-wit with one eye that Jeremy was totally unprepared for the presence of guests. His mouth came a little way open, then closed as he swallowed. I sat looking at him. The nineteen-year-old face was Griselda's face as I remembered it from long past—large green eyes and fair hair; but salted with some tang absent from Griselda's face, a sharpness, an edge of mockery. There had been none of this in the photograph in my bedroom: it was something new. He wore an open shirt, a sports jacket and crumpled grey trousers, here and there stained. Before he could speak Griselda sat up straight in the candlelight and said in her clear hostess voice, 'Jeremy darling; how lovely to see you: I've explained to Mr. and Mrs. Wilcott about your host being taken ill. How you had to look after him.'

Jeremy picked this up nimbly: smoothed his hair, smiled engagingly, came and kissed his mother on the forehead. 'Oh Lord, yes; poor old Tony; he was *terribly* ill; I had to get the doctor; some sort of colic. One moment he was getting together with a gin; and the next he was green in the face and groaning. . . .' He seemed to feel, as I did, that he was overdoing it. 'I'm so awfully sorry.' He came and shook hands with Wilcott, who was unresponsive; and with Mrs. Wilcott who fluttered at him; said, 'Hullo, Uncle Geoffrey; hullo, Father,' and sat sideways on the vacant chair. His glance slid towards me, as if he still waited for a verdict.

My head swam a little from wine and argument: I wondered how much of this showed. I said, taking care to sound sober, 'Have you had any dinner?'

'Not really. A sandwich.'

'Have some pudding, darling.'

He turned with relief to his mother. 'Oh . . . trifle; thanks, I will.' For a moment, as the plate was put before him, he looked a child again: pleased with the prospect of a large helping.

'Did you bring a paper?' I asked.

''Fraid not. Sorry.'

'We're anxious to know about the speech,' said Geoffrey.

'Oh Lord; that speech. Couple of chaps were making forecasts in the train.'

'It's the question of the hour, after all,' said Wilcott stiffly.

'Well, yes, I know; that's what's such a terrible bore, don't you agree?'

'Not the word I should have chosen,' said Wilcott, still stiff.

I could see Jeremy recognizing that his charm had failed. 'Well, but . . . People go on so.'

'Hardly surprising,' I said, 'within about two feet of war.'

I saw the flicker of his eyelid; the same involuntary movement that he used to make as a child when I was angry with him. 'Oh, but there won't be a war.'

'Why not?'

'Oh, well, we just don't have them any more; it's a word people use to frighten other people . . . can I have some wine? Thanks awfully.'

'Ah,' said Wilcott, still distant, not cosy at all. 'Optimistic and rather sweeping. If it does come, which God forbid, you'll be called up, you know.'

'I don't think so, really; by the time anyone gets around to fighting I'll be past military age.'

'Assuming,' said Wilcott, 'that you're not?'

Jeremy opened his eyes wide. 'Then I go in and have a bash, along with the rest.'

And my dream came back to me, flooding over my mind. The dark trench, glistening with rainy mud, the slippery, unco-operative ground. No light anywhere, and my own movement forward, fearful yet impelled, gliding towards horror, as yet unrevealed. Gliding more quickly, and then the sudden steep fall, and under my hand something that resists me, and which, though I do not want to see it, I am given power to perceive with horrid clarity in spite of the dark: the body decomposing at my feet, the face smeared and bloody, yet recognizable, the fair hair quite unstained: Jeremy's face—

The sound ripped the dream away and made my hands jump. The telephone.

Jeremy instantly put down his table napkin and got to his feet. 'Excuse me, please; I think that might be for me.'

When he had shut the door, Mrs. Wilcott said, 'What a nice-looking boy.'

Griselda, more cheerful now that I was silent and Jeremy home, made some sort of maternal acknowledgement; Geoffrey backed this up with careful enthusiasm: one of the surprising things was that Geoffrey and Jeremy were friends. I was pondering this, when Jeremy came back into the room.

'Someone wants Father.'

'Who?'

'Don't exactly know. A girl.'

'What girl?' I asked crossly, for Griselda was now giving this all her attention.

'Didn't quite catch. Foreign-sounding. I said "what" twice, but you don't like to go on. Karen something. Eever, would it be perhaps, Eever?' He was looking at me with amusement, mildly diverted. I said, 'I don't know anyone called Karen-something-like-Eever. Go and ask her what she wants, there's a good chap.'

After a few moments he came back and slid into his seat, giving a shake of his head. 'No go. When I asked her for details she just said, "Oh well, I don't expect he's the right man," and rang off.'

Wilcott laughed loudly, and Mrs. Wilcott said, 'The right man for *what*?' giving me a coy pink glance down the table. Griselda was still alert, and Geoffrey wore his calm High-Churchman face: not condemnatory, merely removed from this kind of confusion.

I was obscurely annoyed. The right man? It could mean anything or nothing. The small pointless exchange niggled at the back of my mind. I said to Jeremy, 'What sort of girl?'

Jeremy shrugged; he was enjoying this all along the line. 'Who can tell? Young, I suppose.'

'What did she say?'

'"Does a Mr. Simon Calder live there, please?"'

'Well, it all sounds highly suspicious,' said Wilcott, which didn't help anything at all.

'Mm, disappointing,' said Jeremy. 'Mystery with no solution, like a crossword clue you can't solve. For a moment we had her, Miss Karen Whatever, on a tenuous thread out of the thronging thousands of this great city. Now the thread's broken and she's lost among them again. For good.'

All right, I told myself; the young have to show off. I said, 'Some other chap of the same name, I imagine. It must be nearly time for the news.'

We rose from the table in an awkward silence. Mrs. Wilcott dispersed it with a scurry of flattery, but it was clear, what with one thing and another, the evening had been a failure. I caught sight of the flowers in the middle of the table, drooping a little in the heat of the candle flames, and felt a pang of compassion for Griselda.

§

When our guests had gone Jeremy at once slipped off to his room as he had always done since childhood if trouble threatened. Griselda and I were left in the drawing-room. I thought that being married was, in its early stages, going to bed together and having children; but after twenty years it meant being left with the dirty ashtrays, crumpled cushions and used coffee cups: the taste of an unsuccessful evening. And the taste of the savage news from Berlin.

Griselda stood, legs a little apart, a cigarette, unlighted, in one hand. I yawned heavily and sat back in an armchair.

'Got a light, darling?' Griselda asked.

I groaned and tossed her a box of matches. She caught them and said, 'Attentive husbands leap up with the flick of a lighter.'

'Sorry. I'm bloody tired.'

'Poor Simon. Rather tight too, aren't you, darling?'

'Yes, I dare say.'

'It didn't go very well, did it?'

'It didn't have much chance.'

'I doubt if the Wilcotts'll ever come here again.'

'Well, that's something to be thankful for.'

'I should have thought Sonia Wilcott was rather your cup of tea.'

'I like my tea with a little less sugar.'

She gave a lift of one shoulder. 'All the same, Harold Wilcott's an influential person. He could have done a lot for Jeremy.'

'Influential people who can do a lot for other people very seldom do. . . . That's a pretty frock.'

She looked down at it as if to remind herself what she was wearing; made no comment. 'What was all that nonsense on the telephone?'

'I've no idea.'

'Seems a bit odd.'

'Well, doesn't it? However, it wasn't anything to do with me.'

She left a silence after this, then said in a throwaway voice, 'No, well, I suppose it wasn't. Pity, though; it didn't really help the atmosphere.'

'Goodness, you can't *get* an atmosphere at a time like this. Or if you do, it's an atmosphere of jumping fire-crackers.'

'Perhaps if we'd not talked about it, the crisis; if we'd—'

'Oh, come off it. You heard what that madman in Germany said: screaming that the Czechs had got four days to surrender; that his patience had given out; that he'd march on Saturday. You can't pretend it isn't happening. We're playing a kind of grandmother's footsteps, creeping up on war, and we've taken a whole jump forward tonight.'

She stood looking at me. 'No, but there can't be a war . . . Think of the young men. Think of Jeremy.'

'Yes, well, I do,' I said. (And there was the dream again; and Griselda was looking at me as though she knew about the dream, though I had never told her.)

'How can you bear to think of it? Don't you ever remember Prue?'

This was like having an ugly light shone straight into my eyes. I muttered, 'Of course—of course,' praying for nothing more to be said.

'You never talk about her.'

'What d'you expect me to say?'

She flinched as if I had been more cruel than I intended. I looked at her across the room, across the muddle of this evening, across the threat of war, and was suddenly saddened.

'I don't know. I just feel one shouldn't freeze things like that, shut them away.'

Nothing now but a jagged irritable longing for this to stop. But she went on, head down, voice not quite steady. 'I think it's better to face anything like that, talk about it, let it come out. However much it hurts. If you shut it away there's some part of you all the time that isn't quite real. I don't know if you understand what I mean.'

I did, but I couldn't talk about it. She waited a moment, then turned sharply from me. 'I must go and find Jeremy. He hasn't even told us what happened.'

'What happened was that he forgot all about it.'

'It might have been something else.'

'You had only to look at his face. He couldn't have looked more surprised if he'd skidded on a banana skin.'

'I'll go and find him.'

'He won't tell you very much.'

'He talks to me, you know.'

I said, 'Oh good.'

'Are you coming up?'

'No . . . not yet. One or two things I want to do.'

She nodded, giving this no interest, which was reasonable, since she knew as well as I did that I hadn't anything to do except perhaps empty the ashtrays.

When she'd gone I got up from my chair and stretched myself in the empty room. Coal shifted in the grate with the sound of a shuffling step. I picked up the evening paper and thrust it into the waste-paper basket; news, a few hours old, died quickly. Now the ultimatum, screamed from the Sports Palace, changed the colour of the world again: four days left. The room so still and curtained had danger in it. ' . . . to send men like David to their death over again.' I still had no answer: evil, it seemed, surrounded us; I was afraid, haunted, passionate for justice because it seemed necessary that there should be one good thing, something saved from the dark.

Something saved. For one had, after all, let so much go, had no certain place to stand. Griselda and Jeremy: these should form the established corners of my world, yet when I thought of them I seemed to be looking at failure. Our words were broken and uncommunicative, and encounter changed easily into a waspish battle over pin-pricks.

Jeremy disturbed me most. I tried to think of him as the child in the photograph, the image of someone loved, yet we seldom met without an argument, and his cocksure opinions, his contempt for anyone over thirty, his worship of whatever silly creed his latest friend upheld all frayed my nerves.

Yet somewhere behind all this was a child of fun and courage, working his difficult way through the confining egoism of youth. Why couldn't I reach him? Lack of patience? Lack of sympathy? My own egoism, which thrived well enough, God knew? Somehow, I thought, I must make an effort. We were very near to war. And he was nineteen.

§

When he came into the room I said, 'I thought you'd gone to bed.'

'No, I've been talking to Mother. Trying to convince her that even if I'd remembered the dinner it wouldn't have done any good: Wilcott's the kind of large businessman who puts the fear of heaven into me; I wouldn't work for him if he were the last man on earth.'

'Still, she did the whole thing for your sake.'

'Oh, I know, I know; terribly sad; poor Mum. Means awfully well, but it misfires.' He wandered about the room.

'What did happen at Brighton?'

'Just a lot of fun. Tony threw a party last night, and it went on till five this morning. That's why I'm looking my age just now. Today was kind of haywire: I didn't leave Brighton till half past six, and I never gave this dinner business a thought till I opened the door and saw the whole merry-go-round in action, and then of course it hit me the way those things do, a kind of bomb that goes off in your head and says "*There*".'

I gave a grunt. 'Doesn't Tony have a job?'

'He's a writer.'

I raised one eyebrow.

'Sort of free-lance journalist,' said Jeremy. 'And he has some money of his own.'

'Lucky chap. How old is he?'

'Twenty-five. Twenty-seven, perhaps.'

'Not married?'

'No. I told you. He lives with his Mum.'

'How did she enjoy the party?'

'She's away just now.'

I left a silence after this. Jeremy was picking things up and putting them down. He said at last, 'Actually he's had an idea.'

I waited.

'Rather a good one, I think.' He was on the defensive, a little breathless. 'He wants to do a travel book, kind of young man's journey to the old places: Greece and Constantinople and all that. His idea is that I should go with him and take the photographs.'

'By-passing the war as you go?'

'If there isn't a war.'

'It's going to cost something, isn't it? Who's going to pay?'

'We'd share it.'

'How're you going to do that?'

Jeremy leant against the wall and hunched his shoulders. 'Grandfather left me some money for when I was twenty-one—didn't he? You've always said so.'

'Yes, a little. Not much.'

'I thought perhaps if I could take some of it out—say about a couple of hundred—and then pay it back—'

'Pay it back how?'

'Tony says this book'll make a lot of money.'

'Is it commissioned?'

'No. But—'

'Has he any idea how many people think they're going to write books which'll make a lot of money?'

Jeremy began to look sulky. 'Yes, but this is different.'

'It always is.'

Jeremy now looked about ten years old, deprived of an air-gun. 'Tony writes damn well. He's had articles printed.'

This obscurely touched me, but I went on. 'Any man who talks about going on a world tour *now* must be out of his mind. And has he any ideas about the effect of war on publishing? Any views on paper shortage, for a start?'

'Tony says this'll blow over. He says it's just a lot of bluff: nobody intends to go to war, now or at any time. He says he's bored with the whole thing. There was a bit in the paper which said peace prevails and will prevail.'

'I wonder which paper he reads. No, don't tell me, I can guess. Why d'you want to go with him?'

'Because it'd be fun.'

'It seems a bit odd all the same. Asking you down for the week-end, travelling all over Europe with you—'

'Oh, *Lord*.' Jeremy plunged across the room. 'We get on together and have fun. Why can't middle-aged people ever get their minds off sex?'

'All right. I'll take your word for it. But I think the whole thing's fantastic. It's unlikely that you'll get a penny back; that the book'll be published at all.'

'If everyone always thought like that, no one'd ever do anything.'

'One has, all the same, to see things as they are.'

Jeremy's face had hardened; he no longer looked ten years old, but a bitter young man prepared for battle. 'I can't get the money without an O.K. from you.'

'No.'

'And you won't give it?'

'I think the whole thing's so absurd. It doesn't tie in with the facts. Even if by some miracle we escape a war now, we won't in the end. You can't go flinging money away on some scatter-brained scheme that'll come to nothing.'

'You won't give it?' he repeated.

'No. For your own sake.'

'Oh, damn all that.' He looked furious, nearly in tears. Then he turned. I heard him running upstairs, and the slam of his bedroom door.

And that, I told myself, is what comes of making up your mind to understand the boy better. Depressed, I went to the window. The street was oiled with rain, and under the lamp one could see the rain itself falling, like scratches on a film. All sound—the kiss of tyres, the slam of a car door, the drifting formless chatter of unknown voices—had urgency in it. Loneliness too; the sounds were isolated, making no communication with each other.

For a moment we had her, Miss Karen Whatever, on a tenuous thread. . . . Uncomfortably, the girl on the telephone returned to my mind. It began to worry me that I hadn't answered her; the small irritable regret grew out of all proportion. *Now the thread's broken and she's lost among them again.* I should have gone to the telephone; heard what she had to say. I turned it round and round in my mind, as if I could get the moment back; then moved from the window and poured myself a drink.

I stood by the telephone, the white one in the drawing-room, but it was a pale crouched shape, part of the furniture; it had no voice.

2

Tuesday

The offices of the Calder–King Group were in Surrey Street, leading from the Strand. The tall grey building held other enterprises than ours; we were on the second floor, a shadowed stone place which even on a fine day gave the impression of a high-class jail. I walked in, pulling off my macintosh, casting a trail of wet from my umbrella. Lights were already lit, and outside one of the rooms was a pair of goloshes.

My own room looked on to one of those narrow cavernous side-streets which run like multitudinous thin grey bones through the body of London. Lighted, the windows of the office block across the way showed a busy mysterious life: when work palled I would sometimes watch this; it was like a very boring silent film.

The Calder–King Group, to my ears at least a rather splendid-sounding name, meant nothing now: we weren't a Group any more. We had started out as one, Geoffrey and I, in not always easy harness, but complementing each other, perhaps, in talents: he careful, orderly and controlled; myself wilder, imaginative and impulsive.

Three magazines had formed the group: one on the arts and politics; one on sport, with particular reference to mountain climbing which, in theory rather than in practice, held great fascination for me; and one for what we called the intelligent woman: a woman's magazine with bite to it, one which didn't look as though it were the product of a marriage between the Windmill Theatre and a department store. This last, called *Woman in View*, was the only one to survive, and not at all as we had first conceived it: we had been taken over by Fielding Publications, and *Woman in View* was, under their direction and within the vast financial structure of their kingdom, changing from a well-favoured blue-stocking into a seductive young woman, concerned mainly with brassières and make-up, and, as an ultimate by-product of these, children. There remained only one legacy from our original idea: a feature called 'The Month in View': a column of comment on the month's events seen through a woman's eyes, and written with edgy wit by a young woman journalist called Gertrude Kayne. Amongst the love-stories, the deodorants and the hints on jam-making, this alone was a source of pride.

On my desk this morning, in the gloom of rainy light, were the galleys for the October issue, with the proofs of coloured illustrations for the serial. They seemed marvellously irrelevant; the cracks in the world outside gave to the office an air of dark holiday.

Miss Brandon came clicking in with the letters. She and her boy-friend, she said, smothering a yawn, had been in Whitehall till midnight last night and she was, pardon me, ever so sleepy. Did I think there was going to be a war, and if there was would her widowed mother be safe in Wimbledon? I said most likely not: I suggested Wales.

'I'd like to get her somewhere, Mr. Calder: she's terribly jumpy about the bombs. And then, if it wouldn't be putting the office out, I could go into this women's Air Force they talk about. I'd like to do something, and I don't fancy that shade of khaki, and navy always makes me look like someone's aunt.'

She was a nice bright girl with auburn hair and too good a figure for one's peace of mind: I could see her having a roaring time in the Air Force. I gave a small sigh: I allowed myself no more than an occasional compliment and a touch on her arm, but it saddened me to think of her being set upon by a lot of Air Force wolves.

She went on, 'Mr. King wants to see you about advertising space.'

'Ah.' Geoffrey's room was the twin of mine: our secretaries worked in the smaller space between. There was a half-mocking, half-irritable battle as to which of us should go to the other. 'All right. Tell him I'm at his disposal. And take these along to the art department, there's a good girl.'

'Yes, Mr. Calder. Any message?'

'None, except that I think they're terrible. I thought we were still a cut above this kind of He-clasped-her-passionately caper.'

Miss Brandon considered the picture which showed a disproportionate young woman with yards of red hair, leaning back so that she made a sort of hoop in the arms of a young man with a jaw and a dinner jacket. 'We used to do something like that in gym.'

'Good gracious.'

'I mean without the young man.'

'So I should hope.'

She giggled and clicked out, showing nice hips and good ankles.

I turned to the galleys on my desk, but it was difficult to work. Even as one sat here playing around with this fool magazine, the thing was being decided.

I looked up as Geoffrey came in. Geoffrey always managed to come into a room in a way that suggested he'd been summoned to the bedside of a patient who was seriously ill but would in time recover. Except that he was wearing a different suit, he looked exactly the same as he had

32

done the night before: I sometimes doubted that he ever went to bed at all, got his hair rumpled, sweated, grew his beard; perhaps he merely went into cold storage for the night.

I faced him across my desk. I wondered how it was that he always loomed like my conscience: he seemed to bring with him a measuring-rod of probity.

'I sent a message by Miss Brandon,' he said.

'I know. I sent one back.'

He gave a faint smile and left it. 'I wanted to talk to you. I'm afraid you're going to be rather upset.'

After this he was silent for some moments, and I knew better than to say, 'For Christ's sake, what *about*?' I waited.

'We're going to have to cut out "The Month in View".'

'For the next issue?'

'For good.'

'Oh, nonsense.'

'My dear boy, we need the space for advertising. And the proprietors are quite clear where the money lies: not in "The Month in View".'

'But it's so damn good.'

Geoffrey sighed. 'For you or me, perhaps. But that kind of witty comment isn't what the average woman wants, you know.'

'I thought we were supposed to aim a little higher than the great typist mass.'

'It seems we can't and make the thing pay as well.'

'Once that's gone the whole thing'll turn into one more Great Romantic Marshmallow.'

'We have to face facts.'

I said this seemed to be the week for facing facts: writing off both the Czechs and Gertrude Kayne.

Geoffrey shrugged. 'That's the way things go.'

I was surprised that he could accept this so easily. How did he square it with God, I wondered? What did he do about the Czechs and Gertrude Kayne when he went to what he called High Mass on Sundays? Perhaps in his view God was of the same mind.

Once Geoffrey had taken me with him to his church. Clumsily I had tried to follow him in getting up and down, always a few minutes late. There were no pews, only wooden chairs, and I got cramp in one knee. The boys' voices decorated this uncomfortable vigil with marvellous sound, and the ringing of the Sanctus Bell pierced some buried nerve of nostalgia and regret for innocence lost, yet I stayed outside it all, and emerged having no sense of blessing. Geoffrey on the other hand came out with an extra shine on him, like a man who has been exceptionally well shaved. I said, when he made some sort of inquiry, 'It didn't take, I'm afraid.' Geoffrey said he hadn't expected it to 'take': one visit to a church after twenty years' absence could hardly be expected to turn an agnostic into a believer: he had merely opened a door.

He said now, surprising me, 'Have you heard anything more of that girl? The one who telephoned?'

'You mean . . .'

'The foreign girl who rang up during dinner.'

'No.' I looked at him curiously. 'Why?'

'I was merely interested.'

It seemed an unlikely thing for Geoffrey to be interested in. 'I haven't any idea who she is, you know.'

'Yes; I gathered that.'

'Have *you* ever heard of her?'

'No.' He stayed silent and picked something very small off the sleeve of his coat. He seemed to have finished with the girl. 'Griselda didn't look very happy last night.'

This sounded like his mother-in-law act; I felt in no mood for it, nor for a post-mortem on the dinner party. 'Understandable, with Jeremy forgetting the whole thing.'

He took his glasses off, always a bad sign, then said, 'I can't help feeling you're not going quite the right way about handling Jeremy.'

34

The moment when my buried hostility to Geoffrey could openly declare itself was always one of mixed rage and pleasure. 'You don't, eh?'

'No. If you don't mind my saying so, I think you jump on the boy too easily.'

'Oh, dear.'

'Griselda feels the same—'

'Then why the hell doesn't she say so?'

'She does, but she says you don't listen. And it's a great pity because the boy's relationship with his father is terribly important, and he *has* a strong feeling for you—'

'Oh, it's nice to know that.'

He looked at me with controlled patience. 'I can see that I've made you very angry. I didn't intend to.'

'On the other hand, if you start telling parents what they should do about their children—'

'I should have thought, as Jeremy's uncle, I had some sort of right—'

'Yes, I dare say; heaps of people have rights to do things which are damned offensive when they do them.'

Geoffrey kept silence while Miss Brandon clicked in, put a file on my desk, smelt the atmosphere, and clicked out again. Then he said, 'Well, of course I'm asking for trouble, I suppose, but it seems to me, Simon, old man, that you're a bit over-strained. No—no, wait a minute. Other people in the office agree with me—'

The idea of Geoffrey immersed in gossipy discussions on my shortcomings so enraged me that I was speechless. He went on, 'The best thing, in my view, would be for you to go away for a holiday—'

'What a perfectly splendid idea. Where shall I go? Nuremberg? Berchtesgaden?'

He put his glasses on again. 'You make it very difficult to help you.'

'I don't need any help. Thank you all the same.'

35

He made for the door, without haste. 'I suppose you never pray?'

'No, I'm afraid not.'

'Pity. Well, there it is.'

I watched him go. Somewhere about one o'clock I made an effort and went into his room to apologize. The room was empty; his umbrella and raincoat were gone. Pleased, if anything, to be spared the apology, and more pleased to be spared a lunch with Geoffrey, I abandoned the whole thing.

§

I left the office at half past five. The rain was heavier, casting its drear gleam over the street, altering the pace and temper of the crowds. I bought an evening paper from a man hunched in cap and sodden overcoat. His drenched placard read 'Message from the King'. This was, I saw from the paper, 'To be of good cheer; keep cool heads and brave hearts.' I jumped on a bus and stood, crushed by wet tweed and dripping macintosh, uncomfortably tethered and trying to read the paper at the same time. German newspapers had suppressed Roosevelt's plea for peace. The cartoon showed two young men, one German, one English, facing each other. The caption read, 'He says his patience is exhausted, so we must die next Saturday.' Americans were hurrying home: all liners had waiting lists. Lurching uncomfortably through the dripping streets I had the first taste of being in a beleaguered city.

The bus swung out of the Strand; Nelson's Column and Trafalgar Square, a wide wet space, made a pattern that spelled London. The threat on it gave it another dimension. I put the paper under my arm. Now, in spite of it all, the day was becoming the day when I was seeing Kate. This changed the aspect of things, street and buildings and the colour of light and the people who passed by. Not into pleasure only; I moved into a secret country, ruled by different loyalties, composed of guilt and uncertainty. For one could be sure of nothing: her aunt could arrive from Essex; the girl upstairs could drop in to borrow some milk and stay for all the time we had. So confined, so threatened, the business had survived for three years.

I had first met her, surprisingly, in a room in the local Town Hall. A playwright of renown was giving a talk on his methods of playwrighting. Town Halls at eight o'clock in the evening, oneself sitting in a draught, either hungry because one hadn't eaten or with indigestion because one had, made small appeal to me. The playwright, however, did: I have always been a sucker for learning how people make things: watches, sewing machines or plays. Griselda didn't come with me; she said the Town Hall made her feel she had come there to report an accident. I left under a cloud, since my not being in for dinner had upset Mrs. Drayfield.

Kate came into the hall a little while after me. The place was fairly full, and for a moment or two she stood taking her gloves off, looking over the rows of chairs. I watched her with mild interest. She wore no hat and her straight dark hair, drawn from a centre parting into a bun at the nape of her neck, gave her a look of calm authority. She stood undoing the collar of her grey tweed coat, un-selfconscious, happy to take her time. When she saw the empty seat beside me at the end of the row, she came towards it with unhurried acceptance. I smiled at her as she sat down and she said, as if we'd known each other, 'I thought I was going to be late.' I made some remark about there being a surprising number of people here for a wet night, and she turned a placid head over her shoulder, nodded, and said no more.

However, the silence she sat in, even if it didn't exactly burn, had a certain friendliness; and when an anxious little man came on to the platform, dropped a page of notes and said that the playwright would, due to circumstances beyond his control, be a quarter of an hour late, we turned to each other, comrades in adversity.

I offered her a cigarette, and we talked amiably together. She was without coyness or anxiety, so much so that it slightly bruised my pride. I sat crookedly in my chair so that I could watch her: her skin was pale and clean, her eyes grey. Her full mouth smiled easily and a little sadly. Thirty; perhaps more. No wedding-ring; a beguiling figure just discernible beneath her unbuttoned coat, with full breasts and a slight waist. I wondered about her, without quite enough force to ask her who she was and what she did.

The playwright finally came dashing on to the platform twenty minutes late, full of charm and apology. His talk, engaging and funny though it was, blew away from me: I didn't seem to be giving it enough attention. When it was over I moved with her in the crowd to the steps of the Town Hall. Would she like a lift, I asked her: I was going to have a taxi. She said No, quite nicely; not as though she feared assault once we were in it. I watched her as she walked away. I did not expect to see her again.

A week or so later, after a tedious morning in the office, I walked down the Strand at lunch-time and into the National Gallery. This calm echoing hibernation of mute splendour was a perfect antidote to the tuppence-coloured complexities of *Woman in View*: Crivelli's Annunciation and the dusky miracles of Rembrandt put the Calder–King Group well into perspective. I was walking down the long Rubens gallery in search of Mantegna's Agony in the Garden, when I suddenly saw her again.

She was looking at the Château de Steen. She was wearing the same grey coat, and was again hatless. She was lost in the picture. I said 'Hullo,' and she turned and gave me the same warm, sad smile.

She came with me to find the Mantegna. When we found it we discovered also a young man giving a lecture, explaining what was wrong with it. This, I told her, was more than I could take; would she perhaps have lunch with me?

So it began. Not all at once, of course; over lunch I merely began to get her into focus: she worked in Whitehall in a Government Department; she'd worked there for ten years, ever since she left Cambridge. She lived in a one-room flat in South Kensington: at Christmas she went to stay with a married sister: both her parents were dead. I began to build up a picture of a woman, unmarried, self-sufficient: going to lectures and art galleries, drawing from these warmth and stimulation to take the place of love. Or so one supposed. She was not, she said, engaged. I wondered for a moment if she was a Lesbian: there was a mature, casual ease that I had noticed in such women before; the same kind of unfussy good looks. But though she wasn't coy with me, I felt nevertheless an undercurrent of communication, different from the communication where there is no sex.

We met for lunch again, this time on purpose. We sat in a crowded pub near St. Martin's Lane, where I trusted Geoffrey would be unlikely to walk in looking more than ever like my conscience. I asked her about her family, seeming to have a need to establish her in depth. Her father, she said, had been an artist, quite a well-known illustrator; his name was Walter Christian; perhaps I'd heard of him. I hadn't, but she didn't seem to mind. Her mother had worn Pre-Raphaelite dresses and read poetry aloud. 'I was brought up to believe that art was sacred and I should be sinning against the light if I didn't produce some myself. I tried, but nothing came out except a gift for maths which I had to keep quiet about as if it were something rude. I'm left with a huge nostalgia for the whole works—Shakespeare, Mozart, Michelangelo. Mother was a bit bogus, poor dear, but Father was a terribly sweet man; he used to talk for hours about pictures, but without being at all boring; more as if he were describing an adventure. I tried to write poetry to

39

please him, but it wasn't any good.' Her name, she said, was Kate Christian, the sort of name that would do well for a poet, if only she could have been one. As it was she had to use it for signing minutes to her chief at the Treasury.

I had, I said, common ground with her here: the adolescent tangles of *Woman in View* were far removed from my young ambitions: these had been directed towards higher things. This shared concern for the arts gave the beginning of our companionship a feeling of innocence, and its later stages a touch of absurdity. I never mentioned her to Griselda, and indeed at first the whole thing was so high-minded that there seemed no need. I thought sometimes of saying casually, 'I've met rather a nice woman, thirty-ish, works in the Treasury: perhaps we could have her round some time for a drink'; but I put it off, and then it got too late, and there would have been too much to explain.

We began to meet regularly for lunch. This took us through the weeks of that autumn, when there was reflected on the placards of the newspapers, like the gleam from a distant fire, the Italian invasion of Abyssinia. I remember as we walked one evening through the city streets a placard that read simply, WAR. I felt the beginning of dark things. 'It frightens me,' Kate said, taking my arm, 'it's always frightened me. It won't come here, will it? Not again?' Against this threatening sky our meetings shone out with beguiling brightness. She had, she told me, been engaged, broken it off; then had a love affair which ended two years ago. Curiosity and companionship changed to a nagging hunger: I dreamed of her indecorously and often.

The first occasion, though, was an accident. Griselda was out for the evening, and I took Kate to a cinema. Sitting close to her in the warm aphrodisiac dark I couldn't think of anything except how good it would be to see that nice body without its clothes on. The film made no impact at all. My hand blundered towards her and lay on her thigh. After a moment or two she covered my hand with hers and kept it there. By then I was lost in impatience and I muttered while the meaningless nonsense went on moving and dissolving on the screen, 'Darling, please let's go.' She came willingly enough. Out on the pavement I held her arm as though someone had threatened to drag her from me, and said, 'I want to be alone with you—please—please.' She gave the address of her flat to the taxi-driver, and in the taxi I kissed her with an endless blind searching: it was like drowning in her.

Her room, which I was to know so well, on that first time made no impression at all: I was composed of impatience and hunger; wanting nothing but to hold her, acquiescent, receptive, responding. I did badly that first time, hampered by nerves and impatience; in the midst of it all surprised at my good fortune, surprised that Kate Christian whom I had first seen drawing her gloves off in the Town Hall now lay naked in bed with me, pleased with me, not a separate person any more but a body whose warmth and pleasure surrounded me. Clumsy though I was she seemed at the end suddenly adrift in a sea of delight, transformed at my command into a stranger, all that dark hair loosed, her face magnificent and unknown.

I left her that evening exalted, tired, with a thunderous headache (almost the first of them) and a growing guilt about Griselda.

This still stayed with me. I told myself she knew nothing of Kate, had never seen her, never heard of her, couldn't suffer through her. But she was aware of something; she would ask casual questions that had been prepared in advance: my replies were cautious, unsuccessful. The tangle grew deeper, darker, more difficult to cut.

And now Kate, this evening. With the shadow of our brief conversation on the telephone.

But first of all, the other visit. Necessary tonight, and anyway an offering, a placating of the gods.

§

'Is that you, Simon?'

Darkened by long velvet curtains and by the rainy light, the room was obscure: the voice seemed to come from shadows.

'Simon?'

I brushed the rain from my hair and went towards the small figure on the sofa. The face with its familiar distortion was very pale. I said, 'Yes. Hullo, Mother.'

She looked pleased when I kissed her, and put the hand she could use on my arm as I sat down beside her. She said, 'It was so wet I was afraid you might not come.'

'By the look of it we're going to have to go out in worse things than rain.'

'Bombs, dear?'

'Yes,' I said. 'That's why I'm making arrangements to get you out of London.'

'To these people in Devonshire?'

'Yes. Elderly Jewish couple, rich and kind, with a long-standing guilt about being so comfortable, and burning to do something to help. Staff and space: much nicer than here.'

She twitched at the rug on her knees. 'You mean they *want* an old lady of seventy-one who's had a stroke three years ago and might have another? Who can hardly walk at all?'

'Oh, yes. That's the idea. It's a marvellous house: Griselda and I've been down to stay there quite often. Another world. And no bombs.'

'We had bombs last time.'

'These'll be different.'

'Different?'

'More and bigger.'

She gave a little sigh, as if at some foolishness. 'It isn't the bombs I think about; it's the young men.' Her distorted mouth worked a little. 'The idea of them going again: so many of them, and so young.'

'It'll be different; a mechanized war; not as it was.'

'They will be killed just the same. I remember it all so well; sometimes I see Esmond so vividly I can almost hear his voice. David's too. Perhaps, when you're old, the ghosts aren't afraid of you.'

It might be so, I thought. But in this room with its quiet light and Victorian hangings the ghosts were there for me too. I said, 'But you will go? To the country? London'll be very dangerous, you know.'

She sighed and looked towards the streaked window, to the pavement busy with rain. 'Yes, dear, if you say so. But it's a long way. I shall miss you.'

I put my arm round her. 'I'll come and see you.'

'All that way?'

'Yes, of course.'

'I wouldn't know what to do without you.'

She was weeping a little, and as I comforted her, I could not help remembering the past: seeing this in strange perspective.

'And you?' she asked. 'What will you do?'

No point in mentioning the Officers' Emergency Reserve, which sounded like battle. 'Oh, end up doing some dull job at a trestle table, I expect: checking tin mugs or fire hoses.'

She looked at me, handkerchief to her face. 'But how *can* it happen again? How can it?'

'I don't know. Unless you say that it isn't happening again: that the nightmare wasn't over when we thought it was; it's still going on.'

'I don't understand the world any more. It used to be simpler . . . use'n't it? When you were a young man, you and Esmond and your father—all of us at Fennelhurst, before the war?'

And very strong the taste of memory in this London room: the empty lanes and the lifting Downs under the sun. Not twenty-five years in the past, but another world.

I said, 'I dare say it was. Or we thought it was, which comes to the same thing.'

She was still looking across time. 'I never thought it would change, I thought it was going on for ever: I suppose I was very stupid ... well, I was; you can't deny it. I'm a little stupid now, but not so much; the old have a kind of wisdom, it sticks to them in spite of themselves. If I thought about the future at all, I saw you and Esmond making very successful marriages ... even becoming famous in some way.'

I smiled. 'Two very difficult things to do.'

'Is Griselda all right?'

'Yes, I think so.'

'She hasn't got over Prue.'

'No,' I said, ducking my head.

'Such a terrible world,' said my mother. 'Changed and terrible. I wish you still went to church. You used to go when you were young. It would be such a comfort, to have faith.'

'Is it to you?'

'Of course.'

'It wouldn't help me, I'm afraid. I can't see it simply as a harbour: it's such a tremendous thing; if you believe it, your world turns upside down. I don't want my world upside down: I'm too involved with it as it is.'

'I don't understand that. I just believe that in spite of the terrible things—Esmond and Prue and David—we're all God's children. I believe He keeps you coming to see me—'

I patted her hand, and stood up, embarrassed. I took a cheque out of my wallet and put it on the table beside her. 'That's for the next quarter. If it isn't enough, let me know.'

She looked sad as if I'd put some small dead thing in front of her. 'I don't like your doing this.'

I kissed her but said nothing, since it seemed to me that

nearly everything said about money sounded predatory, pious or false, or in some way all three and it was best to leave it alone.

'You're going now?' she asked.

'Yes, I have t-to, I'm afraid.' The small stutter betrayed guilt: the sad room already pressed upon me like a cloud.

'Very well. Turn the wireless on for me: it's friendly in a way, even when it says horrible things.'

'I'll come again tomorrow. If the news is worse we must make final arrangements about getting you out of town.'

'Yes, dear; very well.'

'It will be nice; I promise you.'

She sat there, small and pale, looking towards me as I crossed the room, though I knew that beyond half-way she couldn't see me properly any more, only a blurred shape. I felt a thrust of impotent compassion, a throb of failure. I wanted to cry to the God she believed in, You've given us too much; it's nothing but lies, this talk of your love; you load the world with misery and then tell us to be concerned for it; you tell us to lift the weights, but you've made them too heavy: one can only shrug and turn away.

I went out into the streaming street. The rain ran on to my umbrella with an echo, like the sound of drums. The dusky room still troubled me. As I walked away, hunched awkwardly against the rain, I thought of her sitting quietly there, listening to the cracking of a world.

§

It was only a short way to go. The end of the street, round the corner; another right turn. I galloped into shelter, into the small, modern block of flats. In spite of the bright carpet and the polished look of the front doors, there was something dead about the place, a feeling of a stage set whose play is over, and has indeed not run long enough to inform the place with life. The carpet muffled my steps. Familiar,

45

haunted place: not part of the pattern of home, nor of my mother, nor of the violent headlines: something outside the threatened and crumbling world. I rang the bell.

In the delay before Kate answered it I had time to remember her hesitation on the telephone. I waited. When she opened the door she was already smiling, but at something that had happened before I arrived, not to do with me. She took my hand.

'Hullo, darling; are you soaked? Sorry to keep you on the mat; I was talking to Midge.'

'She isn't *here*?'

'No—no; on the telephone. Saying thank you for last night. A well-brought-up child.'

I had no wish at all to talk about Midge, but Kate went on, 'People are always saying the young are no good, but the ones I've met are perfectly fine.'

I grunted and came into the room. I saw at once that it was in some way different. I looked about me. Blue carpet and white walls; bookshelves and magazines and wireless set; a discreet alcove for the bed: Kate's room. But something different: not so far discovered.

I put my hands on her shoulders and turned her face towards the window. The fine pale skin took on, becomingly, a bloom of light, and her eyes with their calm, candid grey, gleamed marvellously. I stared at her, diverted by this strange arithmetic, whereby the fraction of an inch, making the eyes larger or turning a line of jaw, could achieve the formula of beauty. I told her she looked very pretty, which was an understatement, and took her nice body in my arms. The world of war and *Woman in View* began to fall away.

After a moment or two she took a step from me, a little flushed. I kept hold of her arms, being in no mood now to let her go. Her hair had begun to slip from its austere symmetry as it always did when I made love to her, and this was friendly and exciting at the same time. She put up a

46

hand to pin it back, and I pulled the hand away. 'I like it like that. You know I like it like that.'

She said nothing, but left the hair alone. Somewhere in the room, in her face, in her body was a suggestion of resistance, and this was making me angry and at the same time want her more.

'Come along,' I said, 'come along.' I put my hand through her hair so that it fell away from all its pins. 'What is so nice,' I said, 'is that no one else sees you like this, only me.' Still something puzzling in her face, but through the rising mist in my head, I couldn't see it clearly. I plunged into kissing, as a man drives a car fast in spite of all warning. I said, 'This is the only thing that makes sense. All this. Here and here and here. You and I. Isn't it? Doesn't it?'

She made some sort of answer which I couldn't hear. 'I love it all,' I said. She gave a small sound then, like the whimper she sometimes gave near the end of it, but not quite the same. 'Come along,' I said. The difference in the room no longer worried me, though far off, out of focus, it was still there. Her frock was crumpled now and pulled about: somehow we turned and skidded over on to the chair, and I was clumsy and desperate, all over the place. I was trying to draw my breath and take her as gently as I could to the bed, but then suddenly the little sediment of her resistance dissolved and she began wanting me, and it was the way it had always been, and this was too much for me; she was murmuring and crying into my shoulder, into my neck and I made love to her in the cramped absurdity of the chair, blind and loving and sorry and somewhere still angry at the back of it all.

Bruised, dishevelled and empty, we drew apart. She said nothing at all, though a moment ago her voice had been loud saying my name. The room was beginning to darken and grow cold: she got up and stood for a moment in her stockinged feet with her hair down, looking as if some sort of disaster had hit her, like those pictures of people after an earthquake. Then she went to the gas fire and lit it. She looked thin, crouching over it. The fussy anonymous sound of the flames accompanied our silence. She stayed in front of the fire as if she were praying to it, and then she said, 'I'll go and tidy up.'

It was the first thing she had said since we'd made love. She took her shoes from where they'd fallen and put them on. I grasped her hand as she went by. She smiled faintly, but the whole thing was dead: it was like bad actors doing it.

Later, restored in dress, we sat before the fire with a tray of cold food. Kate sat on the floor with her back against a chair as she always did, and it should have been just the same but it was not. I had pulled the curtains and the room in its tranquil light with the glow of the fire was like all rooms where lovers crouch together, watching the clock. Or it should have been. There was a scent in the room that I didn't remember: as I ate the chicken and salad I was trying to think what it was.

Kate wasn't eating much. So far she had said little: 'Here's a spoon'; 'Help yourself to wine.' Then at last she said, sitting on the floor, looking down into her glass, 'I didn't mean that to happen.'

'Didn't mean what to happen?'

'Our making love.'

'Why the hell not?'

She bent her head farther until I could only see the nape of her neck and her frock which was not fastened all the way up. I wondered if she was crying. She said, 'It's all such a bloody mess.'

I waited. The smell was still troubling me: sweet and reminiscent. I didn't want to bother with it.

'I ought to have said something right away.'

I wasn't liking this at all. I pushed at the food on my plate. 'Said what?'

She curled her legs under her and suddenly looked towards me, her eyes wide, her mouth full and soft where my mouth had been. I said, 'I do love you.'

'Simon . . . oh, Simon.'

She began to cry. I put my hand on her shoulder, knocked my glass of wine over and swore. 'What the hell's the matter? There's nothing to cry about. That was a clumsy business just now, but you enjoyed it and so did I.' I wasn't talking to the point and knew it. She went on crying. Then she turned her head, looking away from me. My eyes followed hers. I saw at once why there was a strange sweet scent in the room. In a shadowed corner a great number of roses spread themselves like a peacock's tail. I looked at them for some moments and said at last, 'I suppose those are a thank you from Midge.'

She was wiping her eyes. I had seldom seen her cry, and part of all this was a different Kate, disordered, unsure of herself.

She said, 'I didn't mean to lie to you.'

'Well?'

'I've met somebody. A man.'

'What a surprise.'

'If you're angry it makes it more difficult. I met him a little while ago.'

'Has he taken you out?'

'Once or twice.'

'Who is he?'

'He's . . . oh, it doesn't matter. He works in another department. He's a widower: his wife died four years ago.'

'I see.'

She looked up at me, her eyes bloodshot, her face marked with tears. 'I think he's in love with me.'

'I make no doubt.'

'You're married. I'm thirty-four. This has all been—'

'Don't let's give a map-reading of what this has been.'

'I don't want to live like this for ever.'

'No.'

'I think, if I go on seeing him, if I go out with him, he'll ask me to marry him.'

'Yes.'

'I want to get married. This talk of war frightens me; I want something to hold on to.'

'Wasn't this something to hold on to?'

'You've got Griselda. And Jeremy. You go back to them. I'm alone here.'

There was no answer, and the pain in my chest might have had something in it of wounded pride. I said, 'Have you slept with him?'

'No.'

'But you're trying to give me the gate? Yes, of course you were, from the moment I telephoned you.'

'It wasn't cut and dried like that. I'd gone over it and over. But all this about a war: I thought of being cut off from you, perhaps never seeing you again. And there was Alec—some kind of certainty.'

'Yes, I see. You should have told me earlier.'

But of course she had told me and blind with desire I hadn't listened: had forced her into the old pattern: those clumsy moments in the armchair came back, like some violent act of duplicity.

She went on, 'And of course, when we made love, it was all the same, I loved you as much: I seem to love you through my body, not only with it. But it isn't any good.'

She was crying again. I said, 'I'm sorry I made love to you. It was a silly way to do it for the last time.'

'Oh, Simon. Simon. Why is it all so bloody difficult?'

Her head was bent to the chair's seat; she was crying loudly, and the tray of supper was an abandoned mess with the spilt wine and the uneaten food. I put my arm across her shoulders, and could not help remembering, as I watched her crying there, the woman who had come into the Town Hall, drawing off her gloves. I said, 'I don't want you to be unhappy. I have loved you very much.' I seemed to be protesting to myself.

'Simon.'

I said some more things to her, but the room was haunted, no longer our place; haunted by the roses, by the image of Alec, whoever the hell he was, by the memory of our last love-making; by the uneaten supper, the difference in it all.

I said good-bye to her. She was dishevelled, marked by tears, having belonged to me, but not any more.

I kissed her. There didn't seem much left to say. I told her that I would always want to know what happened to her, if she was happy; and this seemed to be true.

She hugged me, weeping, exhausted, loving, perhaps a little relieved.

3

Tuesday Night

When I got back to the house it was, as I had expected to
find it the evening before, without light anywhere. As I put
my key in the lock, ducking my head against the rain, I
heard the telephone ringing. The sound drilled through
the dark house, urgent, unanswered. Impatient, I fumbled
with the key. I swore at Mrs. Drayfield, until I remembered
that she had the evening off. At last the lock turned and I
ran into the drawing-room, knocking something noisy on
to the floor as I went. But before I could get to the telephone
the ringing clicked off, and I was left with the tantalizing
silence.

I switched on the light and saw that I'd knocked over a
large vase of flowers. The vase had not broken: there was
just a pool on the carpet and a tangle of chrysanthemums,
bits of petal and bits of leaf. I made no attempt to pick them
up, but stared at the telephone. No need to fret. Most likely
some friend of Griselda's who talked too much asking us out
to dinner on an evening—

Ah. The thought in my mind had been 'on an evening
when I wanted to see Kate'. Difficult to accustom oneself
all at once to absence. Difficult, now that the violent and
sorry scene of this evening was done, for the doubts not to

creep in. Was she, perhaps, bored? Was it true she hadn't slept with him? What about—there was always, after all, somewhere below one's confidence, one's certainty of welcome a trace of humility—what about my limp and the wound in my leg which still showed as a crimson puckering where Alec (whoever he was) had flesh that was most likely unblemished and smooth? In the end you were left in a place of childish doubt, believing nothing, hunched over your mangled pride, your mauled ego, wondering if you'd been loved at all, wondering indeed—and here was the rub—how much you yourself had loved.

As if from the other side of a long and violent play, I remembered my mother sitting in the shadowed room. Disfigured, placid, grateful for the crumbs of company I gave her—was there no choice between the violent manœuvres, the pains and lusts and furious pursuits of middle life, and the sad abandoned twilight of age? She had talked of faith, the retreat, it seemed to me, of those for whom life had no more savour, or for those burned and scarred and too frightened to savour it any more. 'It would be such a comfort,' she had said, but you couldn't, just because your mistress had given you the gate, make a grab at God as if He were a passing bus and you'd been waiting too long in the cold.

'You go back to them,' Kate had said of Griselda and Jeremy, but the emptiness of the house seemed to deny it. I could see Griselda sitting in the stalls at the Haymarket, applauding, pleased, saying the right thing: where Jeremy was I had no idea.

I switched the wireless on to see if we were yet at war, but nothing came through except a dance band playing 'Cheek to Cheek'. I could feel the pain working itself up to concert pitch at the back of my head; the room, uninhabited for the evening had—except for the chrysanthemums—an orderly, alien look: magazines set out as if they were for sale, the cushions plump and prim. No place to bring the wreck and confusion that by now inhabited my mind: I poured myself a drink.

The key in the door. Jeremy? No, the sharp step of high heels.

Griselda.

I looked at the clock. The theatre must have finished early. Too early; I wasn't yet prepared for Griselda: I was only just emerging from the scene with Kate; still entangled in it: struggling to swim clear.

Griselda came into the room. Even the short distance from the taxi to the door had scattered her with rain. She wore a black frock and carried a fur over her arm. I was surprised because when I imagined her in the theatre I had seen her in colour, in the green and gold dress she had worn at dinner last night. In the bright light of the room she looked pale but handsome; mouth and nails brilliant, scent a little too strong: a woman dressed for the theatre.

Her eyes went straight to the fallen flowers. 'Lord, what a mess.'

'Sorry. I knocked it over.'

'Been having a fight?'

'No, I ran in to answer the telephone.'

She lifted her brows, but said nothing. She seemed taut, edgy, not quite in her usual after-theatre mood, which was most often detached but gay, full of a lot of things I didn't much want to hear about, but which rattled on, conveying an impression of impersonal goodwill. Still saying nothing she threw down bag, gloves and fur, and set herself briskly to deal with the flowers. I made some clumsy efforts to help which she ignored. She had the whole thing back in no time, flicked the torn leaves and petals into the waste-paper basket, wiped her hands on a handkerchief.

'Had a good evening?' she asked.

I shrugged. 'I went to see Mother. About moving her from town.'

'Stay long?'

'Not very. I took myself out to have a meal.'

She made a sound of agreement which seemed to say: Yes; what else?

I asked, 'How was the theatre?'

'Oh. . . .' She glanced round for her bag; put the handkerchief back in. 'Well, as a matter of fact the theatre was rather a washout.'

'I'm sorry. Dull?'

'Not so much dull as non-existent: Theresa had one of her bad colds and decided at the last moment that it was too wet to come out.'

'Oh dear.'

'She suggested I took someone else, but it seemed rather mean to do that, so I left the tickets at the theatre in case they could sell them, and spent the evening with her.'

'That was gentlemanly. I hope she didn't give you her cold.'

'I don't think you remember Theresa very well.'

'You mean she's the kind of person who couldn't possibly give you her cold?'

'I don't think you know where she lives now.'

'No, I've no idea.' Though of course it was written in letters the size of my hand.

'She's moved to a house in Broadley Gardens in South Ken, not far from that new block of one-room flats.'

I waited.

She went on, 'Just as I was dashing down the steps into my taxi, I saw you come out of the flats.'

I wondered how long it was since I had experienced an evening so continuously and variously unpleasant. I said, 'Yes, you must have done.'

'Theresa didn't see you: she was lurking in the hall because of her cold. But it made it rather difficult to call after you. Then I got hung up because I'd left my fur in the bedroom. By the time I came out again, you'd gone.' She took a cigarette. I saw that she was trembling. 'I couldn't help wondering, of course, whom you were seeing there.'

I sighed. A lorry went past in the road and the room shivered; I half expected it to crack: the place was fragile, threatened. I said, 'A woman. A friend I've known for some time.'

'I see. Have I met her?'

'No.' I thought of adding, 'No, I don't think so,' but the place I'd come to, ignoble and uncomfortable as it was, seemed to allow only for the truth.

'I see,' she said again. 'I assume you were lovers.'

I was silent.

'I think I've known for some time. Half-known, anyway. Where did you find her?'

'I picked her up in the Town Hall. And then in the National Gallery.'

'Young?'

'Thirty-ish.'

'Very pretty?'

'She was attractive.'

'*Was*,' said Griselda in a light, thin voice. 'Still is, I imagine?'

I sat heavily in a chair. 'I don't know whether you'll believe this, but I'm not going to see her any more.'

'Why not?'

'She's going to be married.'

'But if she hadn't done this, got engaged or whatever it is, you'd have gone on seeing her?'

From this room I could see the other: the secret room, now split wide open. 'Perhaps. But it was getting more difficult.'

'Is that meant to make me feel any better?'

'I don't know. I'm giving you the facts as they are.'

'Not very pretty, are they?'

'No. I'm sorry. But you have them all. There's nothing hidden any more.' (Nothing? Would you like to have the whole thing written out, chapter and verse, for Griselda to read?)

She said, 'When did it start?'

'About three years ago.'

I saw her thinking back. I said, 'It was when you wouldn't sleep with me because of Prue.'

'And so you went out to look for—'

'No; not consciously; it was an accident. I didn't go out for it. Or not at first.'

'D'you call that an excuse?'

'I'm not trying to make excuses. There aren't any, I dare say. I'm sorry you've been hurt. I'm sorry you had to find out now, when the whole thing's done with.'

'With no thanks to you.'

'Well no; chiefly to a Civil Servant called Alec Somebody who sends roses.'

'So you're still jealous of her.'

'Oh . . . yes.'

'Supposing I should say I wanted to leave you?'

'I should ask you with all the power I had to stay.'

'Does that make sense?'

'Perhaps not. I can only give it you, as it is. As I am.'

'For all this to happen because of Prue! As if that wasn't enough—'

I said, 'Ah, no—'

'You won't ever talk about her, but *I'm* going to talk about her! Our daughter, eleven years old; dark and so pretty; d'you remember how pretty she was; you used to rave about her—'

'Please—'

'And she was angry with you because you'd forgotten your promise to take her to the theatre, and you couldn't bear it when she was angry with you. So you spent the whole afternoon telling her about these friends of yours: they had a son of her age and they'd asked her to go on a riding holiday with them. And she was mad on horses. I didn't even know these people; didn't know anything about them, but you said she'd be all right, they'd look after her. You did it to make her love you; you persuaded me against everything I felt, everything I said—'

'Oh, please stop—'

'And she went. I remember packing for her while she ran in and out of the room, talking all the time. And I wasn't happy about it; I told myself not to be silly, but there was a shadow on it and I cried after I'd said good-bye to her. She had a week of it, of the holiday. She wrote and said she was enjoying it, but she was homesick, all the same; I could tell. And then the telephone call came, that terrible call, saying she'd had an accident. And the drive, all the way to Devonshire, not knowing what we were going to find; knowing only that she'd been thrown from the horse, that she was still unconscious. And that ghastly hospital, everyone trying to be kind, but none of it being any good, because they couldn't give us any hope; it only meant waiting; sitting there until it was all over and the whole place was a nightmare, because Prue was dead.'

She was crying loudly now through the words; all the past and all the pain and the shock of this evening came flooding out, and I could feel pain, like an echo in my own heart. In the end I said, 'You know, some day you'll have to forgive me for that—'

'Why should I? Why should I?'

'Because otherwise there's no life.' The words sounded odd; I wasn't certain what they meant.

She stood catching her breath; tear-stained, her hair falling on her face: she had nothing to do any more with the woman who had dressed for the theatre. Stunned with headache, with pity for her, with the whole disaster of this evening, I was aware most strangely of a touch of healing, of some warmth that had not been there before.

§

When we heard the sound of voices in the hall, we scurried into different versions of ourselves. Griselda flew to the looking-glass; I took a cigarette from the box and stood stiffly, as if posing for a photograph. Griselda was putting on lipstick when the door opened.

Jeremy said, 'Ah, both parents,' in a voice that was not quite his own, that was geared to someone behind him in the hall. Griselda turned from the glass, and a dark young man with a silk scarf instead of a tie came into the room, smiled, and said, 'Tony's my name: Tony Clare; I'm most terribly glad to meet you: how d'you do.'

Griselda gave a small polite bleat; I nodded and said nothing at all. The young man continued to smile and look pleased. I was startled that the atmosphere of doom into which he had entered should have made so little impression on him, and even more amazed that this evening which seemed to have been going on for ever, should have more to come.

Jeremy, I thought, unlike his companion, had sniffed the atmosphere well enough: he was walking about the room as though he trod his way through a minefield. Tony had, Jeremy explained, given him a lift home; and Tony, who as he talked revealed a slight stammer, did his best to put us at our ease. 'No I won't have a drink, thanks; oh well, if you insist. . . . I've lived in Brighton all m-my life; I simply adore it, don't you?'

Griselda's violent words about Prue were still in my head: remembering her, I looked at Jeremy. The young fair-headed face echoed his mother's, as Prue's dark-eyed one had echoed mine. I remembered my dreams of him. Did Prue lie at the root of these also? I came out of this to find that Tony Clare was still talking: his voice came through as people's voices do from the next carriage on a long and noisy train journey.

'I believe Jeremy's told you about my project. Travel b-books are usually the end, I know, but I think a young man's point of view is going to be different.'

I said, 'There are an awful lot of young, if you don't mind my saying so.'

'Oh, I know, I know. But they aren't all writers, are they?'

'A lot think they are.'

Tony Clare looked at me with calculation, veiled by charm. He had, it was becoming clear to me, no concern for us; Griselda and I were outside his sphere, too old, not distinguished, not valuable.

'Terribly difficult to explain without sounding madly egotistical, but I just have to say that I f-feel I've got the edge on most of them. I really can be funny—'

'Oh, good,' I said.

He gave this a fleeting, non-attentive smile and went on. 'I'm not an innocent in this business. I've had quite a lot of stuff published and received with good words. Although I say it myself.'

By now, I thought, were I not transfixed with fatigue and the deep embarrassed boredom of listening to someone's self-advertisement, I would have been sorry for Jeremy who was transfixed also in the agonized attention of the young whose chosen friend is making a bad impression in the home.

'Even so,' I said, 'there's the question of war.'

He tossed his head up, as if meeting a familiar challenge. 'Oh, I'm not worried about that. That's all a lot of bluff. There ain't going to b-be no war.'

'I agree,' said Jeremy sulkily.

'That makes two of you,' I said.

I saw them exchange a glance. The young had their own language: one could remember it from far back: children, huddled together like bullocks, bound by the common injustice of being smaller than the authority facing them.

Tony Clare put his glass down. 'I'll have to go,' he said, still charming, still unaware that his charm, as far as Griselda and I were concerned, had died at birth. 'I only d-dropped in for a moment.'

'Are you driving back to Brighton tonight?' Griselda spoke for the first time in a strange social croak.

'Oh—no, no. Staying with friends in town.' He said good-bye to us with a smooth detachment in which there seemed a trace of triumph, as if he'd succeeded in selling us something that wasn't going to work very well. I heard his car roaring off, a noisy young man's sound, arrogant and vainglorious. 'He's gone,' I said more in wonder than anything else, and met Griselda's eyes. In spite of everything, we were for a moment on common ground: Tony Clare was a bad risk, and the sooner he was out of Jeremy's life the better.

Jeremy came back into the room. He looked at his mother as if he were about to ask a question, but she turned away from him, smoothing her hair, and said, 'I'm afraid I don't care for your Tony, darling. Just as well you aren't going on that trip.'

Jeremy swallowed, looked at me, then said, 'Well, I am.'

I said, 'Don't be such an ass.'

'It's all fixed up.'

'It can't be.'

'Well, it is. Tony's going to advance me the money.'

Griselda began, 'That young man—'

'Tony's a great friend of mine.'

I said, 'There's no need to look as if you were defending the Holy Grail. Tony's disadvantages must be as obvious to you as they are to us.'

'You only saw him for ten minutes.'

'Mercifully, yes. You really can't be so silly—'

'There's nothing silly about this. It's an idea, an adventure, something I want to do. You automatically come down on it, just because it's my idea, not your sort of thing, and Tony's my kind of person—'

'Darling, he *can't* be,' said Griselda, near to tears again.

'Well, he is, he's my friend and I like him. If he's not yours, that's just too bad.'

Griselda was beginning to cry, and Jeremy gave her a brooding look. He said, 'I'm only trying to live my own life. Be loyal to my friends. I'm not doing any harm to anyone.'

The trouble with the young, I thought, was that in no time at all they managed to sound like crusaders, leaving their elders floundering in a morass of meanness and compromise.

'And the question of war?' I asked.

'You heard what Tony said—'

'Unfortunately he hasn't the last word on the fate of Europe.'

Bruised, saddened, but still upright against unfair attack, Jeremy said, 'There won't be a war: I'll bet you anything on that.'

I looked at him steadily. My dream came back. There would be a war all right, and Jeremy would be in it; and all this absurdity about travelling round with a smooth-tongued pansy like Tony Clare would be lost in fear when from the battlefield there came no word; lost in grief, perhaps, when word did come.

'And even if there is,' Jeremy went on, 'it'd be exciting, wouldn't it?'

As he said this, the doorbell rang.

'Oh God,' said Griselda, 'there couldn't be anyone else, there really couldn't—'

'A mistake,' I muttered as I went into the hall. 'Someone come to the wrong . . .'

I opened the door on to the rainy dark. At first I thought there was no one there, and knew a moment's apprehension, a twang on exhausted nerves. Then a figure came into the light, and I saw a girl standing there, her dark hair drenched, a macintosh pulled over her shoulders. She held a shabby canvas bag.

'Yes?' I said.

Her face was pale and large-eyed in the sudden light. I had never seen her before.

'Mr. Simon Calder? I'm sorry to worry you so late. I have been trying to telephone you all the evening. My name is Karen Ebert.' The accent was barely traceable; it was just that the words were spoken with care.

('Karen something. Eever, would it be perhaps, Eever?') I said, 'Come in out of the rain.'

In the stronger light of the hall her face was colourless, her eyes bloodshot from the rain. She pushed at her sodden hair. 'You *are* Mr. Simon Calder?'

'Yes.'

'I am sorry to come so late, but I was desperate. I've come a long way.'

I nodded. Money? I wondered. She didn't look as if she were going to ask for it, but you could never tell. I opened the dining-room door saying, 'You'd better come in here; give me your coat—' but just then Jeremy came into the hall, driven, I suppose by curiosity, and Griselda followed him.

So we were all standing there, myself with the dripping macintosh in my hand, when the girl said with a kind of passion, 'I came because I believe you knew my father. I believe you knew him very well.'

Slowly the evening began to flow away; all its long ugly length to twist and slide from me. I stood looking at her, quite still. I began to struggle through to knowledge, buried deep; hear from far back the old sounds, formless as drumbeats, reviving the innocent world. Her face was still lifted to mine, but it was becoming another face, and I was becoming another man walking in a different time.

Part II

Lads, you're wanted. Come and die

Underneath the open sky . . .
Lads, you're wanted.   Come and die.

E. A. MACKINTOSH

1

July, 1914

I was walking along the quiet Sussex road, marvellously un-
encumbered in body and mind, aware simply of the sun,
welcome after the blustery cold, the sound of crickets in the
grass, and the pleasure to which I travelled.

In a letter to his brother, John Keats had once written,
'This day is my Birth Day.' The space in the middle of the
word seemed to me endearing: it put the poet whom I
loved best almost within reach. I pulled a long piece of
grass from the side of the road and swished it through the
air, saying aloud, 'This day is my *Birth* Day. And what's
more, I'm twenty-one.' A bird flew up from the hedge:
beyond this the wide summer day made no response.

I was going where I wanted to go, away from my parents'
house, towards the Rectory. From the doctor's house at one
end of the village on its rising hill, to the other. Already I
could see among the spread summer leaves the square Norman tower of St. Peter's, Fennelhurst, with the yew trees
like a stain on the paler prospect of green.

When I came near to the house I slowed my steps. Pleasure fixed its barrier as well as pain: one was reluctant to
cross into its territory lest the magic should fail. I wandered
idly, as if with no purpose now, glancing at the abundant

roses in the Rectory garden, their petals, wide and open, beginning to fall.

'Simon! Coming to see us?'

I jumped. The old man had risen from behind the hedge like a pheasant. He was short and square: his hair quite grey but thick in head and beard; his steel-rimmed spectacles enlarged his eyes out of proportion to his face, giving him a look of simple moony tenderness which was misleading.

'You want to see David, I expect.' Nothing moony about the voice, which seemed an octave deeper than all other voices: it came from lectern and pulpit like the voice of Authority itself. 'Don't look so startled: I wasn't lying in wait behind the hedge, just gardening. Nothing like digging with a trowel to help one's train of thought. I must recommend it to some of my colleagues. David's wandered off into Yarrow's Field or somewhere to brood about his future.'

'His future?'

'Yes; he has new ideas about it. You'd better go and talk to him.' He waved the trowel and bent again below the hedge. When I had gone a little way he rose again and called, 'Simon! Many happy returns!'

This it seemed to me must have been heard all over the county. I coloured and said, 'Thank you, Rector.'

'And you'd better remind David that his future may be taken out of his hands.'

'You mean a war.'

The wide blue moony eyes were on me. 'Yes.'

'It doesn't seem possible?'

'Death doesn't seem possible on a day like this. But it will come.'

He looked like a prophet standing there, a dark figure, bearded and speaking of the end of things. Then he ducked below the hedge again and I walked on. War? My father maintained that all would turn out for the best: not for the first time the Reverend Harry Birch disagreed with him. War? I felt a catch of excitement in my chest: I had a confused impression of bright uniforms and bugles, David and myself, perhaps on horseback, charging to victory. A coloured dream, a G. H. Henty brought to life and informed with palatable danger.

I wandered on looking for David. Yarrow's Field was a small summit from which one could see the blue sway of the Downs; it seemed to be empty but for the larks, spinning their noise. Then I saw him, lying on his back, arms spread out, face turned to the sun. I called, but he didn't answer. I walked on towards him. The pleasure had found its focus.

§

From the beginning, on that first day when he had fallen down in a lot of horse mess when wearing a white sailor suit for some formal occasion, I had been drawn to his side. I had helped him up, and he had risen, smelling vilely, and given me a smile of great charm. 'Isn't it terrible,' he said, trying to brush himself and making matters worse, 'how these things happen?' He was always falling down or breaking things, smearing his ink or treading on people of authority. All this he accepted with a dignified calm.

At school he found himself alone because the boys didn't know what to make of him. He worked slowly, ably enough, but rather as if his mind were elsewhere. He had a talent for drawing which he did absent-mindedly in the margins of his text-books: mostly animals, occasionally a likeness of a companion, caricatured without malice.

Shy and ungregarious as I was, I bound myself to him, and he welcomed me with engaging, unsurprised affection. Born late to his parents, when they had despaired of children, he was an only son: no twin could have felt himself closer. I had to instruct him in the needful strategy of the world, yet he was wiser than I: one day I would record my pilgrimage. Meanwhile I could bask in a friendship that had survived childhood and adolescence, and the beginning of maturity. If this brought me to the question, should I not now at twenty-one be losing all thought of David, and be obsessed only with girls, I shrugged and turned away.

True, I dreamed and day-dreamed of them, faceless and answering only the needs of my body. But when I met them they were without their magic: too shrill, too silly, too strange. I was at once shy and contemptuous of them; the few scuffling advances I made led nowhere, and I was glad to retreat.

I said, 'David!' being now close beside him. He twitched and suddenly sat up. 'Oh . . . it's you. I was back at school and someone said "*David*" in that voice they always used. What a splendid day for your birthday; must be a good omen. . . . Come and sit down.'

He yawned and stretched himself. His fair hair was darkened with sweat, his face caught by the sun. The nose was short and blunt, his eyes blue like his father's. His length, stretched out on the grass, seemed tremendous, greater than it was. I crouched down beside him and said, 'Your father said you were brooding about your future.'

'Well, I was. Then I went to sleep. It was so quiet and hot. Bees buzzing and things like that. It sends you off.'

'As far as I can remember, practically anything sends you off.'

He grinned. 'Well, I know. All the same, I was awake a lot in the night.'

'I don't believe it.'

'Yes, I was. I was trying to think. Takes time. I didn't get it straight until three.'

'Didn't get what straight?'

'I'm not going on at Oxford.'

Shaken, even appalled, I gave a kind of splutter. 'But you've only got one more year!'

'I know. But I'm just not made for it; not in the way you are. I'm not clever: Latin and Greek seem to me like an enormous maze that I can never find my way out of.'

'You manage them all right.'

'Only just. I'm the despair of my tutors: when I go into their rooms I can see them saying to themselves, "Oh heavens, it's *him* again."'

'They don't—'

'It's your world; you'll get a fine degree and end up as an enormously impressive don, gowned and infallible—'

'Oh, nonsense—'

'Yes, you will. Professor Simon Calder will lecture to-night on . . . I can see it now. But it's all wrong for me.'

'Last term you seemed all right. You didn't say you wanted to go or anything.' I felt aggrieved, left out.

'Well, of course it's a pleasant life. You can't help enjoying it, some of the time. I wasn't even quite sure what was wrong. It only came into focus when I was packing my trunk for the long vac. I suddenly knew I'd give anything not to have to go back again. Not to have to struggle with ink and paper and books for days on end.'

'What d'you want to do, then?'

'I want to be a farmer.'

'A *farmer*?'

'Yes; why not?'

'Don't you have to know a lot of complicated things about crops?'

'I've lived in the country all my life. Crops'll be easier than Greek. I want to grow things, make things; fences and woodsheds: I could always do that. Animals too; I'm at home with them.'

'What does your father say?'

He pulled at a piece of grass. 'Well, I know. That's the awful part, of course. It puts paid to my going into the church, which is what he's always wanted. And yet he wasn't angry at all: he sat looking like God for a bit, you know how he does, and then he said he trusted my decisions to come from the heart, or something like that. I'm not quite sure I know what he meant—I often don't—but I felt rotten and terribly grateful to him at the same time.'

I nodded. 'When I saw him just now he said something about fate taking it out of your hands.'

He grinned, and his mouth turned downwards a little. 'Oh . . . this war-stuff. He's a bit gloomy about it, but I think he must be wrong for once. It doesn't feel like the sort of thing that could happen, somehow.'

Death doesn't seem possible on a day like this. 'And yet it *might*,' I said. 'My father says this business is just one more Balkan scuffle and it'll die down like all the others. And he's usually wrong about everything.'

He was chewing the grass and frowning. I waited for him to speak, but he said nothing. I went on, 'If there is one, I shall try to get into it.' He glanced at me, and a cold finger slid down my back: the words were suddenly larger than my imagining, larger than my courage: the fine dream darkened, and I was afraid. I pursued, quelling doubt, 'It'd be exciting, wouldn't it?'

'I don't know. A war?' He seemed to question the quiet landscape, the lark-lit silence.

'I suppose there'd be horrible things, sometimes. But everything would change; one'd be lost in something much larger than oneself—'

'Is that what you want?'

'Don't you?'

He was leaning on one elbow, still frowning, looking down at the grass. 'No, I don't think so. I like all this. I like sitting here with you. I like being warm in summer and sitting by a fire in winter. I don't expect to be successful: I'd just like to work at something I enjoy, and make enough to keep a wife and children. Grandchildren for the parents: they're always talking about them.' He smiled and threw the bit of grass away. 'A war doesn't seem to have much part in that.'

I sat up, clasping my knees. Beside this statement of strange simplicity I felt myself a tangle of restless strivings, a longing for nameless things, for love, for possession, for fame of some kind, even for glory.

David said, 'Is Juana coming to your party this evening?'

'Juana?' (. . . *enough to keep a wife and children.*) 'Yes, of course; why?'

He scrambled to his feet, brushing himself down. 'Well, it might be a bit awkward. We had a row last night.'

Unmistakable, though not to be revealed: a slight twinge of pleasure. In time I should lose David: I didn't want to lose him yet, and I was afraid of Juana. 'What about?'

'I'm not quite sure. I was talking to her about leaving Oxford, just talking it over, and she suddenly flew into a rage. I do think girls are very odd, don't you?'

I agreed and walked beside him along the quiet path. 'You must have said *something*.'

'I suppose I did . . .' He looked concentrated, perplexed. 'I said I didn't want to make money. And then *she* said what about marriage and a family, and *I* said that would have to wait. And she said it was the most arrogant remark she'd ever heard and I was the worst prig she'd ever met.' He blinked, remembering this; he seemed puzzled by it more than angered.

I said, 'I suppose a mixture of Spaniard and German-Jew is bound to produce something pretty explosive.'

'Mm . . . pretty dazzling too. You're coming back to tea, aren't you? Oh, good.'

But Juana, vivid, it seemed in both our minds, accompanied us and kept us silent.

§

Tea over, David saw me off at the Rectory gate. The tea-table had carried enough food to satisfy an army on the march. When I got up to go, most of it remained. Mrs. Birch, a small fair enthusiastic woman, tore to the kitchen, returned with a large basket and began packing scones and cakes from the table. 'Take these home, Simon: they'll do for tonight, for your party.'

I stood now at the gate. I was a little embarrassed about the basket which, with a white cloth over the top, was reminiscent of Red Riding Hood. David stood looking at it as if in sympathy. 'Poor Mother; she has an idea that so long as there's plenty of homemade food, nothing can go badly wrong. She may be right, of course.' He gave me a pat on the shoulder. 'Go on having a good birthday. See you tonight.'

He turned away abruptly, and for a moment I was puzzled. Then I saw, coming down the tree-shaded lane beside the church, the figure of a girl.

She was fair-haired, dressed in a long cream-coloured skirt and white blouse: in the dazzling light she seemed built entirely of white and gold like an angel in a triptych. When I saw that it was Griselda Sanderson, I thought it would have pleased her to know this. She carried a book in her hand, and her head was down, as if she came away from a disappointment.

I had nicknamed her 'patient Griselda' after Chaucer: she always seemed to be waiting for something in quiet, decorative despair.

She joined me on the road. She looked pretty if despondent, her large eyes green against the pale-coffee coloured skin, her hair shining, drawn into its heavy knot at the nape of her neck.

'Many happy returns, Simon.'

'Thank you.' I shifted the basket to the hand farthest from her, and she began to walk beside me.

'I'm bringing your present tonight.'

74

'Oh, good. Lovely. Thank you.' I was not at my best with Griselda, who seemed to demand a heightened form of response that was beyond me.

She walked farther, then said with her head down, 'Did David see me just now?'

'David? I really don't know.'

'I expect he did. And shot back into the house.'

'Oh, don't be silly.'

'He did.' She seemed near to tears.

'He's awfully absent-minded. He was probably thinking about something else.'

She lifted her head and looked tragically towards the skyline. 'I'm not surprised he runs away from me. When I do see him, I can't think of anything to say. Absolutely nothing at all. I just blush and say yes and no. And yet I can talk to you perfectly easily. It does seem such a shame.'

'Yes, doesn't it,' I said drily.

'I suppose it's because I'm not in love with you.'

'Probably.'

She walked a little farther. 'Does he see a lot of Juana?'

'Why should he?'

'Gracious, my mother and your mother and David's mother hardly ever talk about anything else. How it's unsuitable and all that. Do *you* like her?'

'She's interesting.'

'D'you think she's pretty?'

'Yes, very.' Griselda somehow invited this kind of thrust.

'David did a sketch of her: Mother says he made her look much more beautiful than she was.'

I remembered the sketch. I said, 'H'm.'

'Mother says he'd be much happier with a nice girl of his own race.'

'Meaning you.'

'Well, yes, I suppose so. But it doesn't work out like that. Mother doesn't understand why.'

This seemed probable: Mrs. Sanderson, whose husband

had run off with a barmaid ten years before, now lived in a state of dreamy inattention whose only point of clarity and interest was Griselda. Beyond this, everything was lost in a haze.

'Cousin Geoffrey likes Juana,' she said, still sounding despondent.

'Geoffrey does? I shouldn't have thought she was his type at all.'

'No, you wouldn't, would you? But she seems to be. And I think she rather likes him, if the truth were told—'

'She couldn't—'

'Geoffrey's very good-looking.'

'He's a stick.'

'Well, anyway, he went round to see her soon after lunch, and he hadn't come back by tea-time.'

'Probably wandering in a wood working out an insurance premium.'

'I don't know why you're always so unkind about Geoffrey. He's a nice man, making quite a lot of money.'

'Perhaps that's why.'

We had now come to the small cottage where the Sandersons lived. She said good-bye, adding only, 'David'll be there tonight, won't he?'

Yes, I said, and went on. At twenty-one it did nothing for your pride to walk with a pretty young woman awash with love for another man. What someone ought to say to Griselda, and what I hadn't the courage to say, was that if she wanted David she shouldn't spend so much time on the fringes of the Rectory. Romantic, fatherless, living amongst the hazy inaccuracies of Mrs. Sanderson's vision, Griselda was marked to fall heavily and hopelessly in love. And yet, behind the posing and the poetry books, behind the drooping, 'patient Griselda', I occasionally caught sight of something stronger, a trace, maybe, of the run-away father's more earthy structure.

I had said nothing to her of David's wish to leave Oxford.

She would learn of it sooner or later, and start grooming herself, quite possibly, to be a farmer's wife.

Perhaps he would marry her in the end, after all.

§

As I walked up the path of our own house I could hear voices from the open windows of the drawing-room. The house was Tudor, wide, not tall, a pleasant shape with low windows.

I went into the drawing-room still carrying the basket.

My mother was sitting on the sofa, laughing. Both my father and my elder brother Esmond were standing on either side of her, looking down at her, so that she had the appearance of one holding court. At forty-six she was still very pretty; her hair coppery, scarcely grey at all, her skin fine. Esmond said something I didn't hear, at which she laughed louder, and lifted one hand to take his.

Esmond was twenty-four, a medical student in his final year at Guy's (my father's hospital). He was taller than I and better looking, having chin where I hadn't enough.

My mother's laugh ended on a sigh as she saw me. 'Oh . . . Simon. There you are. Where *have* you been?'

'I went round to the Rectory.'

'Wearing that ghastly jacket; I've told you a hundred times to throw it away; the cuffs are all frayed. And what on earth is that?'

I put the basket down. 'Mrs. Birch sent them.'

Esmond lifted the cloth with mock-care. 'Are they dangerous?'

'Don't be silly, they're tea-cakes.'

My father laughed. His laugh was noisy and sudden, quickly done. He was short, smaller than any of us, even my mother. I think he minded about this; he had a gesture of lifting his chin and stretching his neck; he stood always with

77

his shoulders pulled back, as if on parade. 'What on earth d'you want tea-cakes for?'

'We didn't eat them. Mrs. Birch thought—'

'Very kind of Mrs. Birch,' my mother said, 'but I haven't any idea what to do with them.'

All my embarrassment dissolved; I could now only feel angry that the Birches should be slighted in any way. 'They're homemade,' I said passionately.

'Oh, well . . .' My mother sat back on the sofa. 'Take them along to the kitchen and give them to Daisy. She—'

'Hold on a moment.' My father took the whisky decanter from a cupboard. 'Don't have twenty-first birthdays every day of the week. Time for a drink.'

'James, it's only half past five!'

'Never mind, never mind. It's a fine day. And Simon's come of age.'

I perceived here an effort to get on to terms with me, the son with whom he was so often at odds, for whose chosen world of dons and ancient colleges he had no sympathy; for whose careless dress, unpressed trousers and bulging pockets he had the sharp recoil of a sergeant-major.

I watched the level of dangerous amber stuff rise to a surprising height in the glass. 'Not time for you two lads to start yet,' he said. 'Only old men like me have this kind of privilege. Especially when they're worn out with their patients. Happy birthday, Simon.'

'Thank you,' I said. 'Which patients?'

'Old Louis Meyers, for one. Don't get on with Jews, never did. Don't like his house. If it weren't for his granddaughter —what's her name? Juana—the whole place would be too depressing for words. The old boy rambled on about a war; said it was bound to come, and nothing'd ever be the same again. Lot of nonsense, of course. I didn't argue with him: always agree with my heart-cases; no point in asking for trouble.'

'Is he very ill?' I asked.

My father shrugged. 'Oh, I'd give him a year or two. Not much more. Long enough to know he was wrong about a war. What's the view at Guy's, Esmond?'

'Well, rumours fly about, you know. Some of our chaps are joining the R.A.M.C., and there's emergency planning for the wounded.'

At the word 'wounded' my mother looked up as if some strange bird had flown in through the window. My father shook his head. 'Painting devils on walls.'

Esmond took a pipe from his pocket. 'And Austria's declaration of war?'

'Nothing to do with us.'

'If Russia backs Serbia—?'

'Let them. We can still keep clear.'

'Mm,' said Esmond. 'Well, let's hope so.'

'But there couldn't be a war for us,' my mother said. 'We haven't a quarrel with anyone: why on earth should we fight?'

'Mm,' said Esmond again. 'My experience is that one finds oneself doing things in this life not for any reason but because someone's told you you must. What does younger brother think about it all?'

I put my hands in the tired pockets of my coat. 'If it does come, I'm going to join up.'

My father said, 'Come now; there's no need to talk like that'; my mother was looking at me as if I'd just said something in Arabic. Then she turned to Esmond. 'You wouldn't have to go, would you? You'd stay at the hospital looking after the wounded: doctors would be needed—'

Esmond drew at his pipe. 'Oh, I don't know. Perhaps. All the same, I don't quite see myself standing on the pavement's edge waving a flag while younger brother marches off to war.'

Nobody said anything. I picked up the basket and went to find Daisy in the kitchen.

§

All the windows were open to the warm night. Esmond was at the piano; his dark hair fell over his forehead, and he looked as if he were enjoying himself. So did my mother, having forgotten the small improbable menace stirred in her heart earlier on: she looked gay and pretty, light gleaming on the coppery hair.

'Two sons and both of them come of age,' she said, leaning back with a contented sigh. 'Now I really can't pretend to be young any more.'

The Rector gave her a glance through the distorting spectacles and said, 'Only a woman who knows that she can, Mrs. Calder, makes a remark like that.'

'Rector, you're always so kind to me—isn't he, James?'

'He's a sensible man who knows what to say to a beautiful woman.' This was slightly blurred; my father leaned unsteadily over the sofa. The Rector glanced at him with a kind of reasoned speculation.

Not quite comfortable in the unaccustomed symmetry of my best suit, I carried the jug of wine cup round the room. I filled David's glass. He was leaning on the piano talking to Esmond; every now and again his eyes went to the door.

No, she hadn't come yet. Juana was late, and David was anxious. Strangely anxious for someone who moved as a rule so placidly through the currents of desire and fear. I felt in the midst of it all the touch of unwanted discovery.

Holding the jug in abeyance, I brooded about it. Juana Meyers, eighteen and lately returned from finishing school, lived with her grandfather, Louis Meyers, in a gloomy but luxurious house, a mile from the village. A naturalized Englishman, he had never lost his German accent, but Juana, the daughter of a German–Jewish father and a Spanish mother, now both dead, spoke in the accents of her English nannies and governesses. This was the only point at which she resembled them: she blazed into Fennelhurst, alien and exotic: my father called her the bird of paradise. Very dark, she seemed to be electrically charged:

her hair sprang in twisty vigorous curls, and her wide brown eyes had always a pin-point of light in them. Her smile broke the brown-skinned face into a sudden gleam of white teeth and a look of exhilaration; nobody else in Fennelhurst smiled quite like that. Nor flew into such sudden passions either: 'That girl,' my mother said with an edge to her voice, 'has yet to learn self-control.' 'Yes, she has, hasn't she,' said my father, but more as if he didn't want her to learn it: Juana's powerful allure was evident to every man, even me.

'Simon!' Griselda's mother, Mrs. Sanderson. I went reluctantly towards her. She had Griselda's large green eyes, but her face was too solemn and her nose always a little red. Her dress worn loose and straight to the ankles suggested that she might be going to recite. I thought I could understand why her husband had gone off with the barmaid.

She said, 'What can have happened to them? Geoffrey and Juana? He went to call for her ages ago. There couldn't have been an accident, surely?' Mrs. Sanderson was over-ready to suspect accidents: I said I didn't think so. 'No . . .' she agreed. 'I suppose the girl's taking far too long, dressing herself up. Not like Griselda. But of course Griselda looks lovely—doesn't she?—without having to do anything . . . careful, Simon, you're going to pour that wine cup into my lap.'

'Sorry.'

'See how lovely she looks now!'

I glanced towards Griselda, who'd got into conversation with my father and was leaning nervously away from him; when he was in his cups (and he seemed to be in them now) my father loomed towards young women like a hot predatory sun.

'What I can't help feeling—' Mrs. Sanderson was now turned to David's mother who sat beside her—'is that it would be such a splendid thing . . . Griselda and David . . . if only . . . don't you think?'

'Oh yes, splendid,' said Mrs. Birch absently, looking towards her son. She was fair like him, but her eyes were grey, not blue; she was serene, practical; proud of her husband, whose intelligence she did not pretend to match; most proud of her son, born so late in life; an answer to prayer; a gift from God. I did not feel that she wanted him to marry Griselda.

'She'd make such a wonderful parson's wife,' Mrs Sanderson was saying. I heard Mrs. Birch begin to explain that David wasn't going to be a parson; I carried the wine cup over to him.

As I did so, I heard through the noise in the room, the clatter of hooves and the turn of wheels from the road outside. My hand twitched and I spilled some of the wine on the polished top of the piano. 'Bad luck,' said David and wiped it with his handkerchief. I saw with misgiving that his fingers shook a little.

Juana came in first. Her dress of white silk seemed to be sliding from smooth brown shoulders and over her strong breasts. When one looked at Juana, one was more conscious of her body than of her clothes: it seemed to resent the decorous covering, striving to be admired in its own right. She lifted the skirt from the floor with one hand; she was strangely unsmiling.

Her grandfather came behind her. He was small, bent forward; his face with the large curved nose almost colourless, but for a shadow of deep blue on his temples and about his eyes. *I'd give him a year or two. Not much more.* The dark promise isolated him. He wore, as always, his look of patient indestructible grief.

Geoffrey came last. He alone was smiling; a good-looking young man with smooth hair, on terms with the world. My mother rose to greet them, and in the tangle of welcome, apology and reassurance, I noticed the sharp little appraising look which she gave Juana: the envy for someone beautiful, with so much time.

'Congratulations, Simon. A present for you. No, it is nothing.' Louis Meyers handed me a small box; the thickly accented voice commanded a silence in the room. Within this I opened the box and found the gold and onyx cuff links gleaming on satin, adult, satisfying, part of this day of division.

He sat down beside the Rector. He sat down slowly, like a tired man; I felt pleased and flattered that he had made the effort to come. The threat on him gave to the cuff links in my hand a poignancy; I was aware of new distances, another order of time. Death, at twenty-one so dim a stranger, for a moment moved in the room.

I lingered near him. I heard him say, 'If war comes I do not vant the girl to suffer because of her name. I t'ink on the whole what has happened is a good t'ing.' The Rector nodded, but he said nothing, and his eyes went to his son.

I wondered exactly what had happened, but they seemed to be enclosed together within an adult conclave, and I hadn't the courage to intrude. I tried to listen further, but Geoffrey came and asked me if I were enjoying myself. He sounded avuncular, a little patronizing: he worked in his father's firm, an insurance office in Cornhill, and spent frequent week-ends with his aunt, Griselda's mother, bringing with him a touch of alien sophistication.

I said I was. 'You look as if you were, too.'

'Oh I am, young Simon, I am.' He went on smiling.

'So you don't take the war-talk seriously?'

'Oh, Lord no. Not as far as we're concerned. There may be a bit of excitement in Europe: you know what these foreigners are. But not us, old boy, not us.'

'Good. It's nice to know for certain.'

He allowed the small sarcasm to go unheeded, and asked me what I was going to do with my future.

'Well,' I said, 'now that "peace proclaims olives of endless age"—'

'I beg your pardon?'

'Shakespeare,' I said, willing to show off, 'the sonnets. If I get a good enough degree I shall go back to Oxford and teach.'

'Ah, the quiet academic life. Just right for you, I should imagine. Our paths lie far apart. I should find it too slow, too cut off. I like to feel I'm at the front of things.'

'It depends,' I began, but did not finish the sentence, because I suddenly saw that Juana and David were talking together. She was talking fast and passionately, and he was listening with his head down, not looking at her. I said, since Geoffrey seemed to be waiting for me to say something, 'Juana looks very pretty.'

'Juana looks—magnificent,' he said, and at that moment she turned abruptly away from David, leaving him alone.

He glanced up, meeting my eyes. With no further word to Geoffrey, I went over to him. He gave a small smile. 'Hullo, Simon. Any reason why we shouldn't take the air for a moment or two? In the garden?'

I said, 'None at all,' and led him from the house.

Here in the garden there was darkness, a soft quiet; the scents of summer. The lighted room was instantly strange, its sound diminished, a small companionable place seen from the wide loneliness outside. We walked a little way into the quiet, and then David said, 'Juana is engaged to Geoffrey; did you know?'

I stood still. 'She *can't* be.'

'She's just told me so. That's why they were late.'

I saw it all fitting into place. I sought for words as we walked on. 'But she can't be in love with him. Nobody could be in love with Geoffrey, except Geoffrey.'

He said, 'Women. . . .'

We had reached the end of the garden. The sky was rich with stars; I could smell the earth, and feel all about me a mystery, heightened by Esmond's playing 'Get out and get under' at a distance in the lighted room.

The mystery contained the thought of Louis Meyers, with

his shortened prospect of life. I said, 'Are you so fond of her, then?'

'I suppose so.'

'She wouldn't have been right for you.'

'Who can tell that?'

No one, of course; but I pursued it. 'She's too wild, unpredictable; there'd always be a crisis of some kind; you'd get fed up with it—'

'Perhaps.'

'You wanted to marry her?'

'Oh yes. Yes, that's what I wanted to do. But of course I haven't the money, and I made things worse last night by saying marriage would have to wait. Silly to say that, wasn't it; if you'd been there you'd've stopped me. I ought to take you everywhere like a talisman. As it is, I've lost her.'

I felt strongly, standing there beside him, the communication of his unhappiness. I said, 'There'll be other people. Griselda's very fond of you.'

He smiled and said, 'Poor Griselda.' And that was that. 'There's this talk of war.'

He said on a sigh, 'Yes . . . One could be a soldier, of course. Perhaps I shall. Nothing but men about one, except for some free-loving village girls: out and away, following the drum and the flag . . . But of course, it wouldn't be like that.'

'We don't know what it would be like.'

'And yet one has an idea, a kind of shadow at the corner of one's mind . . .'

'It'd be an adventure.'

'I suppose it would.'

'You'd forget Juana.'

'Yes . . . perhaps.'

We stood for a moment longer in the dusky garden, in the wide beneficent silence.

§

As we came back into the room, I saw Juana, anxiously waiting for us. She manœuvred me into a corner. 'Is David very angry with me?'

'No, I don't think so.'

'Wasn't he talking about me just now?'

'We were discussing the war.'

She looked dubiously at me. I said, 'If you're going to marry Geoffrey, I don't see that it matters whether David talks about you or not.'

'I don't understand him. You think he's fond of you, then he suddenly goes away into a place with walls a foot thick. And you'd do anything to blow it up, but you can't.'

'You have to wait for him to come out.'

'I don't like waiting.'

'Then you'd be no good for David.'

She looked distressed; there might have been tears in her eyes. 'I suppose he'll marry that droopy girl with fair hair.'

'Yes; very probably.'

'You've never liked me, have you?'

'I hardly know you. I think you're very pretty.'

'It's David you like.'

'We've been friends for years.'

'Yes, but you love him, don't you? And you were jealous of me?'

'Not in the least; just perfectly clear you wouldn't have made him happy.'

Now it was plain that she was crying; I felt misgivings moving about at some depth beneath this childish bickering.

She said, 'Grandfather's glad I'm going to marry Geoffrey. He wants me to be safe: he says he's old, and he wants someone to look after me.'

I said I thought she could look after herself.

'He thinks there'll be war.'

I looked across at old Louis Meyer's clown-pale Jewish

face. Juana went on, 'He says it will be sad for him, because of Germany.'

'But he's English now.'

'Our name is German. He says it may be difficult, with a German name.'

A touch of difference, of territory half-guessed at. She said, 'I want to be safe, too.'

'*You?*'

'My mother died when I was born. My father was killed a year afterwards. My grandfather is old; he is a German-Jew who talks like a foreigner.' She was looking at him as she spoke, and her face had softened; she was looking at someone loved. *A year or two, not much more.* 'He says the world is cruel to strangers. And the Jews are strangers.'

I had not before thought of her as someone to be protected. I had looked on her as an enemy; now I saw for the first time that there were no enemies, only people insufficiently known. Before I could say more, my father came noisily towards her, glass in hand. 'What's all this I hear about your being engaged, m'dear? Permission to kiss the bride? Yes, I think so.'

She changed instantly, becoming flirtatious again. My father kissed and squeezed her; I caught sight of my mother's face, for a moment disdainful, as if an assistant had been rude to her in a shop.

Juana turned to the Rector who stood close to her. He said, 'Congratulations, my dear.'

She said merely, 'Thank you,' but her eyes were on him, as if she sought reassurance, or forgiveness, perhaps. His face, bearded and patriarchal, looked on her with kindness, from some distance of wisdom. 'I wish you great happiness now, and in all the years to come.'

The rather stilted words lifted a little shutter in my mind, and for a moment I saw Juana middle-aged, a plump contented woman with children as old as we were now; satisfied, protected, the magic gone.

Then I heard a sharp knocking; someone was rapping on wood. Gradually the room became quiet, and the Rector said into the silence, 'I've been asked to propose the toast. This I most gladly do.'

He gave me a smile then, of great sweetness, and for a moment I wanted nothing more but to love and follow him, live in the difficult climate of his severe yet loving vision.

'As you get older, you find, when you see a young man come of age, two things. You have the tenderness of a father for him: and you have a fear. The fear is not so much for his mistakes and failures, for which we trust God in His mercy will forgive him, but for the harsh places in which his road may take him: places where he may seem to go in darkness and lose that faith which must—if we are to look on the world as sane men—be the only basis of life, the only justification for all things, the only true angle from which to look on the world, and the things beyond the world.'

The room was silent. There was, it seemed to me, none of the embarrassment usually attending speeches in a small room. The silence was like the silence of a truce: as if everyone had laid down his desires, passions, hates and jealousies, and was listening.

'As I drink to Simon now, I cannot put away from my mind that this is a threatened hour, a dangerous time to be young. But I am not going to dwell on this; there are sane men in the world, and the armies have not yet moved. Simon, whom we have loved since he was a child, is twenty-one. We drink to him, and wish him all goodness, and pray that over his future and over the whole world, sanity and peace may prevail.'

Then their voices came saying, 'Simon!' and they were all lifting their glasses. I felt confused, longing to express a love which was filling my chest and lungs, yet without words. It was a love which had nostalgia in it for that which was already lost, for an integrity which it seemed I already knew I should fail. I could see them all in the room, raising their glasses: David and Griselda, Geoffrey, Juana, old Louis Meyers, Mother, Father, Esmond, Mrs. Sanderson, Mrs. Birch, and the Rector himself, all of them given to me, promising all things for me, promising too much. Moved and shaken I said inadequately that I was grateful, and then Esmond started playing 'For He's a Jolly Good Fellow'. My mother came and kissed me, and my father shook my hand. The music and voices were loud, but from the open window a little of the darkness and silence seemed to drift into the room.

§

All Europe Arming. First Shots in Belgrade. On Thursday our newspaper showed for the first time its headlines in heavy type, and this typographical strangeness seemed to carry its own alarm: my heart beat as I read, 'The danger to the peace of Europe has not diminished in the past twenty-four hours. . . . On all sides the Powers are arming on a stupendous scale.'

The skies grew warmer. Esmond went back to his hospital; he would be with us again, he said, on Sunday of the Bank Holiday. My father grew more taciturn as the nations seemed to be proving him wrong, and my mother lost a little of her shine as she always did when Esmond wasn't there. Waiting, anxious for news, we were all restless. Rumours slipped through the village like strange cats; the bright day had within itself the darkness of a monstrous fairy tale, in which, though one feared it, one could not quite believe.

On Friday the headlines were the darkest yet: *Europe Drifting to Disaster; Belgrade in Flames.* As my father sat down to the breakfast-table I said, 'The Russians are mobilizing.'

'Damn fools.'

'We're taking precautionary measures.'

'Good thing too.' But he rattled one hand on the table while he drank his coffee and barked at my mother when she made tentative little enquiries as to what was going to happen to us all.

'In the event of a general conflagration,' I read from the paper, 'this country cannot in its most vital interests ever stand out.'

'No need to frighten your mother, Simon; these newspaper chaps make the best of everything. We're still on this side of the Channel, and likely to remain there.'

Doubt stayed on my mother's face. 'They say such dreadful things. . . .'

'Exaggerated. War between Russia and the Triple Alliance needn't involve us. And even if it does, Russia will probably finish the whole thing off before we've begun to fight.'

'That seems only fair,' my mother said; 'there're so many Russians, aren't there?'

When my father and I were alone in the room I said, 'I've quite made up my mind. If there's a war, I'm going.' (Was it easier to say this now that Oxford would be empty of David? Perhaps.) My father looked at me across the table. The sun lay brightly on the spread newspaper and the dark headlines. 'Odd to think of you as a soldier.'

Stung, I said that this would be true of a lot of men, presumably.

'Maybe. Have to smarten yourself up a bit; no time for poetry and all that on the barrack square . . . come, come, don't look so sulky, I was only teasing you. I expect you'll do very well. I'll write to old Colonel Mander; get you recommended for a commission.'

'I'd rather enlist. That's what David's going to do. In the Artists' Rifles.'

'Oh, don't be an ass. What on earth's the good of turning down the privileges of an officer when you can have them for the asking?'

'I'm not looking for privileges.'

'Of course you are: everyone is. We'll get you a commission, and we'll do our best to keep Esmond at the hospital.' He brushed at some crumbs on the cloth. 'You must do all you can to persuade him.'

'Why?'

He gave a small turn of his head, as if to see that the door was shut. It occurred to me that his confident assertions of peace were not quite the truth of him. 'It's a question of your mother. What I mean is, old chap, I don't doubt —even if this ghastly thing happens—that you'll come through all right. It can't last long—six months, if that: Germany can't afford longer.'

'Well?'

'Doctors'll be needed at home. Get this into his head. Then whatever anxieties your mother has about you, she'll know that Esmond is safe.'

He looked at me across the table. The strong light showed clearly the puckered lines about his eyes, the reddish blurring of skin: scars of middle-age, of whisky, of sadnesses unguessed at. For a moment, having youth, I was the stronger and able to pity.

'All right,' I said, 'I'll do what I can.'

§

That evening I had dinner at Louis Meyers's house with Geoffrey and Juana. The house had the bleak, impersonal costliness of an exhibition: the chairs might have been contained by ropes preventing you from sitting down in them. Long green curtains hung at the windows, and the rooms seemed full of an aqueous light. The dinner, though splendid with salmon and wine, had a shadow on it.

'Oh yes, there vill be a war, and it vill bring great anguish to all. To all,' Louis Meyers said, filling our glasses with pale wine. After that it was difficult to be gay. Indeed, gaiety had seemed missing from the first: Juana was constrained, on her best behaviour; Geoffrey was acting the part of a lucky young man who has won the girl of his choice, but did not seem quite to be it. Overawed by the luxury, and the sad alien dignity of my host, I was not at ease, talking with care, hearing my own voice.

The evening only came alive when Juana lost her temper.

Mrs. Corham, the housekeeper, shopping in the village, had met with trouble. The greengrocer had said something about 'the Germans you work for'. 'And she came home *crying*,' Juana said; 'nice, sweet Mrs. Corham, *crying*. I wanted to go straight down and tell the greengrocer what I thought of him, but Grandfather wouldn't let me; he said it would only make things worse. But can you imagine anything more filthy and horrible? If anyone says it to me I shall hit them.' Her grandfather was shaking his head. 'Yes I shall. Why not? If people are cruel and stupid they deserve everything they get. And they're going to get it from me, whether they like it or not.' She was flushed with anger, perhaps with wine; a dark twist of hair had fallen on her forehead; her hands trembled. Geoffrey was looking at her . . . with disapproval? No, I thought; more as if he were calculating something.

'Injustice is part of the world, my dear.' The sunken, heavy-lidded eyes had a sorrowing wisdom. 'You vill have to learn that, to accept it. Othervise you beat your head against a vall until your strength is gone.'

For a moment they faced each other, the old man and the girl; he in acceptance, she in rebellion. Then she turned away, sudden tears in her eyes.

I felt the pressure of disturbing things: even now, within our own homes the prospect of war seemed not to be real: but here in this house it was true, and the world shifted, nothing certain any more.

It was still light when I left the house. Geoffrey stayed behind; I walked alone. The stretching fields were quiet, having here and there amongst their shadow a warm gleam from the fallen sun. I was glad to be out in the air, away from the house with its uncomfortable trace of sorrow. My head sang a little with unaccustomed wine; the warm evening silence seemed to wait the rise of a vast curtain.

Suddenly I saw a figure moving ahead of me. A woman, walking with her head down: Griselda. Drifting about the silent roads like an unquiet spirit. She turned as she heard my step.

'Oh . . . Simon. I thought for a moment . . . Did you enjoy your dinner?'

'I don't know if enjoy's the word. The house smelled of doom; and Geoffrey seemed totally out of place, like a modern-dress actor caught up in *Hamlet*.'

'Have you had too much to drink?'

'No, I don't think so. I've just got a sort of post-prandial euphoria.'

'I wanted to ask you something, but it's no good if you're like that.'

'I'm not like anything; just enjoying the walk home. All the better now I've met you.'

'Oh, don't be silly. I wanted to ask you something serious.'

'I'm serious,' I said. 'I'm terribly serious. I'm the Mass in B Minor and *War and Peace* and the Book of Common Prayer: I'm all the serious things rolled into one.'

She walked in silence.

'I was joking,' I said.

Her voice came, muffled. 'Mrs. Birch told Mother that if there's a war David's going to go to it.'

She made it sound like a fancy-dress ball. I said, 'I think he is.'

'Can't you stop him?'

I met squarely the thought that I didn't want to stop him. I said, 'He'll do what he wants to do.'

'I can't bear it if he goes.'

93

'It won't last long.'

'People can get killed however short a time it lasts.'

'Perhaps there won't be a war after all.'

She turned her face up. 'Wouldn't it be wonderful? Then David would stay here, and with Juana out of the way he might get to like me.'

I remembered David saying 'Poor Griselda'. I swam now in compassion: for Griselda, so loving and unregarded; for the whole of humanity, bruising its heart on the stones of life. I patted her shoulder; it felt slight and vulnerable under my hand. 'He'll like you,' I said. '*Everyone* will like you; you're a very sweet girl.'

We were walking now on the path that led across the fields. Tall trees shadowed us. The sky still had a lemon light, and here and there the undersides of the leaves were touched with it as if with a golden rime. We sat down on the bank, and against the fading light the midges hung a grey murmuring veil. Griselda said, 'Is he very unhappy about Juana?'

'He's hurt.'

'We're all hurt. It's that kind of world.'

'It's a splendid world.'

'And what's more, I'm awful. Because I'd rather he went to war than married Juana.'

I was startled to have my own thought so handed back to me. 'That's only natural.'

'No, it's not. It's perfectly horrible.'

'Perfectly horrible things are.'

She turned to look at me. We sat in a warm green shadow with the land darkening about us and the sky still pale. In the shadow her eyes were large, the colour of the shadow itself. I put my hand on her waist, bent and kissed her. She made no movement away, and I began to twist her body closer to me. For a moment she was with me, stretched against me while I sought her mouth, and the green bank and the trees spun away as my heart beat. Then she made a furious movement, a wild impatient muscular struggling, such as children make when you try to embrace them when they are not inclined.

I let her go and she sat up angrily, smoothing her hair, pulling at her dress. Then she got to her feet, stumbling a little as she caught her heel in her skirt. I stood up beside her. She looked at me. There were tears in her eyes and her mouth trembled.

I said, 'I'm sorry.'

'I didn't like that.'

'I'm sorry.'

'I don't like being kissed by men who don't care about me.'

With this she turned away. The words had an absurd dignity: it was difficult to believe that Griselda at seventeen had much experience of being kissed by anyone.

When she had gone I flung myself down on the bank where we had lain. Stirred by the brief encounter, I was unsatisfied, hungry, restless. I wanted everything and nothing; I wanted to possess, to enjoy, to be king of some territory as yet undiscovered: I wanted to be supine, receptive, letting the world roll over me. All I knew was that I seemed insufficient unto myself: that not only my body but my soul and spirit were incomplete without some other close to me whom I loved.

I turned, restless as a sleeper on a hard bed. I thought of David. Roused and unsatisfied, I thought of him with love, and the love seemed a heavy thing, dangerous, without hope, denied everywhere; for me the essence of myself. I was divided, without certainty, wanting the integrity of David's father as he drank my health, and wanting also a love that I could not have told him of. I stayed there while the colour ran out of the world.

§

In the blowy sunshine of that Sunday we all went to church. A copy of the *Observer* which had fought its way down to us in spite of confusion on the railways announced that 'The nations sit in the darkness of the eclipse and wait for the storm of destruction . . . they await a horror without a name'. Did we so, I wondered, as we went towards the ancient square-towered church on its height? My father had the appearance, as he always did at a quarter to eleven on Sundays, of a brave man going unarmed amongst hostile tribes; my mother looked charming in a large hat and carrying a parasol; Esmond had the gay good-humour of a young man who is perfectly willing to pray if it'll make everyone happy. David too; he had said to me once, 'I think God exists, but if He really enjoys Matins He must be even farther away from me than I've always imagined.' But when I listened to David's father, when I knelt in the small church with about me the stone traces of the centuries, when at early service the words of the Communion were interwoven with the lowing of cows from the fields, I believed it all: I was suddenly at home, knowing not with my intelligence but with some deeper instinct that only with this dimension did the world make sense to me.

The church was full, and the moment I stepped, last of the family, from the warmth of the day into the quiet cool crowded shadow, I felt the question there, the dumb acknowledgement that one sees in cattle when they huddle against a wall before the storm comes. War, being woven of death, was a mystery, and faced with a mystery one sought the answer here.

When the Rector climbed into the pulpit, I thought that my father was already asleep: he had a military way of sleeping, upright, with his eyes tight shut. My mother had her head on one side, as if she expected the sermon to be in some way a compliment.

This it in no way was, not to any of us.

It was possible, the Rector said, though today the church

was crowded, in a short time it might be empty: not because the men and women had all vanished, but because they were boycotting him.

My father woke with a sudden little twitch as the resonant voice boomed these words, and my mother pulled nervously at her gloves.

'Because,' the Rector said, 'if war comes—and it seems now that it must—the danger, greater even than the danger to the flesh, will be that we gradually become strangers to ourselves, to the vision which we know to be the truth of us, to the sanity of men who see the world, not from the egotism of immaturity, but from the wide, upland prospect of reason and charity.' We would become, he said, gradually swept away by a current of false hatreds, easy self-justifications, blinded loyalties; we would become the inhabitants of a smaller world, from which the one quality essential to life was being excluded. And that quality was love. This we were in the gravest danger of losing, and the danger was at its greatest, here at home.

'Yes, at home,' he said. 'Because the soldier, whatever pains and terrors surround him, is strangely in less danger from this loss of love, because when men live cheek by jowl with death, they see the truth of things. Even amongst pain and death, he can say, having love, we are more than conquerors.'

When he paused, he looked tired, and the blue distorted eyes seemed to be gazing out over horizons irrecoverably lost.

Without gesture, only leaning a little way over the pulpit, as if he tried to get nearer to us, he wove the pattern of his sermon on this theme, returning always to the threat that lay over us, greater than the threat of war.

'There's only one way, of course, to resist the tide of hatred which threatens to overcome the world, and that is to be conscious always of that deeper level of existence where we can none of us sit in judgement on the other because we are all members, one of another: and the condition of that level is love. In the name of the Father . . .'

As he came down from the pulpit, peering short-sightedly, he looked as though he had little hope that the world would hear him. He knelt in his stall, head down on his arms, like a man who asks forgiveness for failure.

§

The crowds were thickest in Whitehall. The noon light gave the scene a curious starkness; the great buildings stood with shortened shadow while the people in summer clothes waited for news, for the end of their habitual world, for the unknown. The pallor of dress, light frocks on the women, white shirts on the men, made the prospect of war loom strangely: had all these people, dressed for fine weather, come to the Dark Tower?

On the morning of this Tuesday—decreed a second holiday—I had brought David with me to London. Excitement and rumours: the organ notes of the leader-writers—'The shadow of an immense catastrophe broods over Europe: a new twilight of the gods is upon the world'—made it impossible to stay in Fennelhurst where the lanes were quiet.

Look, I kept saying to him, look: a lieutenant-colonel in khaki, going with rapid authority into the War Office; look, the Horse Guards are in khaki too, dressed for action: everything is changed. He turned his head, smiled, came with me in friendly obedience; remained inattentive. Last night he had seen Juana, and her shadow was on him. What did she say, I asked. 'Oh . . . nothing. How people talk when they see you off at stations.' The foot-thick walls again; himself gone behind them. I was like a parent who drags a half-unwilling child to a fairground, pointing, exclaiming, ineffective.

The crowds and the newsboy running. The surge of people

towards him; the ha'pennies falling to the pavement: *Belgium refuses German Ultimatum: King of the Belgians appeals to King George for aid.* See how the tide comes up, how the enormous and terrible things grow in the sun. . . .

Yes, I see.

And we shall be part of it; as young men we shall go into battle; and you will be with me; come along, come along—Behind the drum and fife, Past hawthornwood and hollow, Through earth and out of life The soldiers follow. . . .

Very well, I'll come.

We shall be together and you'll forget it all, forget Juana, forget loving and pain; be lost in the great thing, you and I together.

Yes, I'll come.

We wandered all day. The crowds poured on, grew thicker. 'The people!' he said. 'They look so excited.'

'So am I.'

'It makes you want to tell them the truth.'

'And what's that?'

He laughed. 'I don't know.'

After dinner we went again down the great highways. *At eleven o'clock (midnight, continental time)—if there is no reply from Germany—we shall be at war.* Jostled, shoved by the crowds who, as darkness came began to take among themselves the pouring, fiery excitement of the flambeaux which reinforced the lights. Even David now was part of it, his eye kindled in the drifting light, and he laughed when a girl called to him, 'Is it cold up there?' As the darkness deepened and the aftermath of sunset changed to such colours as might be painted on stone, and the flames of the flambeaux were like animals leaping, I felt the pressure of an excitement almost not to be borne: an expectancy, a feeling that the time for some momentous spectacle was nearly come: the minutes were flying past and soon—yes, soon—it will be here.

It? For most of them, pushing towards the Palace, it was indefinable: war, the word was, but war just now as the ultimatum ran out, was a passion, a climax, a wonderful desired thing.

They were singing, cheering, abandoned, cast away with joy.

We did not sing. Caught by the excitement as I was, I saw clearly David's father, kneeling in despair after his sermon, and I had a sense of exile, of being lost in a climate of gay savagery, having turned from the places of reason and love. I looked at David. His hands were in his pockets, his chin sunk a little: he watched it all with a bemused attention, combined with a sort of wisdom, as if he'd already heard a whisper of how it might be.

'Three cheers for the Navy—for the Army—for the *King* . . .'

Flags waving. Hats in the air. Men and women dancing. Night all about us now.

2

July, 1916

Now it was coming close again. Nothing much to be seen, and only an echo, in the tired silences as the train limped and halted and the trucks clanged together, of the sound of guns. But among us was the knowledge of it, the smell, the difference in the air; and to me, after long absence, its familiarity had a strange welcome.

This was the journey south, to the territory whose names were only beginning to be known: Beaumont-Hamel, Thiepval, La Boiselle. A warm day slipping out of the sky; the carriage was hot and stale and our small company there restless, yawning, touched with an apprehension we did not speak of. Indeed we had all been silent for some time, the impulses of talk seeming to have died as the journey came near to its end. Then the train, having ground a few yards farther, stopped once more, and the young lieutenant sitting opposite me grinned and said, 'Do all the trains do this?'

'Most of them. No need to worry; we'll get there soon enough.'

'I suppose so.'

'Make the most of it: not very luxurious but better than anything you're likely to get from now on.'

An officer in another corner of the carriage who seemed

to be lost in a book said without looking up, 'Hear bloody hear.'

The young man smiled. 'This is my first time in France. I thought I'd never get here.'

'Yes, we all thought that once.' (More than eighteen months ago: the Base Camp at Harfleur: the dark excitement of being there: the beginning of it all.)

His eye ran over my uniform with its look of use. 'You say you were at La Bassée? . . . What was it like?'

I thought about La Bassée. I said, 'We didn't have steel helmets.' He seemed to be waiting for more. I looked back to the Cambrin trenches. I saw the confusion, the formidable uncut wire on whose steel-strong branchy malignancy the men struggled and died, easy targets for the guns; I remembered three words from a training manual, in case of stoppage of a machine-gun: reload, relay, resume. I remembered pain, and sudden darkness over it all. 'It was raining,' I said. 'The gas swung round on the wind and gassed our own chaps. And something went wrong with our bombardment: I believe we ran out of shells.'

'The papers said it was a good show. Said we'd beaten them back.'

'Oh well, maybe we did. Nobody ever tells you what's really happening. And I was lucky enough to get shot through the chest early on.' (Showing off; playing the old soldier; but we all did it. Somewhere far distant was a shy young man roving the lanes of Fennelhurst, overborne by his father: ingenuous as this boy before me. Scarcely recognizable now; war had forced a hot-house maturity upon us all; I might have been forty years old.)

He blinked at me; respectful; uncertain.

I said, 'It wasn't as bad as it sounds. The worst part was being kept hanging around a lot of dull places at home for what seemed like a century.'

'You mean you're glad to be back?'

'In a way. I had a bit of luck. When I went before my

medical board I found a splendid old bird who knew my father. I wanted to get sent down here, and he worked it for me.'

An officer who'd seemed to be asleep said with his eyes still shut, 'Anyone who *asks* to be sent down here must be out of his mind.'

I remembered Colonel Sir Allen Kent. 'Of course, my boy, of course: work that for you all right. Pretty unhealthy spot just now, between you and me; something blowing up on the Somme, but if that's where you want to go . . . Work that for you easily; rather short of officers just at the moment; no trouble at all.'

I said now, 'A friend of mine's down here. I haven't seen him for a year. A man I've known all my life.'

'That must be rather fun.'

A schoolboy's phrase, a schoolboy's voice. I looked at him for a moment or two in silence. Again I felt a generation distant from him; as if, long before it was possible, I looked on a grown-up son.

The dusk was heavier now: the fields and villages beyond the train windows taking on the sad mystery of a place heard of but not known. We were coming near to Amiens. I pulled a bulging valise from the rack; this part of the journey was nearly done.

§

By ten o'clock I was in Guillecourt. The young subaltern had been swept away, absorbed by the strenuous confusion at a railhead: somewhere between a sergeant shouting orders, a staff officer exchanging opinions with another staff officer and a group of men arguing over their packs, he had disappeared into the anonymity of war.

The village was placid and leafy; a stream wandered through. Beyond the trees I could see the ground rising darkly, like the Downs at home. War seemed a hazy improbability, until your ears caught the distant inquietude of the sky. Excited, expectant, I walked through the black and purple dusk, a lance-corporal by my side. He was middle-aged, not inclined to talk. The little he said seemed to suggest that he knew a great deal more about war than I did, three stars or no. Probably this was true. His name was Marlin. I said, 'Lieutenant Birch is here, isn't he?'

'Yes, sir. A very nice gentleman.' The words were guarded.

'Popular with the men?'

'Oh yes, sir. Very popular. Very friendly sort of gentleman.'

I waited.

'Well, he don't seem to be frightened, sir. This puts them off a bit.'

'Puts them off?'

'Well, yes, sir; after all it don't seem natural, not to be frightened.'

'I should have thought they admired it.'

'Can't really explain, sir. Some officers are brave, and that's all right. But Lieutenant Birch don't seem to *expect* to be shot at. You can't say that's normal, can you, sir, not out here.'

'Perhaps he's thinking of something else.'

The Corporal gave me a glance, but said only, 'Maybe, sir. Then there's that dog.'

'Dog?'

'A mongrel that got left behind when they evacuated the village. Lieutenant Birch took it over; couldn't make more fuss of it if it was 'Aig 'imself.'

'He was always fond of animals.'

'Ah well, sir. Nearly there now.'

I couldn't help wondering, as we walked on, what the men of this new battalion would make of my promotion to Captain over the heads maybe of others more likely. The Corporal could probably tell me, but it would have been out of order to ask him.

He turned a corner of the road and said, 'Headquarters "B" Company: here you are, sir.'

The farmhouse, like the rest of the village, seemed to show few traces of war. The broken windows were stuffed with mattresses; beyond this there seemed little damage, only the lifeless look of all these places from which their owners had fled.

'In here, sir.'

The room seemed crowded with men and candlelight and shadow; with camp beds, rumpled, unmade; belts, tunics, pistol holsters, bottles, glasses, razors and a few tattered books. The men all looked up at me, and by the time I'd got used to the light I saw that there were only four of them, and that one of these was David.

He got to his feet, seeming in the small room to reach almost to the ceiling. His face was brown, shadowed, leaner than I remembered it. He looked as though he had just had the first week of convalescent holiday after a long fever. A dog, half collie, half something undefined, rose as he rose and barked.

'Simon! They said you were coming, but of course I didn't believe it: some other chap of the same name, or wires crossed somewhere; what a surprising war. Pleasant things happen, even here. Be quiet, Joffre; this is your new commanding officer.'

I was a little shy of him, of the difference in him: yet to find him here, in this candle-lit cave at the fringe of battle, set me at peace with the world. He still, it seemed to me, carried his unchanging sanity like a talisman: not a true soldier, as he accepted all things he accepted this to which I had beckoned him.

'These are the other officers—pity we haven't anything better to offer you, but these are what we were issued with— Mike Ewart, George Gann and Bill Spencer. Captain Simon Calder.'

They each summed me up. Ewart, young, not long out of

school, snub-nosed, wide-eyed, with frank interest and speculation; Gann, grey, nearing forty, with the mild accepting look of experience: his 'How d'you do' was unenthusiastic, but friendly. Spencer, on the other hand, merely nodded, keeping his eyes on me for a moment or two longer than the others. He was thin and dark and did not look pleased.

'Fine,' I said. 'Since you'll all know a great deal more about what's going on than I do, I'll trust you to make it plain.'

David patted my shoulder. 'If you think chaps like us have the faintest notion of what's going on beyond the next billet . . . Oh, the great attack's coming, of course: we're going to win the war, but I don't think anyone's very clear how. . . . Come along, the Colonel wants to see you.'

I walked the dark leafy road with David by my side. It still seemed odd: the surroundings and habits of war were familiar; David himself was familiar, but together they were strange. I said, 'What sort of colonel?'

'Nice enough chap. A Regular. Has a deep distrust of the New Army boys, but one can't really blame him. No fireeater, thank God; heaven save us from them. But I'm afraid he believes in the war.'

'Believes in it?'

'Well, thinks it rather splendid. Has to, I suppose, since it's his job. Gets pleased when our boys capture a ditch somewhere. Thinks it all right for men to be soldiers.'

'Don't you?'

He said lightly, 'No.'

We walked on for a few moments in silence. Did I think it all right for men to be soldiers? Perhaps not, but the rumours of the coming battle stirred more than fear in me: I was eager for it, as if some deep truth, some clarification of life were to be found there.

He said, 'What news from home?'

'Oh . . . plenty.' But it was suddenly hard to focus; like

trying to recall people and events from childhood. 'Your parents send their love, of course. Your father isn't very popular just now because he doesn't get up and say that God's on our side, killing Germans as fast as He can.'

'He's a brave old boy, isn't he? I often think of him, out here . . . rather wish I could do something to make him happy. Marry and have his grandchildren, I suppose: bring them up in the fear and nurture of the Lord. More news?'

'Old Louis Meyers died—did you know?'

'Yes . . . I heard.'

'Juana's left the house: there was trouble, before he died: a lot of nonsense about him signalling with lights to the Germans; some damn fools broke his windows.'

He gave an exclamation as if to say, It's an idiot's world now.

'No one's heard from Juana. The house is empty. No one knows where she's gone.'

He said nothing.

'Last I heard of Geoffrey he was in Mespot. I gather they're not married yet.'

He said, 'Mm,' walking with his head down. His voice was without colour: I couldn't tell how deep an interest he had here. I went on, 'Griselda came to see me. She's nursing now in London.'

'Good for her.'

'She's grown up; quite sensible and efficient suddenly: I don't think she's going to turn out like her mother, after all.'

'Good for her,' he said again. 'Have they patched you up all right?'

'Splendidly, thank you.'

'Poor old Simon. D'you know, I've been through the whole of this idiot business so far and never done more than tear my left buttock on a rusty nail?'

'For Christ's sake, shut up!'

'But it's true.'

'You don't talk about it, you bloody fool.'

'Bad luck?'

Within the warmth of the night, cold twisted in my stomach. 'You just don't talk about it.'

He chuckled, paused to whistle to the dog, walked on. The evening now was heavy, warm and dark. From the deeps of it came the little musical whine of a mouth organ; the magical lazy sound of men's voices talking at ease, themselves unseen; at some distance was the bang of a piano chord and the muted clapping like the clapping of ghosts. All these were louder than the crumpled thunder of guns at the rim of the sky.

He touched my arm. 'This is it,' he said. We had come to a pretty whitewashed house with shutters at the windows and a dark shabby pelt of creeper down one side. 'Battalion H.Q. I'm anathema to colonels: not smart enough, too friendly with the men: I don't think they much care for the dog, either. Come along Joffre: we're for home.'

Colonel Prine was sitting at a table with a cup of coffee and pages of a report in front of him. He greeted me with a certain melancholy which surprised me: colonels in my experience had a professionally cheerful trench-side manner. 'Calder,' he said, 'Calder. . . . Oh yes, the Brigadier told me all about you, didn't he.' He paused to drink from his cup, and perhaps also to remember what it was the Brigadier had said. 'You asked to come out here . . . join your brother, wasn't it?'

'No, sir; my brother's in the R.A.M.C. somewhere near Arras.'

He looked at me as if I were purposely making things more difficult. 'Ah . . . no; not your brother then. Just as well: had two brothers in my last battalion both killed in Gallipoli: better to keep them apart. Lieutenant Birch, wasn't that it? Yes, I remember now. Well, you're lucky: the Captain of "B" Company went down with some astonishing disease—measles, I think it was.' He sent a rapid glance over me. 'Extraordinary thing; I hope you won't do the same.'

'I've had measles, sir.'

A faint smile drifted across his face. 'Oh, good. You've come just in time for what may be the decisive push. The French, as you may have heard, have been going through it at Verdun: now it's our turn. The idea is that we blast a way by weight of shells and men to Bapaume, so that the cavalry can go through.' He looked at me as if I were going to be responsible for the whole thing and he didn't think I was going to be able to manage it.

I said as cheerfully as I could, 'Yes, sir.'

'The thing is to keep the men well up to scratch while they're waiting. *And* give them some training, God knows: they come out here scarcely knowing one end of a rifle from the other. No easing off: they've got to be prepared to move at any time.' I felt the little twist in my bowels, the familiar thrill of excitement and fear, the echo from the thing that waited. 'I think that's all, Calder. I'm having a word with the officers of the Battalion tomorrow at half past eleven. Report to me then.'

I saluted and went out again into the road. The night still smelt of summer, but my ears seemed to catch more loudly the distant guns.

§

The men were obedient but reserved: they waited to judge, when it came to the test, what sort of company commander I would prove to be. I was anxious to know too; eager to win their approval. But I came a bad second to George Gann, whom I felt sure they would have preferred to lead them. There seemed no reason, except for the boundless illogicality of army life, why he did not. He bore me no malice, however; only Spencer stayed hostile; and his hostility grew. He showed it by delaying always a palpable moment before he carried out any order I gave him; more particularly, as time went on, by calling David 'Teacher's blue-eyed boy'. David paid no attention to this at all: went on playing with the dog, sketching the village, the men, the heavy, shrouded guns. But I felt my temper rising. Tension in the confined and shabby room increased; might be dangerous.

Spencer had worked in a bank: the war had released him from a tedious job and a too respectable home; he was now a ready frequenter of the brothels round about: he knew them all, and at a word would give his rating of the women there: 'Five-star, old boy, the *Etoile Bleu*: you take my word for it.' I told myself that if he went on like this he stood a good chance of getting V.D. and being sent down to a base hospital before my mounting irritation could explode.

We spent weeks in preparation for the attack: we took harmless mounds of earth far behind the lines: we consolidated trenches where no enemy was; we had bayonet and rifle drill; we were, the Colonel said, 'being made into an instrument to inflict the heaviest blow on the Central Powers this war has yet seen. A blow that may well prove final.'

Some of the men believed it. Corporal Chivers, a small dark man, always full of rumours ('prick him and he bleeds them,' David said) had decided that he did. 'The Jerries are worn out; they're scraping the bottom of the barrel. Wore theirselves out killing Frogs at Verdun, poor bastards. Now we just go through and clear up the mess; roll 'em up, that's all we have to do. The Victorious British bleeding army, that's us. You wait and see.'

Our Battalion still in reserve, we waited. We waited through the five days of the opening bombardment which made a sky of noise under which we lived and moved; deafened, irritable, breathing and thinking noise; we waited through the first of the attack, ourselves still in quiet water, out of the whirlpool, weary of the sight of men burdened by packs and rifles, marching to a distance whose savagery seemed to offer so little hope of return.

The rumours came back: we'd captured Montauban, Fricourt and Mametz Wood; there'd been heavy fighting at La Boiselle. 'And we got a new weapon, mate; a huge thing, like a house; going to scare the daylights out of Jerry: you won't see him for dust.'

But as well as the rumours, the wounded came back. The beaten and bloody men; and the men whose flesh was whole, but whose wandering stare and loose lunatic walk betrayed the wound in the mind. The weather, after tempestuous summer rain, was stripped clear of all cloud, sea-bathing weather, the heat of July.

And still we waited. Our turn would come. I began drinking more heavily: the whisky bottle became a golden thing, a loved and pleasurable release from tension and fear.

The heat grew denser: the threat of terrible confusion hung over us like a dark disturbed wing. The roads were strangled with men and guns and lorries going up to the line, men and ambulances coming out of it, to rest, dressing-station or hospital: they met, ran into each other like rivers meeting, boiled, struggled, slowly emerged.

Once as I stood by the roadside, smoking, nervous, impatient, wishing for I knew not what, a corporal from a Scottish regiment, his tin hat askew on his head, his face and uniform streaked with dust, his eyes too wide, halted in front of me. He stood swaying; I thought he was going to fall. Then he said, his voice strained and shredded, like a child's on the verge of tears, 'It's no battle, it's murder. They told us the guns had blasted a way through the wire, but when we got there the wire was as good as new and so were the Jerry machine-guns, it was just like walking into a trap: our lads were killed in hundreds. Hundreds of them were killed all in a few minutes. You don't ask men to do that, to walk into death.' The tears began to run down his face: he looked absurd, terrible, a messenger from the dark edge of the world. I offered him a drink, but he turned and stumbled off, wiping his nose with his hand.

Shaken, I went back into our room and took half a glass of whisky. The air was close, smelling of men and dust and war. David wasn't there. The dog was moving restlessly around, sniffing for him, and I could see on the table David's sketch-book, open at an unfinished drawing of a weary soldier, resting at the roadside : pencils and rubber lay beside it. The small belongings had a sharpness, a poignancy ; one had seen too many such, to be collected, parcelled up, sent home. . . . Spencer was reading a magazine ; Ewart and Gann were playing cards.

I stood with the glass in my hand. 'Where's David?'

'Gone to smell the syringa,' said Spencer without looking up.

'What the hell d'you mean by that?'

'Absolutely nothing at all, nothing at all.' He still didn't look up. A little silence had come into the room.

'You're being damned insolent ; talk properly when I speak to you.'

Spencer raised his eyes. His thin face was composed, hostile, sober. 'We all have our different ways of showing affection, don't we? Some of us like a straight how-d'you-do in bed with a nice girl who'll put her legs apart, and others like something else—'

My hand, spread open, had caught his face before I could stop myself. The silly tilt of his head, the feel of his bony cheek under my hand, sobered me. A voice in my own mind said, 'That was a bloody silly thing to do.'

§

Later in the day the Colonel sent for me.

He looked more melancholy than before. I saluted and stood before him. He pushed a tired hand over his hair and said, 'Well, Calder, this is an extraordinary story I hear.' His look said, First measles and now this. 'Lieutenant Spencer tells me you struck him in front of brother officers.'

It sounded, I thought, rather grand and improbable, like a scene out of Anthony Hope. I said, 'Yes, sir. I'm sorry.'

'It's not the kind of conduct I expect from a company commander. Have you any explanation?'

Difficult. I said, 'I'm afraid I just lost my temper, sir.'

'It would be more useful to a tired man, Calder, if you'd speak the truth.'

That 'tired man' surprised me. I said, 'Lieutenant Spencer made an insulting remark about my relationship with another officer.'

'Was there any truth in it?'

'None at all, sir. Absolutely none at all.'

He looked as though he caught some over-emphasis in my voice. I went on, 'Out here, in this life, one values friendship. Why the hell not, sir? What else have we got?'

'Quite, quite.' He looked sadder, embarrassed, not unsympathetic. 'However, there's absolutely no need to hit Spencer.'

'No, sir. I'm sorry. I think we all find the waiting a bit of a strain. Hearing the fighting going on. Hearing the rumours. Still doing nothing.'

The Colonel sighed. 'Well, if it's any comfort to you, I have orders here from Brigade H.Q. Tomorrow we move up into the line to relieve the Welsh. You'll attend here for orders this evening at 18.00 hours with all other officers. We move tomorrow night. Now perhaps you can stop hitting Spencer and hit the enemy instead.'

I walked back along the country road. Tomorrow night. The silly episode with Spencer went down before the prospect. Stories of the first days of fighting were dark with death; some said twenty thousand men had been killed on the first day alone. I tried to think of twenty thousand men such as myself, all with hopes, affections, fears and desires and with as great a will to live, but the vast number was meaningless: it made a factual shape in my mind, no more. Twenty thousand men could be killed in a day ('go to their graves like beds'): of what significance then was this fragment of animated consciousness, myself, lately ticked off by the Colonel? None, it seemed, and yet I greatly wanted to live, though all about me men in their thousands died. The enormous disproportion hung over me like a canopy of depression: it seemed to give the lie to all one's small gestures of humanity: these were surely a sham; in the dark places of truth one was concerned only to survive.

Only? I caught the familiar whine of the mouth organ. No; sometimes the tough cheerful courage of the men as they endured all things touched me, became something larger than myself in which my own fears perished. Sometimes it would be more to me that David should live till the end of the war than that I should live to see him do so. Sometimes death slipped its mooring in the mind, changed its shape; became not sharp, bloody extinction, but a place shared, of wider and deeper prospects, wherein the irritable and craving ego could dissolve and ride at ease.

Yet as I walked back to Company H.Q. I became suddenly oppressed with the fear that, in this coming attack, David would be killed. David, not I. Superstitious as we all were after years of war, I saw ill-fortune in those words to the Colonel—'I think we all find the waiting a bit of a strain.' As if the end of waiting would be ease. I could see the whole thing played out in some lurid theatre of my mind: myself waiting in the dug-out, while David went out on patrol into No-Man's-Land in the dark. I could hear the sudden sharper burst of fire amongst the blundering roar of heavy guns: hear the cry of 'Stretcher-bearers! Officer hit!' and feel the dread with which I waited: see, as the men came awkwardly down into the trench with their burden, David, too long for the stretcher, wearing the uniform of blood and pallor, of approaching death.

By the time I got back to H.Q. I was so cloudy with dread that I was startled to see David lounging at ease, unshadowed by omens. Heavy with my sense of doom, I told him the news. He stretched himself and scratched the dog's ear. 'Oh Lord, so they've drawn our number out of the hat after all; I thought they'd lost it.'

§

After the meeting of officers at Battalion H.Q., we sat in our room, the windows open. The Orders were simple. We were to move up into the line tomorrow night, starting at 20.00 hours. We were to make for a map reference which as far as I could judge was slap in the middle of the German lines. This point was somewhere to the east of Montauban. We were to relieve the front-line trench, 'A' Company were to relieve the support trench, and the other two companies were to be in reserve. Once there, the objective of 'B' Company was to capture at once a small wooded mound, known as Thurston Wood, from which heavy machine-gun fire was holding up our advance. This captured and consolidated, the way would be open to Longueval, Guinchy and Morval. It all sounded splendidly clear and straightforward, and we knew from experience that it would be nothing of the kind: we would get lost—everyone got lost in the dark—we would find unexpected pockets of German machine-guns, ready and waiting for us: the formation of trenches would be nothing like it appeared on the map; and there wouldn't—this was most certain of all—be any break-through: we'd be shot at, bombarded, confused, receiving most likely at our darkest moment a message from Brigade about the proper care of equipment.

Moonlight lay about us in the room. Spencer was jumpy, covering it with a long story of a seduction in Amiens: Ewart was perhaps listening—he was young enough to be impressed and stimulated. Gann was sorting his equipment, giving whistles of mock-wonder every now and again. David sat on his camp bed mending a sock, paying no attention to Spencer's startling obscenities, the dog at his feet. The dog was looking at him as if it waited to be told something. I poured whisky from the bottle, noting the tremor of my hand. The image of David dead still oppressed me. He was too tall: so easy for that head to show above the parapet, and a sniper to pounce like an evil leaden bird. . . .

I saw the Rectory at Fennelhurst, where the news would come: the heavy shadow on it, the empty room. I saw Juana, though I did not know where she was, stricken, remorseful . . . or perhaps quickly turning away. For a moment she was very clear in my mind, with her beauty and fine clothes: nothing to do with the world we lived in now.

I looked down at the map: a tranquil design of trenches and roads where the dead and dying were. Where we would be tomorrow. I felt again the twist of apprehension: I was on trial; I had to lead them; I might fail.

David plunged his needle into his sock. 'Why don't we go straight away? What are we supposed to do tomorrow?'

'Now don't be silly, lad,' said Gann drawing at his pipe. 'Don't you want another day's life, given free? A whole bloody day? Christ, you don't know your luck. And what we do tomorrow is, we make our wills.'

I said, 'We pack up the picnic baskets and say our prayers.'

'And of course,' said Gann, 'Bill Spencer here'll have to make another little visit to the Maison, unless of course he's run the well dry, which I should think is more than likely.'

Spencer denied this, practically with diagrams.

David pricked his finger on his mammoth needle and swore. I said, 'I should give that up, if I were you. What's a batman for?'

'I rather enjoy it. And I'm fond of these socks; they bring me luck.'

'Oh, shut up,' I said.

He glanced at me, amused. 'Something restful about darning; you should try it some time. Only the risk of a slight flesh wound.'

'Never cared for it,' said Gann. 'Tried it once but the wool makes a knot all by itself. Bloody silly; you wouldn't think it'd know how.'

Ewart said, 'The moon looks watery. Suppose the weather changed and someone cancelled our orders . . .'

'No such luck,' said Gann. 'We've got to go and relieve those poor bloody Welshmen, what's left of them. Not that I care for Welshmen, particularly. Dirty in the trenches, so they tell me. But it's our turn now.'

I got up and began to pace the room. David went on clumsily mending. Perhaps it was only the moonlight that made Ewart look so pale as he listened to Spencer's interminable enterprises. '. . . this mam'selle was just about the hottest thing this side of the Equator: didn't even wait for me to get my clothes off. . . .' Gann was whistling the phrase of a tune, the same one, over and over again: after a few irritable moments I managed to place it: 'I don't want to be a soldier, I don't want to go to war. . . .' The road outside was loud with wheels: gun limbers and lorries moved through the dark up towards the line. *Our turn now.* 'I just want to *hang* around Piccadilly *Un*derground. . . .' I said to David, 'What d'you want to do when it's over?'

'When what's over?'

'The war.'

'Oh.' He looked surprised, as though he hadn't thought about it. 'Start learning to be a farmer, I suppose. Make a change to grow things, wouldn't it?'

I nodded. The answer didn't satisfy me; I was pursuing an unattainable certainty. 'Where?'

'Near home, I suppose. Within sound of Father's sermons. There I shall till the ground and grow old and bore the young with stories of the Great War. How I lost my left arm.

Shall I lose my left arm? Who can say.' He ran one hand into the sock to test the hole. 'That ought to survive if the rats don't get at it. How about you?'

I said I didn't know. War had taken the colour from the classical austerity of university life. Perhaps I'd be an archaeologist; travel to the strange parts of the earth; dig up ancient tombs—

'Ours most likely,' said Gann. 'What a damned awful row those lorries make out there: too much unnecessary noise in this war; Brigade ought to issue a directive. What's Ewart going to do?'

Ewart's face lost a little of its pallor. He was going to play cricket, he said. He'd already played for Middlesex; made seventy-four against Leicestershire once. His father'd coached him every evening in the summer when he came home from work: he was a civil servant in the post office.

'All I want,' said Gann, 'is to go home to the wife and kids. Girl and boy, eight and six. Pretty, they are, really nice. Quarrel sometimes, of course, but they're fun. You ought to try it, you fellows: kids are really something. Surprise you all the time. Especially girls. Come and put their arms round you and whisper to you, and their hair smells nice like out of doors on a fine day. Good to see them again.'

I thought of Gann, the only one of us, if we were all killed, of whom something would persist, whose blood and flesh would not quite perish here, but would survive in these children who would remember him, perhaps with pride.

'Maybe you'll see them sooner than you think,' said Spencer, for a moment taking his mind off the white thighs and splendid breasts in Amiens. 'I was talking to the Adj. yesterday, and he said the prisoners we get now are an awful weedy lot; Fritz's coming to the end of his rations; can't stand much more of it. We'll soon be rolling them up.'

The words dyed my thoughts the colour of hope: might it

be true? In spite of the wounded and the dead, and the stories of most bloody fighting, there were rumours also of a German retreat. The sight of cavalry riding in splendour one evening down the road inspired wild talk of victory.

'Before the end of the year, perhaps,' said Spencer.

'Before the end of the year,' David repeated. For a moment we were all silent, as if the Angel of Peace himself had shadowed the room with his wing.

Then—'Shouldn't count on it,' Gann said.

§

That night I lay, turning, pulling the blanket about me. Every kind of nonsense was shifting about in my head; it was like watching a dozen plays at once . . .

Tomorrow night. 20.00 hours. North-east of Montauban. 'B' Company to the front-line trench; 'A' Company in support. Watery moon. You don't ask men to do that, to walk into death. I like these socks, they bring me luck. I don't want to be a soldier, I don't want to go to war. It is fear, O Little Hunter, it is fear. That mam'selle, she was the hottest thing this side of the Equator. If it's any comfort to you, tomorrow we move up into the line. Thurston Wood, heavy machine-gun fire. Take the wood, take the wood, oh God, take the bloody wood. . . . It is fear, O Little Hunter, it is fear. Now God be thanked who has matched us with his hour. God is on the side of the big battalions. Where is God in all this? Nowhere, nowhere any more: the church at Fennelhurst, filled with the mystery of the sacrament, and a young man believing all things. Lost now.

What's left, then? Everyone has to have something: you can't exist in all this alone: if there's no God there has to be something that'll do instead . . . love, perhaps. Perhaps even Spencer's encounters between the grimy sheets are a kind of love, a protest in the face of the swollen and blackening corpses from Thiepval to La Boiselle, from Pozières to Martinpuich. A protest of frenzied life. You have to have something . . . I turned again. The guns seemed louder.

Well, I loved David. Unlike Spencer, the years of war had purged me, sickened me of lust. Too many Spencers standing in queues by dingy estaminets: too many crowded V.D. base hospitals, too much obscenity in words, so that the act of love was diminished and muddied. My dreams were black with nightmare but not with lust, and my love was violent but not to do with the body. David's presence eased my world; his charitable calm made sense of things. For as long as we were here, bounded by the confines of destruction and misery and death, he was all I wanted, the place from which life came.

And as I turned and threshed, the foreboding of his death grew larger, became an unreasoned fear that set my heart thudding and the sweat on my forehead. I saw it now in a charge against machine-gun fire, now by a sniper's bullet because he wouldn't duck low enough in the trench (Get down, David, get *down*, you fool); now by a shell which scattered the fragments of men's bodies as if they were bloody rags of clothing, hands and legs and arms, within a moment nothing human any more.

They mow the field of man in season. Heavy machine-gun fire. Take the wood, small wooded mound. Relieve the poor bloody Welsh, what's left of them. Blast a way to Longueval, Guinchy, Morval, Ligny, Bapaume . . . blast a way to Berlin. You don't ask men to do that, to walk into death. *Stretcher-bearers. Stretcher-bearers.* Small wooded mound.

Dizzily it blurred together, swung and was changed into unquiet dreams, at whose edge the guns beat like a menacing sea.

'Sir! Captain Calder, sir!'

I woke, dry of throat, half-way between a cough and a snore. The room was still dark. A young orderly from H.Q. was bending over me, one hand on my arm. Coming from some nameless place of dark pursuit and threat, I instinctively pulled my arm away.

'Message from the Colonel, sir. Orders've been changed. The battalion's got to move within half an hour.'

I groaned an acknowledgement, swinging my legs down from the bed. The hands of my watch pointed four o'clock. As I pulled on my boots I thought that this was part of the pattern of war: no fear, for the moment, of death, merely discomfort, jarred nerves; violent awakening in the small hours, a sense of hurry and confusion: a nightmare obstacle race.

David, Spencer, Ewart and Gann were clumsily pulling on boots, strapping belts and holsters, hanging themselves about with field-glasses, wire-cutters, periscopes and a great deal more. Together we went out into the road where the still dead of morning was given over to sound, movement, urgency. Some of the men were sleeping in an orchard behind the house; I paused to watch the Sergeant as he roused them; he walked among them, shaking a sleeping arm or shoulder. Crumpled, blurred with sleep they rose from the ground: it was like some strange dark judgement day. Their mumbled cursing made an obscene yet unemphatic accompaniment to it all: lantern light shone on sweaty foreheads, tousled hair, unshaven chins: on stained puttees and tunics, on packs and rifles and drinking mugs.

Grotesquely shaped, heavy with curtailed sleep, the men were lining up in the dark road, platoon by platoon, company by company; transport lorries and wagons behind. The vast movement in the dark had the feel of menace in it. The air was moist and heavy; the moon had gone. There was a time of waiting about; a cold time of impatience, dread and desire for sleep. I walked down the length of the Company. The talk in our room a few hours ago seemed far off. Gann had said, 'Don't you want another day's life given free? Another bloody day?' Now the day wasn't there any more.

I saw David who as second-in-command walked at the back of the Company. The dog was running round his feet and whining; he was encouraging it towards a house on the other side of the road. 'Go on, Joffre: I've arranged a fine billet for you: a kind Sergeant in that house over there; a lucky bastard who hasn't got to move on. . . . You wouldn't like it, old chap, where we're going.' The dog still looked miserable.

'This means trouble,' said Melville, O.C. of the Company forming behind us. 'Some poor sods up there've been cut to pieces and sent an S.O.S. back to Brigade.' He was fastening the buckle of his belt and his fingers shook.

I said, 'More likely someone just decided we needed exercise.'

'It's no good, Joffre; you can't come with me; you must make do with the Sergeant: nice man; comes from Lancashire. . . .'

I said, 'Well, good luck.'

'Lots of good luck all round,' said David, still attending to the dog. I turned away. In the distance the sky beat with a pulse of light, as though the heart of the earth itself throbbed in fever. My head was cold and prickly; nausea moved in my stomach. I had never felt less that I wanted to trudge the weary miles towards bloody fighting, perhaps death.

Here we go, at last. The length of us spans the whole village: a shadowy company, heavily burdened, leaving the ease of Guillecourt, the quiet leafy days of parades and musketry drill and route marches: these have been snatched out of our hands. Now we are moving nearer to the guns, a company of men like so many others, scarcely distinguishable from them, the recurring pattern.

And while darkness dissolved and the noise of guns grew louder—as if it were this with its violence which changed the sky—I felt strangely inhabited by the being of some other man: someone dead, or someone still alive, who would come after me: identity wavered and dimmed. Wearily we strode on. The country was changed, given over to some god of destruction: houses were no more than heaps of stones; trees slaughtered and blackened by shell-fire; a village whose heaps of wood and stones did not reach above one's shoulder, as if a fist had come down upon it all. I tried to believe that men and women had lived here and children had played in the street, but even the echoes of life had gone: nothing remained. We passed our heavy guns beneath their camouflage nets; their firing turned the world deaf.

Now we were meeting the men coming back from battle; now the road was filling with ambulances and walking wounded, and everywhere the bright blood, soaking through field dressings, running from open wounds, coloured the day with fear. By now the road was no road: in the first dawn drizzle we were trudging into the authentic confusion of war.

And the shells coming over, weighting the sky with noise, with approaching death; the ground flowering with dirty orange smoke. Crumps—coal-boxes—coming fast now: orders shouted, urgent angry voices, coming through the smoke and the noise. We stumbled on. Suddenly it seemed there was no one in front of us: 'A' Company had disappeared, sheltering perhaps in ditches and craters, perhaps following some different track through the desert of death and confusion. I hesitated, and heard the voices of the men: 'Where the hell d'we think we're going?' 'Dunno, mate; lost me crystal ball.' Further ribaldry on this, but the joking nervous, dying away. Spencer suddenly at my side, urging me forward: he'd met a wounded Welsh runner, our trenches were beyond that small mound—there, on our left. A lull in the shelling; the drizzle heavier now, solid and desolate. It shone upon the men's steel helmets with a grey glister, like the shine on wet Sunday pavements. Their faces beneath were sometimes resigned, sometimes bitter, sometimes, as I shouldered my way through the halting and bewildered advance to gather the Company together, miraculously friendly, even forgiving. I said, 'We're going up into the front-line trench—there, not fifty yards off.' The men shifted, moved together. 'Trust our bleeding luck; next time I'm going to change me sex and nurse the wounded.' I looked on them all with an abortive pity: this was my first command, and the absurdity of telling these men to do anything—most of all to go into the death-ridden places ahead of us, made me turn quickly from them.

But they came. Into the heart of the shelling, reviving now, over the broken ground. Into a world where the dead lay like commonplace things; I saw the men look towards them. The dead are familiar, but their mystery remains and one's eyes go to them. One on his back, tranquil save that there are no legs on his body; one on his side: he might be sleeping but for the evil colour of his face, darkening, almost black . . . what a piece of work is a man.

The light is a little stronger, but the rain in the warm air has formed a mist ahead of us: thank God for the mist. Here, a desperate and welcome refuge, are the trenches. The poor bloody Welsh, the men we are to relieve, are already pushing by us as we make our way into the trench. The rain grows heavier but the light brighter. Our men, pushing against the tide of soaked, weary, shattered soldiers, halt and stumble against each other. There is a dead man across their path: newly dead, he has been shot through the loins and seems to have a red cloth seat to his trousers. Of the men going out of the line some go dream-like, only their eyes betray them: brilliant with fatigue and horror, like eyes that have looked upon burning cities and open graves.

An officer of the outgoing company, swaying with weariness, a nerve twitching in his face, greets me as if I were a raft in a tremendous sea. 'We've lost nearly half our men. Scarcely an officer left. We were sent up to attack the wood, but it's alive with machine-guns. Supposed to be supporting fire on our left flank, but bugger-all we saw of it.' He wiped his face: he had a wound in his hand which left a mark of blood on his colourless unshaven cheek. 'Now we've been warned to expect a counter-attack: that's why they got you up here double-quick: we could never hold them.'

The shelling does not diminish: is it the prelude to an attack? The rain continues too, but there is a heavy warmth behind it: the day to come may be hot, strengthening the sickly smell of the dead, of the refuse, of this forsaken place at the end of the world. The mist still holds. While a cook brings us a ration of rum and has managed, God knows how, to brew some sort of tea, tasting of fish, onions and chloride of lime, but tea, and a slice of bread covered with marmalade in whose substance is something gritty (sand? sugar? coffee?) I find myself beguiled by the mist, and an idea begins to nibble at my mind.

Whether Fritz knows we've been marching through the night, he'll guess there are exhausted men in these trenches; the counter-attack will come soon. Could anything be done under cover of the mist? On the exhausted nervous energy of men not yet relaxed into sleep? If the mist holds? Could I, with a few men, move silently up to Thurston Wood from the flank and surprise the machine-gun posts there into surrender? The fantasy of exhaustion, or a flash of sense?

I call David, Spencer, Ewart and Gann. Huddled in the chalky trench, they listen.

'It's crazy,' says Spencer.

'What happens if the mist lifts?' asks Ewart.

'A few more officers returned empty,' says Gann.

David is silent, looking at me as if he were working it out in his head. Spencer says, 'You need to get an O.K. from the C.O.'

'I haven't the faintest idea where he is. And there's no time.'

Gann says, 'I think the risk's too great.'

'But if we stay here we meet the counter-attack at Fritz's own time. And the whole battalion comes under fire.'

'I'm for it—' this is David at last, 'though there's always the chance of getting shot up by our own men.'

In the event, I go with Ewart and Gann and six men who volunteer. Their faces are very clear to me, and their names: Ferham, North, Carey, Kendal, Lane and Miles.

Under my orders, David, as second-in-command, is to stay in the trench: in case of the mist lifting, he is to order heavy covering fire; to follow me at the arranged signal, if I succeed. Leaving him behind has moved him to his rare anger, but he cannot disobey.

On to the firestep and over the top of the trench. There is again a lull in the firing, and we go in the most careful silence. If map reference and compass are correct, Thurston Wood is about 200 yards away to our left. Indeed, I can see the smudgy outline of its trees, like a gigantic thumb-print. The mist still holds, the rain keeps on. A shell goes over, to burst some distance away.

The ground over which we go silently and in such fear is evil: it might not any longer be part of the friendly earth: its surface is dug with holes as if some herd of gigantic beasts had rooted among it: and scattered everywhere are the dead. In the mist one comes on them so suddenly; one's foot strikes something different from the churned earth, the yielding but resistant flesh. The smell does not warn one: in the warmth the smell is everywhere. The day is scarcely up, but the bluebottles are already droning obscenely: it is like the sound one made as a child, blowing through tissue paper on a comb.

What will come of this? A court-martial? A medal? Death? Am I trying to prove myself in my first command, is there within myself a person who sees this as daring, splendid, clever? If so, God help him. Is it perhaps an insane effort to keep David safe? If so . . .

Is the mist lifting? A little thinner? We are making no noise. I feel the Mills bombs in my pockets. The thumb-print is coming nearer. We are moving closer to its flank.

The barrage has quietened on both sides, as if it paused for our endeavour. The rain is nothing now, merely a dampness in the air. The day will be hot, a summer's day. A day for swimming, for lying at ease—

A rat, swollen from human food, scuttles from under my foot. I scarcely see it; my heart is beating fast and there is a singing in my ears that has nothing to do with the guns. I am sweating as if from high fever: my clothes are soaked with rain and sweat. Has the mist changed? I am aware of Ewart and Gann, and the men behind us. The trench where David is seems suddenly far off. I remember myself as a boy, swimming out to sea, turning to find the shore diminished, cut off, seemingly impossible to regain. I stumble and recognize, almost for the first time, extreme exhaustion. Since the orderly shook my arm in Guillecourt all those hours ago there has been no respite: only the rum ration and the gritty marmalade. This I can still taste in my mouth. I start to yawn, but this is fear, not weariness, because now we are very close. The firing revives a little.

Can we have come so close, all safe? Am I dreaming this? No, it is real: the sweat on my body, the dryness of throat, the sense of absurdity: What am I doing here? Is there a catch in it? Shall we all be dead in a moment? As the mound comes closer, I see Fennelhurst and the quiet fields and my father and mother at the breakfast-table. I wonder where Esmond is now.

A strange quiet: but the mist? The rain has stopped, and the air is somehow bright, though without distance. If the mist clears we shall fail, we shall all be killed. This will lie on my head, but I shall have no knowledge of it. Unless . . . but one has long ago lost all sense of God, of a world beyond this. . . . Not one sparrow shall fall without your Father . . .

The mound is clear now. I can just see the shapes of men on the mist. We move closer. I can hear voices, German voices of men like myself—but the pattern is now that I have to kill them, or be killed.

We are right upon them. I lift my arm to give the signal; we throw the bombs. Storm now instead of quiet; the exploding bombs, cries of pain, shouts, a rifle fired. Blind now, seeing death close, but almost as a friend, I run upon them: I fire my revolver and there is a sudden difference in the shape of a man. One German, though wounded, is at his machine-gun: *reload, relay, resume*; I hear the bullets chatter like teeth and a cry; then the gunner himself is hit. A man, he is North, I remember, goes forward with his bayonet fixed; he has killed a man before he himself is killed. I am firing crazily, continuously, drunk with firing, with wild dreams, with a throat like sand-paper, with no reason any more. I blow on my whistle for David to follow, bringing up the men. The mist is only now beginning to lift: we can take the mound before it clears: we can take Thurston Wood. This is victory, triumph, banners fly out in my mind: perhaps it is the end of all things; the end of the war. Those Germans left alive have their hands up: the insane ruse has succeeded, the blessed mist has kissed us with good fortune.

Our men are coming up from their trench. Revolver in hand, I look behind me in a sudden stormy quiet. There are new dead on the ground: Ewart lies on his side, sobbing; I can see the tears on his cheeks: he has been shot in the stomach. Gann seems to smile at me, but then I see that the smile is a stain of blood from his mouth, a stain which grows wider as he does not speak and the colour changes to the colour of the grave in his face. Carey is wounded, oh pray God, only wounded; his shattered arm stains his tunic, but this could be a blighty one; he could be safe.

David comes up with the men. He looks about him, but says nothing. For a moment his eyes catch mine and I turn away. The distant guns are firing heavily again like beasts woken from sleep. The stretcher-bearers are here, to take away the wounded and the dead. The day is coming up, warm and fine, and the mist has nearly gone. The day smells of blood.

We have taken the mound. I must get a message to H.Q.; we have taken Thurston Wood : the machine-guns are in our hands. But I stare at Ewart who is silent now; mercifully silent, not crying any more, done with pain and with the days of sunlight, done with it all; at Gann who will not see the children he talked of again. The sweat and rain on my body begin to feel cold in spite of the heat of the coming day. We have succeeded and David is safe, but the haunting begins.

3

July, 1917

All day long the gun limbers, the lorries, the men had been going up the road. Despatch riders ripped by, lifting the dust, sounding important, as if they carried news. But there wouldn't, I thought, be news yet. The companionable sound of horses, the clink of harness and the cough and whinny seemed to belong to some different order of things. The air was grey; the familiar pattern on the sky, the torn tower of Ypres, was dark with promise of rain.

We had come north. Thurston Wood was a year away: a small bloody enterprise of no account; we were forced in the end to retreat. We had endured the icy winter in the Somme trenches, those that were left of us. Quiet in its strait-jacket of ice and snow, the place was haunted by the great company of the dead: I was glad to leave it. Finding myself so little hurt, so comparatively unharmed, I felt that the gods had erred: this mercy must have been meant for someone else. Discovering their mistake they would no doubt in time correct it. Meanwhile I was glad to come north, to the Ypres Salient, the Mecca of this war, over whose ground they had fought since the beginning, so that all the names were darkly familiar: Potijze, Langemarck, Hooge, Zonnebeke, Passchendaele.

The howitzers had been firing so continuously that the present lull assaulted the ears like a silence. Against this silence the churning of men and mules and wheels on the road came strangely; one could hear scraps of crude singing, and the shouts of command from a hop-field where some luckless men were being smartened up in musketry. One could even hear the rumours.

'They say we got five tha'sand heavy guns . . . they say we're blowing the Jerries out of the ground. . . . Well, that's what they tell us, mate: when the brass hats *tell* us we're winning the war, it's not for us to disagree with them, is it? . . . You want to be careful what you say, mate: no point in getting shot for treason when you can get shot perfectly well going over the plonk. . . .'

I stood looking down the filled and pounded road. About me the stretching fields were crowded to the eye's limit with encamped men, stores of ammunition—huge honeycombs of violence—guns, horses, mules, field-ambulances, the vast paraphernalia of war: a nation on the move. The German Taubes which flew often our way must have carried long ago the news of the attack that was coming. The attack on the height of ground which, shaped like a lengthened womb, half-ringed the Salient beyond Ypres and sent upon our men below continuous death from its guns. The height whose apex was Passchendaele.

I wandered on. Taylor and Corham, two men of my own company, were sitting together on the ground smoking, exchanging desultory bits of conversation as if they swapped cigarette cards: they seemed at first glance as much at home, as much at ease, as if they sat outside a pub on a fine day. But it was impossible not to paint behind them the back-cloth of the fighting they had known and survived, the fighting to come; the shadow of death.

Taylor, in his forties, grey-haired and a grocer, looked up.

'Not a very nice day for an outing: think it's going to rain, sir?'

'Oh certainly: it always rains.'

'Jerry rain. . . . I reckon God's on their side, don't you, sir?'

I shrugged, without comment. Corham said, 'You shouldn't ask the O.C. things like that; it's secret and confidential.'

I smiled and turned away. I was glad to stop talking. I admired their courage; I could see the poignancy of this murderous exile from their life of work and chatter and children and aimless summer ease—but I had nothing to say to them, for I had nothing within myself. The hothouse maturity of a year ago had gone sour: I went through my duties; I censored the mail, I heard disputes, I listened while the Colonel exercised either his spleen or his command, but within my head was a dull greyness such as covered the Flemish sky.

The men said I drank too much: they said, some of them, that I'd been out too long, that I was one of those whose usefulness was past: who had survived in body, but whose nerves and stamina were bitten through, ready to crack when new strain came. I did not think this was true. I was dried, empty, on the far side, it seemed to me, of sanity: when I looked in the glass something seemed missing from my face: thin, a yellowish brown, already lined, it had a blankness which I found disconcerting, as if a friend had passed me by as a stranger. But I did not think I should fail. My body obeyed me, as I obeyed my commanders: and in place of fear was a certainty that I should be killed before long. I was afraid of pain, of how the wound would come, but death itself seemed now merely a logical end, a place so filled with men that it could not be lonely.

Two things made sense here in Bredenhoek on the road to Ypres: whisky that I drank steadily in quantities which would have startled even my father; and the prospect which, in the face of all things, marked this day with the almost forgotten trace of hope.

I walked farther down the road, searching the gun limbers and lorries and the companies of men for the hope, as if one man alone might be discovered there.

My fear on the Somme that David would be killed had now irrationally passed. I believed him to be charmed, specially cared for. The wound in the thigh that had taken him home before the end of the Somme fighting was part of the pattern. They said now that an officer's expectation of life in the front-line trenches was three to four weeks, but I believed that he would come through. I was as crazily sure of this as the fortune-teller is of his prophecy or the compulsive gambler that his number will come up. This I believed in: and in nothing else.

Now he was due back from leave: I watched for him.

Bobby Cartright wandered towards me, flicking his cane against his leg. He was a subaltern, newly come from England. He was so like other young men I'd known: like Ewart on the Somme, like a young man, nameless, dimly remembered, in a train carriage going south, that I found it hard not to see the ghosts standing behind him. Indeed, except for a few closely known, I saw all men not quite in focus, not as themselves but only briefly inhabiting a place between the death of men who had gone before them, and their own.

Cartright said diffidently, looking at the vast encampments, 'It must be the largest army in the world.'

'Except for the one facing us, I suppose it is.'

'They say at home Fritz is almost played out.'

'We're both almost played out. But we go on.'

He glanced at me. 'All the same ... I don't really see how we can fail this time.'

I smiled briefly and said nothing. I could hear the men's voices in my head: 'The first twenty years are the worst, mate.' 'Haig's got a plan: he's going to kill all the Germans *and* all the Allies and just leave 'im and the Kaiser to have a nice tea-party.' 'Wave good-bye to them, chum, you don't get leave from there—only to Heaven: must be a dreadful crush upstairs; they'll have to build an annexe.' Different voices from a year ago, stripped of all illusion, unsalted with hope.

I said, 'I used to feel like that, before the Somme.' I could see, standing here, the leafy summer dark in Guillecourt; the men whose names even were fading now; the different days, before hope died. Now under this heavy sky the tireless tide went on: men, mules and guns, moving up towards Ypres, to the hungry and threatening distance. The men still sang, but there was a difference in their singing.

Cartright was looking a little crushed: I was sorry for it but had not the energy to redeem it. He said, 'Yes, I suppose so.'

Doyle came up to us: he was a schoolmaster, pleasant, human, cheerful: a man of thirty or so with prematurely grey hair, a plump face and the lazy manner of one who expects no evil from anywhere. 'Watching the Lord Mayor's Show? Must be the longest in history.'

'Cartright thinks we're going to win.'

'There now.' Doyle patted Cartright's shoulder. 'He's young yet. Ah, here comes Spencer: the dark gentleman of the sonnets.' (This was his nickname for Spencer; I'd forgotten why, if there was any reason beyond Spencer's black hair. I had some time ago decided that in this war Spencer was my old man of the sea: wounded on the Somme he had been sent back to England; spent about six months on a course; but was now, inexorably, back with us, again under my command. Perhaps the dispensation that kept David beside me gave me Spencer also as a penance.) 'Hullo, Spencer. Think it's going to rain?'

'Well, of course. And this means trouble: the ground's no good if it's wet: isn't that so, Simon?'

'The ground's always wet.'

'Yes, but this is different. Low-lying; it'll soon be flooded and we'll get stuck in it, tanks and all.' He pulled a packet of cigarettes from his pocket. 'I was talking to Naylor of the Cheshires: he's got hold of a rumour.'

Only Cartright looked interested; Doyle and I had supped full of rumours. Spencer went on, 'Apparently there's some great bloody army somewhere else, acting as a decoy. Making Fritz believe we're going to attack farther south; drawing his men and guns down there so we'll have a cushy time of it.'

'And what's all this supposed to be?' I made a gesture to the road. 'A special matinée for the General?'

'Naylor said it was going to be easier for us.'

'If you believe that you'll believe anything.'

'It's a damn good idea. If it isn't true, it ought to be.'

'I should tell the C.O.'

'Anyone feel like dinner in Pop tonight?' Cartright was perhaps pouring oil on troubled waters. 'It could be our last chance . . . would it be all right, sir?'

I felt Spencer's eye on me; I said, a little irritably, 'Yes, yes; why not?'

'I'll come too,' said Spencer. 'Quite good hunting in those parts.'

I opened my mouth to speak and closed it again. I wasn't in truth happy about two officers going off to Poperinghe for dinner, and I could see that Doyle had his doubts about it too, but Spencer always set me off on the wrong foot.

Cartright said a little shyly, 'No good asking you, sir, I suppose?'

Surprised, touched, I said, 'No, I'm afraid not; the Colonel might want me to go and hold his hand.'

'And of course,' said Spencer, 'Birch is due back from leave, isn't he?'

A small sizzle of temper ran up in my head, but Doyle broke in cheerfully, 'A lot of poor bastards coming back from leave.'

I said, 'Leave's all right for a day or two when you can

sleep and wash and eat. After that, the bloody nonsense people talk makes your spine crawl.'

'Talk,' said Spencer. 'You don't have to talk: get a nice girl and find something better to do.'

'Some of us lack your stamina, old boy,' said Doyle; 'we have to talk for a bit to fill in time.'

Cartright was looking interested, as if for him this territory was still unexplored. I wondered what he would say had I told him that in this third year of war I was virgin as he most likely was at nineteen.

'Enjoy your dinner,' I said. 'Get back early. Maybe a lovely surprise for us tomorrow.'

I looked away from Cartright's face which was startled for a moment into fear.

Then I turned and saw Geoffrey walking briskly towards me.

§

Nothing in this war was truly surprising, but I looked once or twice at Geoffrey to make sure I hadn't imagined him.

'Simon! What a piece of luck. I thought I should have to go hunting all over the place.'

I took him into the farmhouse which served as the officers' billet. Its walls were crumbled and eaten: its roof mostly gone, covered now with tarpaulins. We sat in a room with broken windows and the gritty dust of war over table and chairs and camp beds. Ayres, an officer of 'D' Company, a young man, curiously solitary, was reading *The Mill on the Floss* in one corner. He nodded as we came in and paid no further attention.

I thought Geoffrey looked thin, somehow changed. He was a captain: Town Major, he said, in Bondières, a few miles to the south-west. 'I heard you were here, and I managed a lift in an empty ambulance going up to

Vlamertinghe. Wonderful what a town major can do. I'll tell you everything that's happened; I've been having a pretty nasty time, as a matter of fact.'

I nodded, constrained by the effort to disguise my fall of heart at his presence when David was due.

'I got scurvy out in the desert, of all the foul things to happen. I lost a couple of stone, as well as having a lot of filthy symptoms that I won't tell you about now in case I spoil your dinner.'

'Poor old Geoffrey.' I was trying to get at something which seemed to be new in him: something at the back of his eyes—he was the same Geoffrey on the surface; underneath, a cornerstone of certainty had been removed. 'Have a drink.'

'No, thanks.' He took out a cigarette case; his fingers were yellowed and shook slightly. 'I got sent home at last; I had a long spell in hospital and a good many weeks' convalescence. Then a medical board finally passed me as fit for fairly light stuff; but believe you me, it's not all that light in Bondières: planes coming over all the time.' He looked a little offended, as if this were a breach of etiquette. 'It's so long since I've seen you, I thought I'd come up here and—and—well, wish you luck and all that.'

I filled my glass. 'That was friendly.'

'One doesn't like being left out of the big push, but if you'd had scurvy, old man, you'd know you weren't much good for anything. It was bad luck, you know; most of the officers escaped; only the men had it, as a rule.'

'Poor old Geoffrey,' I said again. I thought that if luck came into it, it was better to have scurvy and miss the great push, but I didn't say so.

Geoffrey glanced towards Ayres who continued to read in a little tent of concentration. 'I don't know if you knew— Juana and I aren't going to be married, after all.'

'I'm sorry.'

'Yes.' He lit his cigarette with haste, as though he hadn't

much time. 'No quarrel, nothing like that—just a . . . a friendly agreement.'

Now he didn't look at me as he spoke. I said, 'What happened to her? No one at home seems to know where she's gone.'

'No. She's in London. Before he died the old man had rather a rough time, being German, and Juana was very bitter about it. She's changed a lot; you'd hardly know her.'

'I suppose everyone's changed.'

'Yes.' He said it on a sigh.

'Or if they haven't they must be lunatic and blind.'

He swung a box of matches round in his hand. Outside in the grey air the noisy cavalcade went on. In the room with Geoffrey surprisingly there and Ayres hunched, reading, the past drifted, the time before the war: all of us innocent where now we had knowledge. I said, 'If you stay, you'll see David.'

His head came up sharply, and his eyes met mine. 'David? I thought he was on leave.'

'He's due back today.'

He looked, as Geoffrey seldom did, suddenly overthrown. 'I thought he wouldn't be back for a day or so.'

I shook my head. For a moment or two Geoffrey was enclosed within his own thought; then he gave me a quick little smile as if to say, Don't you believe it, I was with you all the time; and glanced at his watch.

'It's bad luck, but I shan't be able to wait for him, I'm afraid. Got to get back; a whole lot of billeting problems to deal with.' He stood up and I saw him put on the old Geoffrey again; it almost fitted him.

'It was good to see you,' I said, encouraged by his going.

He gave a small smile, and we went together out into the road. With the stretched encamped fields and the movement, it was like coming to the edge of the sea. He held out his hand. 'Good luck, Simon.'

'Thanks.'

'Tell David I'm sorry to miss him.'

'I'll do that. How are you going to get back?'

'Oh, there's a transport chap in Vlam who'll look after me. Good-bye.'

'Good-bye, Geoffrey. All the best.'

Puzzled, I watched him go, his uniform a little too well-brushed, his boots unmuddied. He had brought a mystery with him which for a little while shifted about in my mind as I waited for David.

§

'So it was a good leave?'

'Absolutely splendid,' David said. Candles burned on the rough table and half revealed his face to me. I poured whisky from the bottle he had brought. We'd finished dinner; outside it was beginning to be dusk and the guns were livelier.

'And you saw them all?'

'Oh yes, everyone.' There was a shine on him, a lightness I couldn't account for; he was like a man who had just heard tremendous but secret news. 'My father and mother; your father and mother; everyone's father and mother. I listened to Pa in the pulpit; he was very fine: I don't think I've ever admired the old boy more. But the church is almost empty. A lone voice, I'm afraid.'

'Did you see Griselda?'

'Oh yes, everybody. It was fun. Even Mrs. Sanderson was fun.'

Jealous of his leave, I said, 'I couldn't wait to get away from it.'

'Back here?'

'Everything else seems unreal.'

'Oh, I don't think so. People talk nonsense sometimes, of course, but there's less of it—the casualty lists are so long: not a street that hasn't lost someone.'

'Maybe. Father goes in for a lot of armchair belligerence which I find hard to take.' (But I could see them as they had last waved me good-bye: my mother in tears, my father looking older, a disappointed man on the sideline of history.)

David asked, 'How are things here?'

I shrugged and poured more whisky. 'As you see. And hear. Sooner or later we shall all go up that road there. If God is with us—as they say—we shall go a few miles farther into the Salient. If not, we shall go back. Either way, a lot of men will be killed. Perhaps this is what the top boys aim at: kill lots of chaps. Gives them a feeling of achievement.'

I saw him glance at me across the table. I could hear the bitterness in my own voice; feel myself at odds with his mood which seemed to be one of deep happiness. He said, 'When did you last have leave?'

'Six months ago.'

'I think you're due for some more.'

'Oh Lord . . . don't you join the Calder's-for-Colney-Hatch brigade. I can do all that's required of me; I can get lost in the trenches and shot up by our own guns same as the next man.'

'I think you've had more than your share.'

'I've been lucky. I'm still alive. How many of those who came out in '14 can say that?'

'I dare say. But the dead don't have to go into the attack.'

'No.' The candles shivered in the room and the dark crept in. I was touched again by the certainty that this time I should be killed. A certainty from outside? Or a wish within myself, an exhausted survivor, too haunted to cope with life any more? It wasn't important. I said, 'I don't want to go on leave. The curtain's going up. One wouldn't want to be left out.'

He was still looking at me as if he tried to read something in my face beyond my words. I said, 'Would you?'

'Oh . . .' he smiled, turning so that his face moved out of

the light, 'No, I suppose not. And yet—how wonderful when it's over. Oh, wonderful.'

'Will it ever be over?'

'Oh yes. Yes. D'you know, I've got a feeling it'll be over very soon. Sometimes when I'm half asleep I can *see* it being over—printed in the papers, all that sort of thing. Sounds daft, I know, but we're all a bit daft now. Have visions, hear voices. My oracles tell me time's nearly up.'

I poured myself more drink: I saw him watching the level in the glass but he said nothing. 'I can't really see a world outside the war; I can't imagine it.'

'There is one.'

'But we can't just go back; pick up things as they were. Nothing will be the same.'

He stood up, and a fantastic shadow of his great length sprang on the walls. By a trick of candlelight his face from gaiety changed to cadaverous sorrow. His absurd shadow curtsied and grew as if it mocked him. 'Some things will. Animals, for instance. None left out here now except rats. Back home there are dogs and cats running about and hedgehogs on the lawn.'

'After three years of fighting I want something more than a hedgehog.'

'Well, there's living and having children. Remember Gann at Guillecourt?'

'Yes, I remember Gann.'

'That's the sort of thing.'

He stood there smiling at me. I was swept by the absurdity of his being part of this great mindless machine: one of those exhorted to drive the bayonet three inches—not more because one had to get it out again—into the German in front of him. I drank from my glass, not wanting to think about Gann. The whisky, taking longer than it used to, nevertheless began to work: the haunting grew less. The guns seemed louder now, as if each had frenzied the other: the candles were jumping and the shadows like monstrous plants driven by a wind : outside was the sound of armies. I said, 'What happened on your leave?'

'What d'you mean?'

'Something has.'

He didn't answer, but his face was alive with memory. I said, 'D'you know who was here today? Geoffrey. And when he heard you were coming he dived off like an eel. Why?'

'Probably I bore him to death.'

'He's broken it off with Juana.'

'I know.'

'Have you seen her?'

He was turned away from me. 'Some time I'll tell you it all.'

'Why not now?'

I seemed to speak in anger, and he was looking kindly at me, from his happiness. 'A whole heap of reasons.'

I sat there hunched, baffled, excluded. Then the door opened and Perks, an orderly from Battalion H.Q., looked into the room. 'Captain Calder, sir? The Colonel wants to see you.'

I got savagely to my feet. 'Oh hell.'

'Perhaps this is it,' said David. 'Time to be going.'

'Shouldn't think so.' I said to Perks, 'Is this a party for all company commanders, or just me?'

'Just you, sir.'

'Trouble then,' I said. 'The Colonel doesn't send for me alone to tell me interesting secrets . . . all right, Perks; let's go.'

§

Colonel Vaughan was sitting at ease after dinner, smoking a cigar. The Adjutant and the doctor sat with him. The room was small, showing marks of dereliction, the window boarded up, the walls stained and peeling : yet it contained a surprising relic of other times, a huge carved dining-table.

There seemed to hover some echo of the family who had sat about it on evenings undisturbed by war.

The Colonel took a mouthful of coffee, then said, 'Ah, Calder.'

I saluted. Colonel Vaughan allowed a moment or two's silence. I watched him through the cigar smoke, feeling conspicuous standing there, at odds with the post-prandial atmosphere of old boys together. The Colonel was a man in his mid-forties, with oddly girlish features : small nose, small mouth, large dark eyes. Nothing feminine about his manner, which was abrupt, precise, uncommunicative. They said he was one for the women, and I thought it might be so : you could see the closed precision of that face changing to practised gallantry. The doctor, with the whisky bottle squarely in front of him, was looking at me with a smile that didn't quite focus ; the Adjutant, a friendly young man called Bill Sterne (nicknamed Bond Street Bill because of a languid, high-bred air), gave me the trace of a wink.

Colonel Vaughan said, 'I understand, Calder, that you allowed two of your officers to go into Poperinghe for dinner this evening.'

'Yes sir.'

'I'm at a loss to understand how an officer of your experience can be so lax in discipline. Why weren't they sent to me to get permission ?'

'I didn't think it was necessary, sir.'

'Had they come, I should have refused it. Before long the most momentous onslaught of the whole war will be launched against the enemy. Who knows when orders will come ?—Tomorrow morning, perhaps ; and I want my officers fit and ready. And in the face of this you show no regard at all for proper discipline. What kind of example is it to your men ?'

'The men haven't made any complaints, sir.'

'No, *I'm* making the complaint, Calder. Some of you young officers who've been out here since the beginning get a damn sight too big for your boots; you think you're in command of the whole Battalion. Well you're not: I am.'

I said, 'Yes, sir.' Bill Sterne was looking into his glass as if he'd seen a fly in it; the doctor seemed to be asleep. Anger was beating in my head: the frustration of the scene with David fed this small ignominy before the Colonel.

He seemed about to dismiss me; then he said, 'I'm aware that officers like yourself have been under considerable strain. But the mark of a good officer is that, strain or not, he doesn't let his standards fall. That'll do, Calder.'

In a rage I flung myself back to our billet where David was placidly waiting, smoking a pipe and looking through *The Mill on the Floss*, which Ayres had left on the table.

I said, 'Of all the bloody nonsense. Fuss about nothing. Are we fighting a war or running a boys' boarding school? Cartright and Spencer may be dead in a week: what the hell does it matter if they go to dinner in Pop?'

David put down *The Mill on the Floss*. 'I expect the old boy's getting a bit jumpy.'

'Jumpy be damned; he was cruising on cigar smoke and baiting a junior officer. An old-time sport like pig-sticking.'

'He isn't worth getting so worked up about—''

'A whole string of clichés about discipline and the respect of the men.'

'Colonels have to talk like that, the way actors put on greasepaint.'

'I don't know why the hell you're taking his side—'

'Now don't be an ass,' said David with an affection that could not reach me. 'He's got his problems, same as everyone else—'

'Yes, but we don't sit behind the lines, resting our backsides on comfortable chairs, we have to—'

'We have to get shot at; so does Vaughan sometimes; he did something frightfully dashing at Messines, I can't remember what—'

'I don't care what the hell he did at Messines: he's a domineering fuss-pot without a grain of imagination—'

'Come and sit down and stop getting so excited—'

'I'm damned if I will!' Anger existed in its own right, and I clung to it with childish force, as if its arid heat were in some way nourishing. 'I'm not going to be ordered about by a lily-faced womanizer who talks to me as if I'd written a rude word on the blackboard—'

'Come on, old chap. Sit down and have a drink—'

'I don't want any bloody drink,' I said untruthfully and swung round to face Perks again. He stood with his mouth a little way open. 'Well, what the hell is it now?'

'The Colonel wants to see you again, sir.'

'Dear God; haven't I done my duty tonight as target practice?'

Perks ran his tongue over his lips and did not answer. 'Go on, Simon,' said David. 'Perhaps he wants you to make up a fourth at bridge.'

Trembling, I went out again into the road. Though still held in my anger I could see the end of it in sight, the waste-land, the ashy after-taste of rage. They said animals were sad after the act of love; men were most sad, I suspected, after anger. Again Perks led me into the Colonel's H.Q.

The room was changed. Bill Sterne and the doctor had both gone: the Colonel was alone. It seemed that they had both left in a hurry, for the cards were down on the table, prepared for three-handed bridge. (I thought of David's words.) The Colonel had a small pink telegraph form on the table in front of him.

He cleared his throat and said, 'Yes, Calder.' His tone was changed also. I waited. He went on, pulling a glass towards him and pouring whisky into it, 'Here. Have a drink.'

'No thank you, sir.'

He didn't look annoyed, merely tired. 'Go on; take it.' He pushed the glass towards me. 'Sit down.'

Puzzled, I sat on a wooden chair. The silence in the room was surrounded by the sound of guns. The oil lamp on the table left the fringes dark. The Colonel looked down at the scrap of pink paper. He seemed genuinely perplexed.

He said, 'I've just had this from Division. They asked me to communicate it to you. It's a message from Major Comyns, O.C. at the base hospital at Etaples.'

I waited. He cleared his throat again. 'Your brother, Captain Esmond Calder, R.A.M.C., died of wounds there this morning. I'm very sorry, Calder.'

I stared at him. The room in its uncertain light was sharply changed. I said, 'But I heard from him the other day. He was at a dressing-station somewhere behind the lines. He said it was quiet.'

The Colonel grunted and poured himself more whisky as if he needed it. 'Always a chance of long-range shelling—something like that.'

I drank from the glass. Of all the many deaths, this refused to make sense. I said, 'It's a bit of a shock, sir.'

'Yes, of course. Men killed all the time, but one's own family . . .' He took up his cigar, then put it down again.

I finished the whisky and got to my feet. 'Thank you for telling me, sir.'

'That's all right, Calder.' He looked relieved, a difficult job done. 'Of course, if I'd known about this . . .'

'Yes, sir. Thank you.' I saluted, and he said a little absently, 'Good night.'

Outside in the noisy dark I walked alone.

Esmond. He moved through my mind with ease and confidence: I had no picture of his death. I saw the house at Fennelhurst, a place darkened by news; most clearly I saw my mother, unarmoured against such grief.

Died of wounds. The words were tidy, a formula: she would not, I hoped, look beyond them to some savagery of mutilation and pain. Esmond? No, still I couldn't quite believe it: not the boy who had grown up beside me, with no shadow on him at all.

Died of wounds.

Yes, it must be true; they wouldn't send a message like that to the Colonel, unless it was true. I lit a cigarette. Something had darkened the future, darkened my hopes. I kept seeing my mother's bright head and pretty smile. 'Darling mother, I was so shocked to hear . . . I'm sure he died bravely. . . .' No; what was there to say? She wanted life, not death. 'Try to believe . . .' What? Not in God any more: no God could look on so much misery and pain. 'Father and I will do all we can . . .' But there was nothing we could do: it was Esmond she loved. What, then? I could think of nothing: only the Colonel's face, as he offered me a glass of whisky. It wasn't much, but it was comfort, of a kind.

§

'Listen.'

We lay in our bunks. The room was the colour of dust. No sleep; the guns had doubled and trebled; their noise made an iron echoing in the sky, without rest or cease.

'This must be it. Zero hour. They must be going over soon.'

'Poor buggers.'

My heart beat, as if I were already up beyond Ypres, in the trenches, waiting for the moment of commission, for the climb into the terrible open. The noise put fever in my limbs; I turned and threshed on the wire bunk. Images of Esmond, torn and bloodied, swam through my mind. Two men from my company stood clear, as figures come close at the beginning of sleep: Carter, the bricklayer: knotty, ugly, ageless, always with a fag drooping from his mouth; foul-mouthed, dirty and so curiously and continually brave that one was abashed, as before something of tremendous authority; Harding, a fussy little chemist who had theories about the Zodiac: he said the war would end when Saturn was in the ascendant, whatever that meant. Some of the men thought him a bit daft, but he was gentle, ready with comfort for the young under fire: 'Don't fret, lad; lie down till it's over . . . you'll be all right.' Such men as these . . .

Louder and louder the shelling.

'Our turn soon,' said Spencer.

Cartright on his bunk under the window turned on one elbow, but said nothing. I could see the grey light on his cheek as he fearfully listened. Our turn soon.

David said, 'I keep thinking of Esmond.'

The guns even louder, reaching some absolute of destruction. (Yes, I think of Esmond too. But David will be safe; I still believe that, in face of everything. He may be wounded, but he'll live. 'Some time I'll tell you it all,' he'd said. He'd told me nothing yet, but his deep happiness still contained him.)

'It must be now. They must be going over now.'

'Lord.'

'You may well pray.'

The air was cold, strangely full of activity, though here we lay, like children listening to a story, on our beds. I thought that now, after this long time of war, one was never quite alone, never safe, even in one's safety: some sense of the many who were at the heart of violence surrounded one always. The floor of the room trembled and a glass sang.

'Praying's no good. Look at all the people who pray.'

'It keeps them happy.'

'Not for long.'

The fever of sound drove me from my bunk. I put on raincoat and shoes; let them think I was going to the latrine.

The air was moist and cold: I stood looking across the flat plains towards Ypres and beyond. On the horizon light burst and flooded from the assaulted earth, like corruption

148

from many wounds. *Now they must be going over.* In the heart of that evil light, men were running and dying; yet from here, where you could not see them, the sky had an awful beauty. Our turn soon. I looked over the crowded fields: the world this side of the assault might have been made of stone. The tents began to gleam a little, not white, merely a lessening of the grey. They had about them the still patience of beasts, obedient, unmoving. Within them the men dozed or turned, listened to the sound, contained their fear; like beasts too, made no protest.

Soon.

4

August, 1917

We went three days later. We went in a dusk made darker by a continuous and vertical rain: a rain that had scarcely ceased since the opening day of the attack.

We were going through Ypres itself. The echoing and savaged streets had about them the grandeur of their long defiance; even the rain could not quite dispel it. We went through, the men distorted by their grey-green capes, tin helmets slanted against the rain, rifles slung, rising like lean periscopes from the humpbacked mass. Against all reason the town in its desolation seemed to give us welcome, to know that we did not abandon it. And for a moment, as we went through the Grand' Place, under the ragged tower of the Cloth Hall, I caught an astonishing echo, of the town as it must once have been, in the medieval spring-time of its glory: I saw pale, fashioned stone, pennants and flags; a structure made lovingly by men. Now in this twilight nothing remained but the ragged shapes of destruction, and these men who went wearily through.

On, towards the echoing and malignant sky. Through the Menin Gate, now no more than two heaps of stones, the clamour of its name lost in fear as we went forward on to the wet and dangerous cobbles, chosen target for the German guns. '*Keep apart ; two hundred yards between each platoon.*' The men were silent now; cold, wet, weary and afraid, coming once more into the territory of death.

We trudged by a splintered mass that might have been a gun limber; the horses, their black hides glistening like dark ice in the rain, lying dead. I remembered once hearing the anguished scream of horses wounded and not dead; had these horses screamed so? Men were passing us now; two stretcher-bearers with their load; a Highlander, limping, with blood on his face. The sound of a shell came into sharp focus, a scream of warning, and I was suddenly thrown to the ground as if by a large angry hand; I heard a shout, perhaps of fear, perhaps of anguish somewhere in the rainy fire-splashed dusk behind me. My face was wet, my body bruised and shocked; my head had one name fearfully sounding there.

All my certainty vanished; senseless comfort, now snatched from me.

I scrambled to my feet. The road was a churned confusion of men and wet and fear. I pushed my way through the column. 'Anyone hurt? Is anyone hurt?'

'Couldn't say, sir. Blown me toothpick right out of me mouth.'

'Is anyone hurt?'

'Poor bastard over there.'

'*Is anyone hurt?*'

'Over there, sir.'

'Where, you bloody fool?'

'Those poor sods, sir.'

I looked where Bert Stanton pointed. The stretcher-bearers with their burden and the limping Highlander weren't there any more. Or . . . yes, they were there: the rain pooled crimson on the torn body of the Highlander because both his legs were gone: the stretcher's load and its bearers had left only such bloody wreckage as in a nightmare one would have said had belonged to living men.

I turned from it. I thought I heard a man vomit on to the pavé; only the new ones did that.

'All right. Get on. Leave them, there's nothing we can do.'

I could see David there. He was alive. The superstition, overthrown, grew tall again.

§

We had left the road. The ground sucked and muddied our boots; the blackish substance, because one couldn't see it clearly, seemed more sinister. Stronger now was the familiar smell of the battlefield: cordite, bitter on the tongue, sewage and death. But the shelling seemed to have died: now and again a distant gun, the devil-dance of machine-gun fire like an answer. My own weariness, as I forced my feet forward over the unwilling ground, seemed not mine only, but an echo of the men's behind me. The rain did not lessen; darkness increased. A Very light swung into the sky; swam slowly down in a ghostly green brilliance which showed the wasteland of glistening mud, shell-holes filled with black water and the darker huddled mounds that might have been earth or men. I stared about me; the light died and the murmurous, strong-smelling dark came down again.

I stood, passing the word behind me to halt. 'Harrison,' I said. 'Where are you?'

'Here, sir.'

Harrison was the Company Sergeant-Major, a surprisingly young man with a tired and cynical expression; his attitude in the face of German shelling was that it was offensive in the civilian sense of the word: I found him often a comfort.

'Harrison, I've no idea where we are.'

'Not surprising, sir. There isn't exactly anywhere to *be*, is there?'

'Take a look at the map.' I shone my torch on it. Its sterile and ordered pattern, blurred by rain, bore as little resemblance to the wastes about us as an equation in algebra. 'We've got to relieve some poor benighted Irishmen in those trenches, west of Gheluvelt. And a guide meets us *here*.' I showed him a neat point on the map.

'Pity we can't go home and tell them rain stopped play. Compass, sir?'

I watched the delicate needle sway and turn. 'We should be heading south-east,' I said. In the streaming dark the words seemed meaningless; all directions were the same; all led to limbo.

'This way, then, sir.'

We moved on again; the sense of being lost seemed to strengthen the intractable mud, add weight to one's limbs.

A voice behind me: '*Here* we are: climb on the rafts, boys: float home to Mother.'

'*Quiet*, there.'

The duckboards. Trodden by men and mules, slanting, half-sunken, here and there broken, but welcome, suggesting order, correctness: that we were on the right path even if it led straight to destruction. Still the quiet continued; a nervous quiet; the watery and muddy waste seemed more desolate and menacing because of it.

Suddenly it was broken: the guns grew loud, and our world was lit again by the flash and tremble of light. The shells were close; they fell hissing into the slime, torn red-hot splinters plunging like arrows, quickly extinguished. But here, thank God, was the communication trench. A ditch, rather, buttressed with wooden props and sandbags, striving to return to the unity of mud. Somewhere here should be the guide from the Irish regiment.

I jumped down and crouched there, for it wasn't deep enough. It smelt evilly, and its floor was best screened by the dark. The guide? I made my way on; a rat scurried over my boots; trailing wire caught my foot; the shells were driving their noisy path continuously, shredding one's thoughts and one's breath, so that one lived and moved from sound to sound, from explosion to explosion. I wanted to call to David to keep his head down; he wouldn't take that well: I kept quiet. The guide? One could only follow the trench; sooner or later I must come to him. I began to grow anxious, like a man waiting on a railway platform for a friend who doesn't come. The men had been going through this, without food or drink, for more than three hours. I looked behind me. Humped and streaming, swearing quietly, they were following me. This was worthy of some better enterprise. I floundered on.

A nearer scream of shell; light like some God-forsaken day, revealing ahead of me the hunched figure of a man waiting. I said to Harrison, who was behind me, 'That must be the guide.'

'Looks like it.'

A fallen trench prop caught my foot and I swore; I was moving more eagerly now. Though he must have heard us, the figure did not turn.

'Hullo,' I said into the dark, in a brief quiet within the shelling. 'Captain Calder with "B" Company of the . . .' I was nearer now. The man had not moved. I put out my hand to touch the arm in its sodden sleeve. Instantly the figure, stiffened in death, fell into the muddy bottom of the trench at my feet. By the light of gunfire I could see the blackened face, half shot away. Death was all about us, but this, like the news of Esmond, chilled me. I said to Harrison, 'He can't be our guide; he's been dead some time. I don't know where the guide is.'

'Waiting under the wrong clock, sir.'

'Something like that. We'll have to get this poor bastard out of the way or the men'll tread on him.'

'Right, sir.'

We lifted him away, quickly; no point in standing straight longer than necessary; no point in adding more deaths.

Perhaps the burial parties would find him. I said, 'I wonder where the hell this damned guide is.'

'The fire's been pretty heavy, sir. Perhaps they got him.'

'Yes, I dare say.' Odd, this feeling of emptiness, of foreboding. None of this was new; it was the well-learned pattern of war. Yet I went deeper into misgiving. I said, 'I'll follow the trench further. Perhaps he's wounded. Or sheltering from the fire.'

I said this without hope. The guide was lost to us: this seemed to me a certainty. Labouring on through the trench I found that I had to bend deeper, for the ground was rising. Now it was hardly a trench at all; soon it would be part of the inky morass, the open ground. I could not see the duckboards. The shells still went over. I said to Harrison, my voice strained and harsh above the sound of the shelling, 'Tell them to go back. There's nothing here.'

'Sweet Fanny Adams, sir,' agreed Harrison. 'Come along, get *down*. Put up your umbrellas; we're all going to have a snooze. Pass it along; we're all going to have a lovely rest.'

The men crouched down in the mud. Their heads sank forward, so that each man looked like a huddled monument to his own weariness. I wondered how many of them were blaming me for having led them here. They muttered among themselves: 'If I'd known it was going to be as wet as this I'd've joined the Navy'; 'Pity I forgot me water-wings.' They didn't stand up as one man and curse whatever brute or blackguard brought them here. I said to Harrison, 'Get Lieutenant Birch. And for God's sake tell him to walk double. I've got enough worries without losing my second-in-command. And see if there's any rum going for the men.'

David came, making his way clumsily. We stretched a piece of tarpaulin over the trench and crouched below it. 'Here,' I said. 'Come on, David, pull it your side; come on, Spencer—Doyle—Cartright—Harrison. Now we can look at this bloody map.'

I shone my torch. We crouched together in its frail light,

sodden, faces drawn and dripping, close, lashes and skin and teeth, eyeballs and nostril, the delicate human stuff, no match for splinters and bullets and shell-fire.

'All right,' I said, 'here we are. On the map there's another trench, leading through to the line. I propose to take a couple of men and prospect. On our bellies. I don't want the whole Company wandering out there in the mud.'

'No place for anyone to wander,' said David.

'The shelling's quieter.'

'Won't do any harm to wait here,' said Spencer.

'And the Irishmen?'

'They'll send another guide.'

'We can't count on it.'

David said, 'I think it's a damn fool thing to do.'

'The whole bloody war's a damn fool thing to do.' I seemed to have lost my temper. 'There must be some indication of a trench or a duckboard: as soon as I've found it, I'll send one of the men back to guide the rest of you. I'm going to take Hobhouse and Wicks.' I named two young runners who had stamina and sense.

'All right: but *I'm* going to take them,' said David. 'O.C.s are valuable; O.C.s should be preserved.'

'So should we all,' I said, pushing the map back in my pocket. 'Harrison, get me Hobhouse and Wicks.' I could feel David's eyes on me. Not the moment to tell him there was little courage in this: my fear was of a different colour. I lifted myself from my crouching position, dislodging the groundsheet; anxious to be gone.

Crouching in the trench, the figures came towards me. Hobhouse and Wicks. Their eyes were on me; one grey pair, one brown. Afraid? Yes, but prepared to go. Oh, damn everything.

I explained my plan, turned my back on them and climbed up the sticky side of the trench. Both rain and shelling had almost ceased. I could hear the two men moving behind me like crocodiles on their bellies. The mud now had a strange friendliness; one moved like one of its own animals, belonging there. A damn fool thing to do. Was I perhaps already a little mad? Well, we were all mad.

A Very light went up, its high swooning movement languid as the drift of a cloud. I froze on the instant: soon enough? The shells coming over again, and the cross-stitch impatient rattle of machine-gun fire: directed at us? I felt beneath me a little downward slant in the ground. Were there machine-gun nests hidden, having this stretch of ground below them, making a field of fire? Impotent anger ran through me: nothing was properly organized, thought out: the Staff, comfortable in dry billets behind the line, wrote words on paper, sent messages, maps, sat back and left us to grovel in this murderous mud. Such anger was useless: one had to let it run out, like water from the bladder; it was a waste product, to be rid of.

Then I saw the duckboard. Broken and half-hidden by the embracing mud. A shattered tree, black, fossilized, grew beside it: it stood with an arm out, as if it should say, *No further*. I remembered the stiffened body in the trench. Once on the duckboard I could see the trench we sought for not five yards ahead. The temptation to stand up and run for it was too much: I called to Hobhouse and Wicks, '*Come on!*' The dangerous air skimmed past my face as I clumsily ran: the duckboards sagged in the slime; I stumbled and ran on. Here was the trench; quickly into it; safety now—

The shell screamed, closer than the other shells. I heard a cry behind me; its impact was savage in my chest as if I myself had been hit. Then I heard sobbing, unrestrained, like a woman weeping for a lost child. Hobhouse was beside me in the trench, very white. 'It's Wicks, sir. A splinter right through him somewhere.'

Together we got him down into the trench. All the time he didn't stop crying. I heard my own voice as I had called, '*Come on!*' Shouldn't have done that; shouldn't have stood up out there; going crazy, perhaps; not to be trusted any more. I said, 'You'll be all right, Wicks; we'll see to you. Any stretcher-bearers here?'

The men in the trench, stupefied with lack of sleep and five days in the line, looked on him with the remnants of pity, but there weren't any stretcher-bearers. They had no O.C. either; he'd been killed that afternoon; the last of their officers. A sergeant, snatching a sodden cigarette from his mouth, his face wet with strain and moisture from nose and eyes, said, 'We're supposed to be supported on the right flank by a company of Highlanders, but it's my opinion they've legged it, the way they usually do. And half the men are sick: dysentery, trench-fever. Ye've not come a moment too soon, sir.' I nodded. Beyond the parapet I could see the bodies of the dead. Wicks was still crying. I knelt beside him, doing what I could for the wound in his hip, while I listened to the Sergeant. The Jerries were about seventy yards ahead. Orders to attack were expected, but so far they hadn't come. Looked as if we'd get them. There were some particularly persistent machine-gun posts concealed on high ground to the south there, making all movement perilous. He didn't know what had happened to the guide; he must have been wounded or killed. Nice lad. Name of O'Malley.

I nodded. The shelling had quietened. I said to Hobhouse, who crouched, looking broodingly at Wicks, 'I want you to get back to the Company. Guide them here. Tell them about Wicks: the stretcher-bearers must get him to the nearest Aid Post.'

'Yes, sir.' He was still looking down at Wicks.

'Keep to the duckboards. Be as quick as you can but don't take any risks.' As if the whole damn thing wasn't a risk.

'No, sir.'

He turned and began to climb out of the trench; his figure looked lonely, obedient, moving clumsily. I shut it out of my mind and said to the Sergeant, 'My Company'll be along soon. Show me the line, and get your men out.'

We pushed past huddled men; as I came some of them lifted weary heads to look up at me; their eyes were red, moist, patient, drunken with lack of sleep, with sickness. One or two smiled, recognizing the chance of relief.

'All right,' I said. 'Take them off.' (And what was I doing, letting them go before my own Company arrived?) 'I trust Fritz won't try an attack in the next half-hour. If he does he'll find me and poor Wicks here and he'll get a lovely surprise.'

Muttering, heaving themselves up, shouldering packs, rifles, water bottles, the men were gradually moving. Their words were few; they were dark shapes of weariness and suffering, akin to the shapes out there in No-Man's-Land, not moving any more.

I watched them go. Wicks had stopped crying: I hoped he was unconscious, but every now and again his eyes opened. I said, 'They'll be along soon. Stretcher-bearers. Get you to an Aid Post. Nice blighty one: peace and quiet from now on. Bit of luck, really.'

'I don't think it's any good, sir.'

'Don't be silly. Leg wound: best you can have.'

'I feel so weak.'

'That's shock.'

He closed his eyes again and didn't answer. The last of the Irishmen had gone. I crouched in the muddy trench, alone with Wicks. The guns were quiet, but every now and again there came a sharp burst of machine-gun fire, like a boy dragging a stick along iron railings. It sounded close. The trench, empty of men, its floor scattered with bully-beef tins, rounds of ammunition, broken rifles, and the tattered hessian of sandbags, was a benighted place, haunted, smelling and silent. I had known trenches, even in their places of extreme danger, with something of comfort. This had none.

I waited there. I trusted the Sergeant wouldn't tell any

higher authority that I'd let him take his men off before my Company had arrived. I went on saying comforting things to Wicks, but I could see the blood soaking through the futile field dressings on his side, and I think I knew as well as he did that he was done for.

And there seemed to come from the noxious mud, or from the shell-torn air, a sensation of loneliness so extreme that had it not been for Wicks, muttering and groaning there, I should have had to rush from the trench and run madly along the duckboards to find other men. Even towards the enemy, for they were men, and any company was better than this towering isolation, the inadequacy of one man alone, having no one opposite him to reflect his humanity. The hermits saw their humanity reflected in God; but here was no God, and one needed other men, else in this place one was nothing, a scattered confusion of conflicting impulses, the spiritual counterpart of the bodies blasted by shells in No-Man's-Land.

I started gabbling to Wicks again, a stream of false comfort; I don't know if he heard. I tried to think of the Company, perhaps by now making their way towards me. A bright evil strip of machine-gun fire stopped my words: I waited, listened. Then I went on talking: I talked of peace, beds, sheets, England, warm earth and quiet, beer and summer. I gabbled faster because his face was so very pale. If I hadn't said '*Come on*' . . . No use in that; if he didn't die now he'd die later: we'd all die, before long, somewhere in the stretches of the Salient below the Ridge. Better so, perhaps, for what would there be after this? Peace, with a vast unhealed wound, the wound of the dead. Better to go into the last mystery knowing only that men can send iron and steel into each other's flesh, and yet show kindliness, forbearance and love: that with one hand they direct the machine-gun; with the other bind the wounds. Fall asleep for ever knowing nothing but the paradox.

A sudden sound from Wicks. A sound too familiar, a

snore, a violence in his throat. I clasped his hand. For a moment it held mine, but the fingers quickly slackened and fell away. I felt them go as one feels a failure, the cancellation of hope.

One more.

I waited then alone. Wicks, R. E., Private, some number like 8/5139. A letter to be written; grief somewhere to be received. For myself, still living, the abandoned trench, the dark, the awareness of his death that absurdly seemed to give me superior knowledge, as if there would not come a time when some man, perhaps now unknown to me, would look down on my body, secure in the knowledge of his continuing life.

I pulled him to the side of the trench and, lying thus, he seemed to be turned from the world in some sorrow. . . . Had the Company lost their way? Was I isolated here? God, make them come. . . .

My own breathing sounded harsh, panic-driven. But then I heard movement, voices, the pressure of company on the air. I stared towards them in the dark, thirsty for them; they came like a blessing; how beautiful upon the duck-boards are the feet . . . Alone here a man would go crazy; but they've come.

§

On the rim of distance was a pulsing light and the undertone of gunfire, but here we seemed to exist in discomfort but most strange absence of danger. With David I had prospected as far as possible to right and left; there seemed no trace of men supporting us. The foreboding of this place crawled beneath my skin. The very quiet had a menace of its own: what brooded and spawned within it?

'Not much of a trench, is it?' said David, looking at it rather as if he'd been sold a dud.

'Bloody awful.'

'Wonder how long we're going to stay here?'

'That poor Irish bastard said they were expecting orders to attack.'

'How splendid; what are we supposed to attack in: boats?'

We were rolled in our groundsheets, huddled into a corner of the trench. Extremity of exhaustion didn't seem to bring sleep. The men were collapsed in those positions of weariness which resemble death. Gunfire, still distant, was as little troubling as the sound of the train when one travels by night. These moments, like all moments of peace within the war, made the whole thing absurd. One could not be sleeping in a ditch, one's skin irritable with lice, surrounded by the dead and by men who would soon be dead, separated by seventy yards or so of mud from an enemy, so-called, who turned and crouched and waited and feared as we did here. This was not a way of life.

I said, 'What are we doing here?'

'Breathing mud. Or fighting a war. Depends how you look at it.'

'A bloody silly business.'

'Well, of course.'

Sodden clothes lay clammily on my skin; I turned and shifted, but no new position was any better than the last. 'You haven't told me about your leave.'

'No.' There was a little silence in the dark. 'It's a long story. I will tell you. But not yet.'

I shivered and pulled the groundsheet about me.

He went on, 'I could hardly bear to come back. The only good thing about it was finding you here.'

'I thought you said I ought to be bundled off home with a keeper.'

He chuckled. 'Even so . . .'

I looked towards him in the dark. Isolated here in this evil place I was suddenly so charged with love that I could not imagine love of any woman being as strong as this.

162

He went on, 'The men are for you, you know.'

'I lose my temper and drink too much.'

'Maybe. They don't mind that. They trust you.'

The words put an ache in my chest. 'To do what? To get them all killed?'

'They just trust you, that's all.'

'God help them then.'

A silence; then David's voice again. 'D'you know what I think? I think we'll both survive it.'

'Second sight?'

'My oracles again. I can *see* us both back at Fennelhurst, growing into rather boring old men, full of yarns about the Salient.'

I had a sudden taste of the far future: the places of old age, wars finished, passion done: *No war, or battle's sound, Was heard the world around.* . . . 'Shall we be old?'

'I think so. . . . Lord, this mud does stink. D'you know the men here I envy most? The ones with children.'

'Isn't it worse for them?'

'No, I don't think so.'

Silence then, fringed by the surf-boom of the guns. I tried to think what it would be like to have children, but I could form no image of them. Part of my own flesh, yet separate, grown from the seed of my body; they moved in an unknown world, featureless and shadowy, teasing because in spite of the incapacity of imagination, they might one day exist.

And a child of David's? This was stranger still.

A cold, aching sleep seemed to take hold of me in the reasonless way of the trenches: I dreamed of Esmond. I was standing in the garden at Fennelhurst, aware that he was dead. But suddenly I turned to see him; he had come noiselessly over the grass. Large relief swept me; I said, 'Does Mother know?' Then the relief began to fade, for he said nothing, merely stared at me, his face distorted by grief. He had terrible news, and fearful of hearing it, fighting to wake and not hear it, I gave a grunt and was back in the trench; Esmond was dead and had no news to give me.

The air was moist and grey. David wasn't there. I made my way down the trench, pushing past the legs of hunched and dozing men. I found him talking to Harding the chemist on guard in a bay of the trench. Harding said, 'All quiet, sir.' He looked cold and earnest; his eyes watered from the strain of looking.

'Fine,' I said. 'Are the stars in their right courses?'

'Wouldn't like to say that, sir.'

'What about Lieutenant Birch? His birthday's in October.'

He wrinkled his forehead. 'Which day?'

'The fourth.'

'That makes him Libra.'

'Lucky or not?'

'Oh, I'd have to work it out, sir.'

The dark dream was lifting off; fear was different in company. Harding beat one hand against his side. I said, 'Stand-to in about ten minutes. Then a rum ration. Then breakfast.'

He smiled. 'That's right, sir. Porridge for me and two eggs. My wife makes wonderful porridge. Have it every morning. And d'you know, sir, it's a funny thing, but it must have rained sometimes at home, mustn't it? I mean, near Wembley? But when I think about the breakfast-table I always see the sun on it, I can't see it anyhow else. Nice blue china and a white cloth and the big brown teapot and the morning paper. Nicest meal of the day, I always said. The sugar was in a bowl which said "A stitch in time saves nine"; when I wanted the sugar I'd say to my wife, "Pass me the stitch, love."'

'We had a jug,' said David, 'which said "Look before you leap . . .". When's your birthday, Harding?'

'End of July, sir.'

'Like me,' I said.

'Really, sir?' He looked pleased. 'We're both Leo, then. Both lions, as you might say. . . . Think it's going to rain again, sir?'

I glanced at the sky. Its increasing pallor showed no sun. Harrison was calling the men to stand-to, and all along the trench they were moving, preparing for one more day.

§

The day that grew from that grey haunted mist was nervous, irritable, jagged with bursts of gunfire. The rain began again, hesitantly at first. Half-way through the morning Hawkins, a signaller, came to tell me the field-telephone was cut. This seemed of a piece with the isolation of this place, but I didn't like being cut off from Battle H.Q. I crouched by Hawkins as he listened, for surely men would be sent from H.Q. to repair the wire but he kept shaking his head. 'Nothing, sir.'

I said, 'They'll mend it when it's dark.' If they didn't, I'd have to send someone to look for the break, but not yet, not with the machine-guns so lively and so close. 'Tell me the moment you hear his master's voice; they may have news for us.'

'News, sir?'

'The big attack that's going to win the war.'

He turned his eyes to the glistening swamp. 'In that, sir?'

Afternoon. The day was unlike any day I had known, even in these years of war. There had been other days in the front line, nervous with gunfire, having no certainty of action about them. Mud, rain and desolation were old company. Yet this was different. My own weariness? The fatigue that David had spoken of, the stretched nerves, the jumpy unstable centre of one's being? Perhaps it was only this. This, and Esmond's death, and the dead man waiting upright in the trench.

Tea, tasting of petrol and onions. I watched the men drinking it in mugs. Curious, so close to death, how the small necessities of life persisted: up to the very edge of it men gulped their tea, munched bully beef, relieved themselves, smoked the coarse cigarettes. One would have thought there should have been a limbo when, aware of death so close, men shuffled off desire for food and drink and all the needs of the body whose intricate flesh might in a moment, in the twinkling of an eye, become bloody and obscene refuse in the receiving mud.

Later afternoon. A wish now for some definite news, for some purpose to be explained to us. Anything would be better than to sit in the sluicing, shelving mud, from time to time under fire, having seemingly no purpose here but to be killed.

Towards five o'clock there was a lift in the rain. Across the level wasteland a diffused light spread, just somewhere touched with colour, so that one looked for greater certainty, a sign of returning sun. The watery shell-holes were suddenly lit, having the haunting melancholy of mountain tarns, and the chaos of mud was given form and symmetry by light.

And the shells began coming over again. They were falling behind us, but near enough to change the atmosphere in the trench; glancing down I saw the men's faces beneath their dripping helmets, tightened once more, paler, dark-eyed, meeting the onslaught as best they could, containing fear and the places beyond fear behind a shaking hand and a twitching eyelid.

A five-nine landed closer than any yet, and at first when I heard the disturbance in the trench, I thought someone had been hit. Then I saw the young strange soldier making his way clumsily towards me.

§

He had the drawn, old look of all men who have made their way through heavy fire. 'Captain Calder? Message from Battle H.Q., sir.'

I took the crumpled paper and read it in a corner of the trench:

'At zero time, oo, tomorrow morning, you will attack Remus Alley. Barrage will lift at oo hours. First wave will go over the top. At plus 8 wave will double to objective. Bayonet if necessary. Consolidate.'

I said to David, 'I think Battalion's gone out of its mind,' and handed him the message.

I watched him as he read it. I said, 'We've no support on either flank as far as I can see. We shall be exposed to machine-gun fire from the moment we move. And the men who aren't shot will sink in the mud.'

He glanced at me, his face alert, traced with grim amusement, acknowledging the prospect. 'They promise us a barrage.'

'Which'll finish off the few of us still alive. I'm going to question the orders.' I took my Intelligence pad and explained our position as firmly as I could. When I glanced up I saw David watching me. He said, 'We'll go just the same.'

'I'm damned if we will. I'm *here*, looking at the mud: I know that we're out on the end of a branch line, like a lot of fool sparrows at the end of a twig.'

'I expect it looks a good idea on the map.'

'The Colonel isn't a complete ass. Facts must mean something to him.'

'Probably not his idea. Someone in Brigade, I dare say, or even Army Corps.'

'Well, facts have got to mean something to them too.' I had a rage inside me that was going to resist this command to the limits of my power; I wanted David to share it. But there was a strange wisdom on him, a calmness that I resented; that seemed to say he knew more about this than I did; that he knew how it would be.

I gave the young runner who'd brought the message a tot of whisky. He had a cast in one eye which made him look as though he were seeing into a distance, of space or time. He drank the whisky and coughed; his eyes ran. When a blue dusk swamped the sky and the mud, I sent him back to Headquarters. He was frightened to go, but his fear did not move me enough; I was set upon saving the Company from destruction, and nothing mattered beyond this.

When he had gone there was nothing to do but wait. After stand-to the cooks produced something that they called soup. It tasted like (and maybe was) water in which the dishes of the whole Company had been washed several times over, but there in the benighted place it brought a moment of comfort. The dusk began to lose all colour; the sky was overcast, showing no stars. The guns, though not quite silent, were quieter now. How long before a message came?

Darkness totally down. One more night. Some comfort in the masking of desolation by the dark: the day laid too much bare to the eye. Star shells and signal flares coloured but could not define what lay under the dark. Weariness and fear in equal parts kept one in yawning wakefulness. The field-telephone was still dead. No messenger came under cover of the dark from Headquarters; we had no news. I poured more whisky.

'Supposing that poor bastard of a runner's copped it?' said David.

'He won't have. It's been quiet since he went.'

Still we waited. I got up and pushed my way over the legs of the men down the trench. Few of them slept. The current of waiting ran through them all, jerked their heads up as they fell forward, as if someone had pulled a string. I gave them false cheerful exhortations of hope. I thrust my way on, aware of time moving forward through the night. In my head I could see the globe turning, having just now the continents of the west away from the sun. Though the dark seemed consistent, unending, this was a journey all the time: the remorseless day slid inch by inch nearer as we turned. If there were a God, I thought, he would cover this torn and desecrated earth with darkness until it was healed.

Still no one came; the telephone was still silent. The air had the lifeless cold of the small hours, silent except for the distant heaving sound of gunfire. I returned to my hollowed place in the trench, wrapped myself with my groundsheet; it might be possible after all to sleep. Tense as I was with waiting and listening, exhaustion like fumes began to cloud my head. . . .

'Sir! Captain Calder, sir!'

My heart gave a long vibrating twist; I was awake, out of the doze, looking into Hawkins's face through a darkness that was not quite the same darkness.

'The wire's been mended, sir. H.Q. on the line.'

I gave a grunt of acknowledgement. I could still feel the twisty, unpleasant beating of my heart. It was twenty to four. The cone of darkness was slipping away. The guns vibrated like a man stamping in anger. I put my ear to the field-telephone that had been dead for so many hours. Against the noise of the far guns I heard the Adjutant's voice. Bond Street Bill.

'Hullo, Simon. Look here, the Colonel says he's damned sorry but the order's got to stand.'

'No, it can't—'

'Don't be an ass—'

'Bill, the whole thing's nothing but a bloody farce. We haven't a hope—'

'I know, old chap, I know. The Colonel's done his best; he's been on to Brigade.'

'Brigade haven't the dimmest notion of what it's like up here—'

'Too true, old chap, too true. No mud in their drawing-rooms. But the order stands. I'm bloody sorry.'

'I see.'

'And what's more, you've got to send out a patrol before it gets light to gauge the enemy's strength.'

'We shall know that soon enough.'

'Those are Brigade orders, old boy. Not my fault. If I had my way we'd all go home and play bezique. I may have said before, I'm bloody sorry. I have to ask you to synchronize your watch with Brigade time: it's exactly 3.48 ack emma *now*.'

'Right.'

Across the frail and bombarded wire there was a moment's silence. I could see Bill in Battle Headquarters; myself here. My throat was dry. Bill's voice came again, 'Zero hour will be seven-thirty.'

'Right.'

A little flutter over the wire as if he'd coughed. 'Good luck, old man.'

'Thank you. Good-bye.'

I hung up the telephone; the light companionable voice was gone.

§

I said to Cartright, 'We've got to send out a patrol. I'm afraid it's your turn.'

'Yes, all right.'

He looked frightened. I drove on because there was nothing else to do; we moved now in a close climate of fear, consistent, palpable as smoke. 'If you can get some idea of what we're facing, you'll be damned helpful to us; it could make all the difference.'

He nodded as if he believed me, as if he didn't know that nothing could make any difference.

'And for God's sake get back before our own barrage starts. We don't want you shot up.'

'All right,' he said again, and pushed his way down the

murky and glutinous trench to collect his men. I had an impulse to call him back; make him stay here in such safety as there was; tell Brigade what they could do with their orders. But the long habits of war lay on me like an iron cage, the rebel was contained, watching with amazement and disgust. Anger, being voiceless, had changed to a cold clenched knot in my chest.

With David, Spencer and Doyle I went through the plans for the attack. They asked questions, and I answered irritably, as a parent who isn't sure of his own knowledge answers a child. Nothing could shift from our small Company the sense that the Staff had put a pin in the wrong place, tossed the wrong coin, and that we were the losers.

David was trying to light a cigarette, swearing as the matches died. Spencer sat hugging himself; his eyes were watery and bloodshot, his body shivering; fever rather than fright, I judged: a problem to be met here. The day was sliding nearer, bringing the quicker beat of the heart, the unstable, apprehensive bowels. I stared over the sandbagged lip of the trench to the swampy slime beyond. A wind drove suddenly, carrying a stronger smell of corruption, old gas, high explosive, fear. Benighted ground: to receive us soon? Why no, something would prevent it; orders would come; the worst wouldn't happen. . . .

The small dream perished, leaving the cold, the inimical night whose darkness in fading brought the appointed hour nearer, certain, inexorable, like death. . . . A feeling of movement suddenly: a fallen picket-iron? A man somewhere close, friend or enemy? . . . No; nothing; silence but for the wind and the distant guns and the cough, the murmur, the little human sounds of men waiting.

The day nearer. The patrol hadn't returned. I said, 'Why don't the bloody fools come back?' but no one answered me. I said again, 'Why don't they come back?'

Like an answer came the confident inhuman efficiency of machine-gun fire. I said, '*They must come back.*' My mind, weary with waiting, fastened on this, became obsessed with it: news from the patrol could give us hope; they'd tell us something; they'd change the colour of fear—

Doyle gave a sudden snort. 'Lord, I was asleep.'

'Good dreams?' David asked.

'Can't remember. Some bloody nonsense; they always are.'

'Last time I slept,' said David, 'I dreamed of Victoria.'

'Girl?' asked Doyle.

'No, the station. Bloody waste of time: war's rather like a railway station, with mud and the enemy thrown in.'

'You'd think you'd dream of spring and birds and all that sort of caper.'

'Ought to be able to indent for the right kind of dreams. Comforts for the troops.'

The cold clenched knot in my chest had not moved. I looked at them, from one to the other: from Spencer to David to Doyle: back to David again. In the slow-growing light he looked weary, muddied, enduring. *What a piece of work is a man.* I said, 'We have to leave an officer behind.'

They were silent. The trench wasn't much of a place, but it was better than the air above it. I looked towards David, having a small hope here, but his face was full of angry resolution; his glance slipped to Spencer and back to me again.

All right; Spencer's ill; men have had to go over the top with worse than that. . . .

But if I leave David I shall go towards possible death remembering the anger in his face.

I said, 'I'm going to leave you, Spencer'; and could have cried out in protest. My eye fell on Doyle: he gave a small lift of his brows as though he'd thrown a ball at a coconut and seen it miss. Should I have left Doyle? David? No time for it now: shells were falling nearer, and the patrol had not yet returned.

Now our talk fractured and died; we were not listening to

each other: we were listening to the shells. Were they finding the range of the trench? Did this mean a German attack, or that they'd got wind of our attack that was coming? You could hear them as they came, louder, and louder; the sound as it increased uglier and more dangerous, more like a cold knife in the bowels. The soupy and viscid ground flowered upwards into shapes of orange water and flame; within the trench was a vibration, a strange liveliness, like a train going at speed— A shell closer than any yet; the watery earth falling down on us, lumps of it like heavy rain. . . .

And then, as there seemed to go up from us all a silent protest, a prayer: 'Oh God, make the buggers stop'; most strangely a silence, a letting up; time to breathe, to hear the racing heart beat slower; to see Doyle, careful and wary as if he walked a tightrope; David, pale but grimly amused—

Sounds in the trench. The light grey now; the familiar stone-grey of dawn; the air very cold. Men's voices; a feeling of turbulence, of alarm: 'Poor bastard. . . .' 'Get him to the Skipper. . . .'

Cartright stumbled and fell in front of me. He stayed there on all fours, his head down, drawing in great breaths as a child does after a storm of weeping. I said, 'Where are the others?'

He shook his head, still gasping in air. 'Couldn't get—any of them back. I tried. I did try.'

'Grimes? Fielding?'

'They're dead, I think.'

'Lecker?'

'I don't know . . .'

'What did you find?'

David said, 'He's badly wounded.'

I saw the blood spreading on the back of his tunic. 'Bandage him up; do your best.' I had a driving need, surpassing all pity, to find out what he knew.

He gasped, 'I feel so cold.'

'We'll warm you up. What did you find?'

For a moment his eyes were lifted to mine, bewildered with pain and with my brutality. Dimly I saw that David was kneeling beside him, cutting away his tunic.

'It hurts terribly. Am I going to die? I think I am.'

'You're all right; we'll have you sent back home. *I want to know what you found.*'

'We got—almost the whole way. We could hear them talking. The Fritzes. It does hurt. Can I have some morphia?'

'For Christ's sake give him anything he wants.' I was only half aware of David's face turned up for an instant to mine.

Cartright gasped out, 'Wire in front of the trench—tough wire. Machine-guns—worst of all.'

David had cut his tunic away, and the torn flesh was clear, a wound above his shoulder blade, bleeding on to David's hands, on to the ground, on to the discarded and useless tunic.

I thought, One more.

'Where are they, the machine-guns?'

David turned to look at me again. Cartright was shaking his head, but whether in answer or in pain, I didn't know. 'High ground to our left . . . suddenly.'

'Didn't you freeze when the lights went up?'

He nodded or perhaps merely bent his head nearer the ground. He was whispering now, and I had to lean close to hear him. 'Lecker was wounded . . . couldn't keep still . . . they fired on us. . . . Oh God. . . .'

David stopped his work and looked, not at me, but at Cartright as he lay on the muddy floor, face down as if he slept.

One more.

§

Seven-twelve.

We are all prepared. The men have been served with some sort of breakfast, have eaten the bully beef and biscuits either with absent-minded haste, or with a long slow chewing as if they found it hard to swallow. They've had the harsh, friendly rum. The day is without colour, heavy with the promise of rain.

Watches synchronized; the thin hand like an insect's leg kicking round.

My thoughts rattling stupidly on, now clinging to the tracks of sense, now skidding off. All orders correctly given? Gas-masks at the alert; the speed at which we are to cross the muddy and murderous ground . . . The speed . . . How far is St. Helena from the field of Austerlitz? . . . A little trust that when we die . . . Dear Mrs. Calder, I regret to inform you that your son Esmond . . . your son Simon . . . Both my sons . . .

Dear Mrs. Birch, I regret to . . .

No, I won't think of that. I should have made him stay behind. (Yet with what hope? May he not be wounded: the best passport to safety?) All the same I'd rather he'd stayed: there's something about the air above the trench that gleams with evil promise. The trench, slimy, cold, noxious, has the look of safety, a place we do not want to leave. . . . '*It's a long story. I will tell you. But not yet.*' He's said nothing: now there isn't any more time.

But there will be time; later there will be time.

The shells from our own guns going over, but the barrage lacks power; it speaks with an uncertain voice. Cartright said the wire was strong; this will not destroy it.

Do we all know our jobs? Doyle, David and Cartright? . . .

Ah. No, Cartright's done with fighting: his body lies in the mud behind the trench. Cartright and Wicks and Gann. . . . They have one face; they are the dead, with their thousands for company. *I regret to inform you that your son, that all your sons* . . . It is fear, O Little Hunter, it is fear . . .

But there is a place beyond fear, a strange place on its further side; though the worm of terror twists, one is now almost numbed; waiting; watching the insect's hand. . . .

Seven-eighteen.

Twelve minutes more. A scrap of time: *time was: time is: time is not.* The men move and cough; speak occasionally; move their rifles an inch or two this way or that: when I give the signal they'll come—why don't they throw down their rifles; refuse to go? But they'll come, in obedience and fear. . . . If one's heart and brain weren't dried and empty one would weep for their courage and their small prospect of life.

It's still not too late. I could refuse to lead them out of the trench. . . . But the seconds go past, and I know that I shall follow the pattern, moving blindly, without hope, trying to smother the knowledge that someone's muffed the whole thing.

Not a trace of sun. The word August sends an echo in one's mind of deep grass, moist with its own shadow, and the blade-bright glint of afternoon on summer streams. Here there is nothing to show any season: torn trees in a desert of mud; nothing grows here but death. (And the garden noisy with birdsong, dew heavy on the grass; the beginning of a summer's day. . . . Distant; a place out of another life. To be seen again?)

Seven-twenty-six.

I regret to inform you that your son . . .

If I die now, I shall leave no son. I shall die virgin, not having known the coupling of the flesh that everyone makes such a song about. Bodies so bloodily dissected by splinters, bullets and shells have destroyed the flesh's hunger: this is the ultimate end of the body: mangled meat of entrails and limbs and genitals, spread shamelessly to the sky. There is left only a raw ache of feeling, a need to love, the sensation that perhaps belongs to an amputated limb.

David?

Yes, he is there.

Our own shelling reaching its crescendo (but it is still not enough; go on; go on; this is our only hope). The German guns heavily replying: are they prepared for us?

Seven-twenty-nine.

And the insect's leg kicks the seconds away: one, two, three, four. . . .

You'd think it'd be hard to move, to go up into the air, but terror is contained, a parcel one carries with one: the mind is drugged, not working truly any more—

Time is.

I am up above the trench.

The streaming death is all about us while the pulverized and slimy ground drags at our feet. Machine-gun bullets slice and sting the air: already the men are going down; one sees them with the eye, not the heart; the thing begun has to be carried through: this is all now. . . . The second wave, led by David, swarms from the trench. . . .

He is there now.

You must move on.

The bullets come like familiar things, tamed, so close, so strangely close, by one's head, by one's side, into the ground beneath one's feet—and yet one lives. Moves on. A little trust that when we die we reap our . . . Too many men are going down; they fall as if this were the purpose of man, to receive the bullets in his flesh, to slip in anguish to the mud: Harding, the chemist, close behind me, screams like a torn animal and drops; he clasps one hand round my leg; there is blood running from his throat. I have to go on, but his hand grips strongly and it's difficult to move . . .

We're both Leo, then. Both lions, as you might say.

On, towards the German wire. In the mist of noise and death it looks strong, untouched by the guns. On. It's as if one dreamed; landscape of sound and death flow past one, not fully apprehended. Shrapnel, greenish black, falls thickly: towards it, into it, as into a sea. The thin evil whine

177

of bullets never ceases, yet some of the men miraculously go on, against all natural laws, like Christ walking on the water. The smoke from a burst of shrapnel close at hand suddenly destroys all sight, and I move alone in a strange stinking fog. Slowly the smoke clears. And as if it had wiped a slate clean the vast stretch of doomed mud is almost naked of upright men. The place belongs to the guns, to the burst of shrapnel, to the bullets which possess the air.

A man comes stumbling up and I shout to him to get down: there is no hope for us; we must lie in shell-holes till dusk; then, if we are still alive, crawl back to our own lines. There is a man still moving on and I shout to him, wave to him. He falls, but whether in obedience or because he is hit, I do not know.

Suddenly I stumble; it is as though I had run with my full force against an iron box, maiming my shin. My right leg has suddenly no power; it collapses like a rope of rags. Down in the mud; I press my hands on the yielding stuff, trying to rise, but the pain comes then, vivid, electric, absorbing.

I shut my eyes against it, against the world. Time dissolves into a roaring place, half dream, half truth: pain and the sound of guns are woven into some personal structure of my own. For how long? I do not know. Something draws me out of this half-dream; it's the sliding rain, running like cold blood. There's a shell-hole a few yards to my left. I begin to crawl towards it; at once the machine-guns open fire again and the bullets sing.

But the shell-hole. With a thrust of my arms I am over the lip, rolling in. I roll on my leg, and the pain makes a red mist in my head. The mud is turning from its firm stickiness into something thin, like dark gruel: it is in my hair, my nose, my mouth. There are the bodies of men in the trench, flung like discarded things into a pit; sprawled, abandoned, waste of uniform, boots, hair, skin: all so carefully fashioned; no use any more.

At first it seems I lie there alone with the dead. But then I hear a sound, like a whispering in my ear. There is some-one else in the shell-hole; someone still alive. Alive and close to me. I put out a hand and touch the man at my side; it is he who is speaking. 'Where are you hurt?' I ask; 'I've got some water here. . . .' I can see him, through the pain and the stinging water in my eyes; he is lying forward, head upon his arm. I feel for my water battle, but it isn't there. Morphia tablets? No, I seem to have been stripped without my knowing; my uniform is ragged, torn, un-familiar. The man is still whispering, but I can't hear what he says. 'Are you all right? Are you badly hurt?' Savage with pain, I grow unreasoning, angry: 'Damn you, what's the matter? I can't hear, damn you, I can't hear.' I give a thrust with one hand and he rolls over. There is a torn place in his chest; the opened flesh gleams and the blood is dark; his face is frozen, grey, but I can see that it is Harrison, that look of quiet cynicism caricatured in death. The whispering is the work of the rain, collecting in a fallen helmet, over-flowing with small sibilance into the shell-hole.

No, there are only the dead.

David?

In the attack, in the pain, I had almost forgotten him. In the brutalizing anaesthetic of fear everything had been lost but some mechanism of movement and survival. Now the old sensations begin to return.

He must be dead. Why should he be left alive? The long fantasy, held since the Somme, perishes before the savage arithmetic of this day.

This is the truth of things, with hope gone. The rain has ceased. No sun, but a firmer light defines the mud, the water, coloured dark; the men who lie with me here; the empty world. My trouser leg is heavy with blood; blood runs over my boot, oozes from the boot itself: I watch its journey, concentrated on this; I do not want to look further. Pain dries my throat, my tongue is large and

179

sticky; dry, dry. Only the water in the shell-hole, foul with death. Men have drunk that before now. . . .

What time is it? Afternoon, perhaps. Even late afternoon; the guns are quieter; the day's tide at the ebb. The shell-hole is a place beyond the rim of the world, beyond the reach of comradeship—

And now, stronger than pain, stronger than thirst, is a longing for living men. The isolation which I'd known in the trench, waiting with the dying Wicks, is intensified, becomes unendurable, like a sound too close to one's ear: why can't I run, burst from the shell-hole, into the upper world into the gunfire, screaming for company? . . .

I must move as best I can.

Slowly, upwards, over the mud.

It is still light, dull, without shine. Crawling over the mud like a worm, like a crocodile, I do not seem to draw the fire. Why not? It doesn't matter. It is difficult to move, and the dead—or the pieces of the dead—are everywhere. Some are not yet dead: they moan and whimper as I draw beside them. 'Got a bullet, chum? Please . . . got one?' No, my revolver's gone: anyway I couldn't do it. Don't know why, but I couldn't. Even though his blood runs to a great distance from his savaged bowels.

David?

No, he's dead. One of the dead. Lying this way, on their sides, on their backs, some with nothing shameful to show, curled, as if sleeping; others violently dismembered, dis-embowelled, betraying all that was private to the merciless air.

Slowly through the mud. Pain, but it seems no longer to make the same impact, as if the brain had tired of it. Weak-ness, so that every movement is made against a weight like snow. Desultory shelling; a dim reminder that somewhere a battle is going on.

Suddenly I see men upright, as trees walking.

Stretcher-bearers. Then we are not quite lost. They come

to me, but I direct them farther on. I can move, and have no great wish to be saved.

A voice in my ear. Lost. A memory.

Simon.

Pain clouds my head; I do not believe in the voice; it belongs to a different time.

Simon.

In a mist, I see David's face. Blackened, shadowed with strain, blood somewhere on it.

Part of the dream?

Simon.

No, he's there. Alive. Most strangely, miraculously still living. For a moment out of the mud I can lift my head and feel the communication, the love and comradeship, the thing that sets even this world on its axis, that even here comforts the heart.

'You're only wounded. Fine. We'll get you into the trench.'

I have words in my head but none of them come, only strange sounds; it must be weakness, perhaps loss of blood.

In spite of everything, he is alive. It is a charmed life, after all. He bends to me, trying to lift me. 'Lean here. Lean on my arm, and we'll get you to the trench.'

He is alive. Against all odds, against all reason. Then perhaps God is good, and there is some hope and purpose, after all.

'Lean on me. Can you stand? Lean on me.'

Alive. Not a ghost. My brain though ragged, distorted, still knows fact from fantasy. A burst of machine-gun fire, like a savage round of clapping. *Quickly, into the trench.* Don't delay for a moment, don't wait, don't give them any chances; not now; not now.

'Here we are,' he said. 'Back home.'

Yes, it is home of a kind, but different, filled with the wounded and the dead, and the few living. Spencer? Yes, he is alive. David has sliced away my trouser leg: the shin is a bloodied mess; of small importance. The rain has started again; through the whispering air comes the single whiplash of a rifle: a sniper somewhere. *Keep your head down, David; for God's sake keep your head down.*

How long before dusk? We are isolated here; the German trenches ahead of us are uncaptured; if they counter-attack, we stand little chance. Yet David's presence beside me gives me a kind of optimism, traces the pattern of things with hope. A message has gone to Battle H.Q.; perhaps relief will come soon.

The dim boom of guns; the harmless assault of the rain; the punctuation of the sniper's bullet, personal, malevolent: perhaps he sees men still moving amongst the dead out there. *Keep down; out of his way; keep down.*

Heavier shelling now; the sky noisy, meshed with dangerous sound. It isn't over yet, but relief must come soon. Soon they'll come and we shall go back, out of the line, and David will be of the company, one of the tired men, embracing sleep and quiet with a kind of exhausted passion.

Heavier shelling still, but pain and weariness remove it a little way from me; it will pass; we shall be relieved; we shall be safe—

And then, from a place of dimmed vision, of skidding consciousness, I hear David's voice: 'My God, here they come!'

He snatches a rifle. Barton on the Lewis gun is ready. Lifting myself on my arm, I can see the dim grey figures, coming close. They seem a small company, as if this were some wild exploit: a dash for the trench by a dozen men. They slither and stumble in the mud, over the dead and wounded. Close. Coming closer.

David leans on the rotting lip of the trench to fire: the Lewis gun splits the air into fragments. One grey figure falls; then another. I grab a rifle: it is sticky with mud, the mechanism clogged and stiff to the hands. Another man has gone down.

And then there is the single sound of a rifle as if someone had sharply flicked a wet cloth in cold air. I feel a bump on my arm. And then David slides down into the trench.

For a moment I believe nothing of it: he has slipped; he is only wounded.

There is a mark just between his eyes; it is not unsightly; not terrible as some of the wounds are.

But there is no life in him: it has in that instant snapped off: nothing can bring it back: he has joined the large voiceless company.

And Barton on the Lewis gun falls too, hit in the throat. Then nothing possesses me except rage and misery: pain and weakness vanish; I lift myself and direct the vengeful gun on the grey figures before us. *Reload, relay, resume.* . . . I fire, the vibration and the banging bite of the explosions waking some echo of pain that seems to have no part of me.

Fire. Fire. The grey figures founder and fall. One comes on, but a rifle's bullet wounds him.

Vaguely I see that it is Spencer who has fired it: and for a second he glances down at David, then looks at me; his face strangely in the midst of this has pity.

Fire. Fire. The gun is a lovely thing in my hands, an expression of hatred and misery. The chatter of iron teeth: relieving, merciful; all there is left. His body is at my feet; I can feel its weight against my leg.

Send it into them. Kill them all. Why should a dog, a rat, a mouse have life . . .? The enemy was repulsed with heavy losses . . . The enemy . . .

The grey figures are gone; wounded, dying, or dead. And I begin to know that they are not the enemy; there is only one enemy, but I cannot name it now.

Distant guns. The muddy waste with its rich harvest of dead strangely silent.

My hands slip from the gun. I look down at David.

Now it is different to look at him: the rage has run out of me. He is part of this pattern; one of the dead. One more.

Careless of snipers or shells, I look over the trench, over the wide waste. The rain has lifted: a trace of light wakens the shell-holes, gleams on a fallen bayonet, the darkness of blood, the bodies of the men who lie there. Greyness, death, water. A moaning from the wounded: perhaps from the Germans I have hit; a wide desolation; man, abandoned by God.

And there is in my head an echo, travelling through an increasing mist of pain, through the knowledge that men, our own men, are coming up towards us, a sergeant, stretcher-bearers, men in good shape, not ghosts, not the dead—and the echo persists like a thin dream: David's father, on that last day, in another world, in the quiet of Fennelhurst church where no murder was done: 'Even amongst pain and death he can say, having love, we are more than conquerors.'

Before me was the field of the dead; at my feet, David's body. And I had no love, even for the men who were tending me, lifting me, promising me, who had no use for it, life.

Part III

Silence; and the faces of my friends

Dim wealds of vanished summer, peace of home,
And silence; and the faces of my friends.

SIEGFRIED SASSOON

1

September, 1938

'Your father?' I said.

The girl pushed the wet hair from her forehead and faced us as one who had learned to face strangers in the difficult climate of opposition. The drawing-room had by now the look of a battle-ground many times fought over. Griselda's fur was lying on the sofa and Tony Clare's empty glass stood on its mat on the table. These things were old.

She sat on a small upright chair, her clumsy bag beside her. Her shoes were shabby, mottled by wet; her clothes—grey sweater and black skirt—belonged to necessity. I stared at her, the echoes loud in my ears, time shifting under my feet. Griselda was tense and fearful, as if some great and unwelcome thing were to be demanded of her. Jeremy just looked surprised.

'Your father?' I said again, because there was only one name in my head, back after all the years.

She said, 'I know it is inconvenient for you, that I've come.'

Griselda gave a brief, unconvincing shake of her head; I said impatiently, 'No . . . no . . .' and went on staring at her. *I believe you knew my father. I believe you knew him very well.*

'I must try to explain. I arrived in England last night—'

'From?'

'Vienna.'

The word fell strangely into the small London room, at this time.

'But your father,' I said.

'His name was David Birch.'

And he might, after twenty years, be here in the room: the blue eyes and the cast of her nose is his, most strangely his: but alive, not wearing the colour of death, as I had last seen him.

'*David?*' Griselda burst out. 'But he couldn't have been!'

'Oh, it's true!'

'Of course it's true,' I said. 'You've only got to look at her.'

'I can explain if you've time to listen—'

'Time,' I said; 'of course we've time.'

'Heaps of it,' said Jeremy. In spite of the dripping hair and the plain clothes, she had beauty: the skin transparent, the naked mouth full and firm. His eye stayed for a moment on the line of her breasts in the sweater, the young moulded legs.

'*David*,' said Griselda, moving her shoulders as if cold winds touched her; 'then your mother—'

'She was Juana Meyers—'

'Was? She's not dead?'

'I pray not. She's in Vienna.'

And vividly Juana came out of the past, darkly beautiful, thirsty for life. But now of course she must be . . . *Vienna*. I saw old Louis Meyer with his pale grief-stricken Jewish face. I saw the heavy armies marching, the Swastika, black on its pool of white, surrounded by crimson: the shadow slipping over the world. I saw the signs on the street benches—*For Aryans only*; and the more savage signs: *Juden Verboten*: the poster of the Jew, his hand full of money and the map of Germany under his arm; I heard again the sinister rumours. Juana?

'What happened?' I asked.

'I was born over here in 1918—'

(Conceived then in '17 . . . on that last leave, from which David had returned, to die in the trench near Gheluvelt. *It's a long story. I will tell you. But not yet.*)

'My mother married after I was born. My stepfather was an Austrian Jew, a prisoner-of-war. He accepted me; he was like that—kind, very gentle. He was a doctor. We all went to live in Vienna. I believe things were very terrible there just after the war, but gradually they got better. For a time we were happy.'

I went on staring at her. 'And then?'

'After the Anschluss, everything was changed. My stepfather wasn't allowed to practise. But a little while ago he attended an Austrian woman who was dying in childbirth. They arrested him at five o'clock one morning. They took my mother too.'

Now there was no colour in her face at all; her hands were trembling. It was past midnight, and by floodlamps they were digging trenches in the parks, in all open green spaces; the crowds waited for news in Whitehall; three days remained before the deadline of October 1st, when Czechoslovakia must yield all that was vital of herself to the engulfing shadow.

She said, her voice rough now, 'They just came and took them. My stepfather was quite calm. I used to think my mother was the stronger one, but when they came it was she who was frightened.' (Juana, sweeping into the Sussex room on my birthday, in the last hours of a different world.)

Karen wiped her cheek with her hand. 'She'd always told me about my father: that you were his greatest friend. She said you loved him very much.'

'Yes, I did.'

'She kept saying that morning, "Remember everything I told you. Go to the German Consulate and get a permit to leave the country: go as soon as you can. You have only a little Jewish blood in you; you don't look like a Jew; you are like your father." Am I like him?'

'Yes,' I said.

'At first I stayed alone in the house: it seemed so—so dreadful to leave them, as if one had just thrown them away. But the money was giving out; I couldn't get any work; the house was empty and I began to be afraid they'd come and knock on the door for me too.'

Suddenly this room seemed beleaguered also, as if it shared something with that room in Vienna.

'You'll stay with us?' I said.

'Come on; do,' said Jeremy, but Griselda's word was not audible, her face enclosed in private perplexity, shut away from us all.

Karen was turned to her in doubtful inquiry. Griselda stayed silent. 'I have a little money,' Karen said, 'some left out of what I was allowed to bring from Vienna.'

A word from Griselda that still I could not hear.

'I have to find work,' Karen went on. 'I have British nationality, so perhaps it will not be too difficult. I will do anything: clean, wash up, scrub floors.'

'If you're looking for a job,' said Jeremy, 'so'm I.'

'Of course you'll stay,' I said. 'As long as you like.'

The room was briefly silent; then Griselda moved sharply as if she'd heard the bell ring. 'We will do all we can to help you.' The words were a statement, no more. 'You must have something to eat, and then go to bed.'

Obediently Karen got to her feet, picking up her bag. She followed Griselda to the door. I saw that the months in Austria under Nazi rule, the daily threat on her house, the arrest of her mother and stepfather, had made her easily acceptant, had beaten away the polite dissembling shell: she was prepared for mercy, felt perhaps, deep within herself, some right to succour.

His name was David Birch. Thought of him was strong now, dyeing all things with memory: the room seemed full of him, voice, smile, the great length that had slipped so quietly down beside me in the trench; in this silence echoed the angry, unceasing guns.

I sat there with Jeremy, not quite seeing him, trying to come to terms with the idea of David's child.

He got to his feet. 'Golly,' he said, stretching his arms wide, 'we've got a refugee.'

§

When at last I went up to the bedroom, Griselda was in her dressing-gown, sitting before the glass. She had creamed the make-up from her face so that she seemed to be drained of colour; her hair was pushed haphazardly from her forehead. She was smoking; apparently just sitting there, doing nothing else. For a moment I saw her as she had returned home, dressed for the theatre, alight and wounded with the new knowledge of Kate. Now she was a different person, stripped of armour.

She didn't look up as I came in. After a moment or two she said, 'What's the time? Something's wrong with my watch.'

'Twenty to one.'

'You'd think it'd be later.'

'Is Karen all right?'

'She's upstairs, in bed.'

I began to undress. 'There was nothing else we could do.'

'A strange girl in the house. What is it going to be like?'

'I don't know. What is anything going to be like now?'

'The spare room's Prue's room: you know that.'

'Of course. Other people have slept there.'

'Yes. . . . This girl is a stranger.'

'So like David.'

'Oh, yes!' She met my eyes in the glass. 'Very like.'

'How could I not ask her to stay?'

'I don't know.'

191

'She's been through hell.'

'Haven't we all?'

'She's very young.'

'A year older than Jeremy.'

'Still young.'

Griselda, hunched on the dressing-table stool, had her hands over her forehead. 'I suppose I feel I've had all I can take; that tonight of all nights I don't want a strange girl in the house, whatever she's been through, whoever's daughter she is.'

'But to come all this way—'

'You want her here, don't you? David's child. Sometimes I don't think you ever loved anyone but David.'

'You loved him too.'

She lifted her head back and put one hand to her throat as if she sought to disguise the little markings of time. 'Oh . . . as a schoolgirl. I cried when I heard of his death, but not with real pain. I didn't know then what pain was.'

I sat down on the edge of the bed. I could feel again the grey waste of those weeks and months in hospital, the days without meaning when I lay watching from some removed place the muddle they made of the torn leg, bored as a man listening to a thrice-told tale. As I pulled on my pyjama trousers I could see the wound now, old, dried, like something salvaged from the battlefield as a souvenir. I said, 'It felt as though there was nothing left. You used to come and see me; I never understood why: I must have been boorish and dull.'

She put out her cigarette; gave a small smile. 'You were a wounded hero. There had been nothing but the war for so long: war and death: in a way one wanted to think about them because anything else seemed unreal. And you'd been through it all; you'd been beside David when he'd been killed; you were part of it.'

Looking at her hunched before the dressing-table, I saw myself out of the war, in the time of creeping disillusion, recovering from wounds but still haunted, so that the backfire of a car could make me fling myself to the ground; the rattle of a window, simulating the echo of guns, set the huge ghosts swarming. Through all this Griselda had appeared, punctuating the grey miasma of a burdened mind with visits of determined cheerfulness. I was . . . grateful? Touched? In the end, gradually dependent, climbing up from the haunted places to an upper climate of ordinary air, of calm, only shadowed by dreams.

As it was still shadowed.

Griselda, taking another cigarette, said, 'You realize that I don't even know that I'm going to stay with you? This girl hasn't changed anything.'

'But she's been hurled into our laps—'

'Like an act of God?'

'An act of something, I suppose.'

'And because of her, I'm to forget about this woman; treat the whole thing as though it had never happened?'

'No. Only believe what I've told you—'

'I don't know what you've told me; I don't know anything any more. Only that this girl's come when I can't face her, can't face anyone—'

'You heard what she said. You know the kind of world she's been living in, afraid all the time—'

'I didn't say I wasn't sorry for her. I know it's all very terrible. But to have a stranger in the house *now*—'

'She isn't a stranger. She's David's child.'

'David.'

'All right: I loved him very much. It was innocent enough, God knows—as far as any love is innocent, and I suppose none is.'

'You think of everyone before me; you always have; you don't know how it makes me feel.'

'I'm sorry. It isn't true.'

'I don't *want* this girl here—'

'Why not? We may be at war in twenty-four hours—'

'No. No. I lost Prue. I can't lose Jeremy. Oh, Simon, why is life like this? Made so you daren't think? Last evening when the Wilcotts were here I was all right; well no, not all right, but able to think I was, and then this evening everything seemed to be stripped away, the whole past dug up, the dead—Prue and David—somehow back again, all the pain back.'

'If we can work through it to something else—'

'I don't want to work through it. I don't want it again. I don't want this girl here, David's daughter, sleeping in Prue's room—'

'What harm does she do?'

'I just don't want her here. I'll help her, give her money, but not keep her here to live—'

'I haven't asked you to keep her. Only take her in for a time, give her some comfort—'

'And what about my comfort?'

'You haven't watched your mother led off to a concentration camp—'

'I've watched other things.'

'I know. I know.'

'But you don't really care. All you care about is this girl—'

'You're jealous of her, and I tell you you're wrong to be jealous of her. Wrong, wrong, wrong. Because . . . Oh, it's no good talking any more. Get to bed. Try to sleep. We can start again in the morning.'

I watched her as she went towards the bathroom, tying the cord of her dressing-gown. I had thought myself composed of guilt and anger, but as I looked at her I was taken by a warmth and pity which I had no words to express.

Alone, I turned the knob of the wireless, searching for news. The National and Regional stations had closed down; I chased through a tangle of strange voices; one came into focus: German. I leaned closer to the set. It seemed, from what I could understand, that unless the Czechs accepted the terms of Hitler's memorandum by two o'clock this coming afternoon, Germany would immediately mobilize. Then the voice dimmed, muddled by other voices; came clear again to say that the sands were running out. After that, martial music, tinny and distorted. I clicked the knob and brought silence back. But the voices went on, over the wires of the world.

The late hour had an odd feel about it as if we were waiting for a train connection on a long foreign journey. Griselda came back from having her bath, and I put my feet into slippers and went out to the bathroom. I paused, looking up to the landing above, where Karen was.

From where I stood I could see the door to the room that had been Prue's room wide open.

Open?

I scrambled up the stairs, stumbling and losing one slipper. Jeremy's door was shut; he must be asleep. I had a second in which to envy the young, who could sleep through anything, rumours of war, the strife of their parents; even war itself.

Then I was on the landing. I said, 'Karen.' The shadowy room was silent. I switched on the light. The bed looked as though someone had jumped hurriedly from it. No trace of the girl, of her clothes, of her bag.

I went through the house, calling for her. No answer anywhere. Breathless, choked, miserable, I went back to the bedroom. I said, 'She's gone.'

Griselda on the edge of the bed looked up startled. 'What d'you mean?'

'Gone—gone—gone. She must have heard what you said.'

'Oh, no—'

'What else. I'm going out to see. She can't have gone far. Only a little way.' I was pulling on trousers and jacket over my pyjamas. Griselda was saying, 'But how could she have heard? I left her in the room upstairs in bed; there wasn't any reason . . .' Then she said, 'I didn't want her to hear; I didn't mean her to hear—'

I ran away from this, down the stairs and out of the house. The street was empty except for newspapers drifting, and an echo of footsteps going firmly some distance off.

I ran under the tall dark sky, through the empty city street. I was conscious of my limping run, ungainly, a handicap. *She can't have gone far. She'll come back: she's hardly any money: she doesn't know anyone: she'll have to come back. . . . Unless . . . No; nothing could have happened; she was shaken and exhausted, but she wasn't the sort to do anything wild; she knew that I wanted her; Jeremy too. . . .*

The end of the side-street; into the wider road. Traffic, lonely, going fast on a dark road licked with moisture. Tall buildings, mostly dark. The withdrawn anonymous world, unconcerned with any man's desires, offering no answer. . . . One person in these streets, in this city. An hour ago, perhaps, she had been in my house, safe: now she was gone. Rage against Griselda mounted and died. Had there been no Kate . . .

It was lightly raining now. I went on, until I came to the great station. Life here, and my hopes rose a little: travellers standing about; people sitting, some asleep, on the station seats.

I looked everywhere. A girl with long dark hair, raincoat over her shoulders, walking away from me . . . I ran, but it was a stranger's face. The all-night buffet? Crumby tables: a few customers: an air of tired aftermath, of a tide at the lowest ebb.

No, she wasn't there.

Now I had less hope. A mirror above a weighing machine showed me myself, greying hair blown, pyjama collar showing absurdly over the jacket, face haunted and a little wild. A middle-aged man, with all his sins on him, chasing in his pyjamas through Victoria Station for the daughter of a man, dead twenty years.

There was nothing to do but to go home.

Could she perhaps have returned there? Run out wildly, then sanity returning, gone back?

I put my key eagerly in the lock. The hall, the familiar smell of the house, envelopes on the table. A creak of wood from the drawing-room; otherwise silence.

No, she wasn't here.

Griselda was sitting up in bed, smoking. She looked strained, a little frightened. I began taking off the clownish jacket and trousers. 'No, I didn't find her.'

'Where could she be?'

'I don't know.'

'How could she have gone so quietly?'

I shrugged. 'We were talking, not listening to things outside.'

'You think she heard what I said?'

'I'm afraid she must have done.' She looked stricken, and on an impulse I bent to kiss her. I said, 'I'm sorry it's been such a bloody day. Let's try to get some sleep.'

For a long time I lay, the old and new things together in my head: David rising to greet me in Guillecourt, in the summer of the Somme: Thurston Wood, the mist and the men who had died there; Yarrow's Field and the lanes of Fennelhurst; the Rector and Mrs. Birch, she dead now, but the old man still alive, living in a cottage near the church, knowing nothing of his grandchild. Kate in her room; Karen coming to this house: *I believe you knew my father. I believe you knew him very well.* The tangled voices, charting the progress towards war.

A sound from Griselda.

I said, 'Are you awake?'

'Yes.'

'Don't cry.'

'What will happen?'

'I don't know.'
'Will she come back?'
'She must. Somehow I'll find her.'
'And the war?'
'We can only wait. Don't cry.'

2

Wednesday

The papers next morning were black with large print, as if danger itself had walked over them. (And the breakfast-table at Fennelhurst; the strangeness of heavy type: the beginning of it all.) *British Fleet Will Mobilize Today. Hope Not Yet Lost, Says Premier. Britain's Mighty Host of the Air.*

I ate breakfast quickly, drinking four cups of black coffee, smoking almost at once. Griselda was silent, eating as little as I did. Jeremy was inclined to ask questions—'You mean she's *gone*? That nice girl? But why? She'd only just come.' We gave him little by way of answer. I saw a headline, *Recruits Needed in Army, R.A.F.* I turned the page. He looked very young, spooning marmalade on to his plate, not certain of his parents' mood. There were other young men in my mind: lying near Fricourt, Arras, Vlamertinghe. He murmured to himself, 'Golly, fancy her going. In the night. Can't we get her back?'

I said, 'I'm going to try.'

I had the day planned.

First to Geoffrey.

The office seemed a trivial and unimportant place. I caught a far and vanishing glimpse of a young man, set for a life of high scholarship. Miss Brandon was putting letters on my desk: I said, 'I'm not staying. I'll look at these and then go. Has Mr. King arrived?'

'Yes, he came early. Looks as though I'm going to get into Air Force blue any moment now, doesn't it?'

'Yes, I'm afraid so. If you'd just got out of Austria and come to England and found yourself adrift in the middle of the night, where'd you go?'

'Me?'

'Yes; what would you do?'

'Gosh, I don't know. Why?'

'I just want to hear.'

'I suppose I'd . . . goodness, find friends, I suppose.'

'If you hadn't any?'

'Goodness . . . die, I should think.'

'No, you wouldn't.'

'Mr. Calder, you make me jump when you shout like that.'

'Sorry.'

'I suppose I'd go to the Police or something.'

'I rang the Police.'

She looked at me, mouth a little way open. 'You mean this is a *real* thing—this happened to a *real* person?'

'Oh yes,' I said, 'she's real.'

'Gosh. I say. What're you going to do?'

'Find her, somehow.'

I went to Geoffrey's room. He was sitting at his desk, head bent, one hand to his forehead, like a man posing for a photograph of a man working. I said, 'Look here, Geoffrey, I've got to take time off. There's nothing outstanding at the moment; I'll deal with it all later.'

'Yes, very well.' He looked a little guarded. 'What's happened?'

'We have a girl in the house. Or had last night. She's run away and I've got to find her.'

'A girl?' He looked disapproving.

'Her name's Karen Ebert. Ring any kind of bell?'

'None at all.' But he was still on guard.

'It was she who telephoned when we were all at dinner.'

He waited. I said, 'She's David's child.'

'*David's?*'

'Juana and David.'

He put both hands over his face. This seemed so surprising an action for Geoffrey that I stood silent. He said at last, 'I was very much in love with Juana. We were engaged, as you know . . . for a time.'

'Yes, I remember.'

He put one thumb between his teeth and began to chew on it, as if some serpent memory had stirred and stung him. It was strange to see Geoffrey doing so many things I had never seen him do before.

'She was very attractive,' I said. 'Her daughter is too.'

He gave me a quick sideways glance, then went on chewing his thumb. At last he said, 'Look. I've never told anyone this before.'

I waited. Miss Brandon's typewriter clattered on in the next room.

'Before I went to France I took Juana away for the week-end.' He chewed further. 'I found that I couldn't make love to her.'

I said nothing, seeing so much become explicable. Pity for him stirred, though I thought it was not the worst that could happen, for a man to be compulsively chaste.

'We broke off the engagement. I suffered very much. She tried to comfort me by saying that it wouldn't have been any good, she and I together, because she'd never really cared for anyone but David.' His face twitched. 'I didn't see her for a long time; I was sent out East, you remember, and got ill. With scurvy.' His voice had an echo here, a sense of affront, and I saw him on the other side of the wooden table in Bredenhoek, leaving hurriedly when I had said that David was coming. 'She came to see me while I was in hospital. She'd written to David, but he hadn't answered.

And then one day when I was convalescent she came, delirious with joy. She'd heard from him; he was coming on leave and he wanted to see her.' He dug a pencil into his blotter. 'She was the happiest person I'd ever seen.'

I waited. Heard from him? Then from the encampment outside Ypres, David must have written to Juana. I could see the field envelope going off, out of that threatened and legendary place of war, addressed in his large hand. Had Juana kept it? Did it still exist somewhere, even now?

'I saw her again about two weeks later, just before I went back to France. David had gone to see his parents. His leave had a few more days to run. I took her out to dinner. I don't think I've ever seen such such a change in anyone. She was terrified. Almost beside herself.'

I eased my position on the arm of a chair. Curious to have tapped Geoffrey's deepest and most painful memory: for the first time in all the years I was seeing him as human.

'She was convinced he'd be killed. They'd stopped printing the casualty lists then, but they couldn't stop the people you met; the endless people who'd lost husbands and sons. And she seemed to *know*.'

Strange that in the time before Third Ypres Juana had been convinced of his coming death, and I of his prospect of life.

'And then she said suddenly, "My only hope is that I shall have his child."'

Again I heard Miss Brandon's typewriter going impersonally on.

'I left her then,' Geoffrey said. He'd stopped chewing on his thumb; he was still and lost in it all. 'At that moment, I mean; I went straight away.' He seemed surprised even now at the memory of it. 'I'd always wanted children, you see— perhaps that's why I take such an interest in Jeremy—and this was suddenly too much. And d'you know, Simon, I never saw her again.'

'Never knew for certain about the child?'

'No. When I heard of David's death, I wrote to her, but she didn't answer. I wrote again, some months later, but the letter came back marked "Gone away". I heard a rumour, after the war, that she'd gone to live in Austria, but nothing certain. She never wrote again.'

'And now,' I said, 'there's still no news.' I told him what had happened in Vienna, and he said, 'How monstrous to take her away!'

'That's the pattern of things now. Until we change it.'

He glanced at me, as if he remembered our argument two nights ago. 'And the girl? You say she's like her?'

'More like David.'

'Do I want to see her?' He seemed to be talking to himself. 'I suppose so, after all these years.'

'We have to find her first,' I said. 'She ran out of the house in the middle of the night. Where would she have gone?'

He stared at his desk. He looked stricken, changed, like a man who has seen his possessions burnt down. 'I don't know. In the middle of the night? I don't know.'

'There are trenches and sandbags and shelters.'

He said, 'Again.'

'I have to find her. We may be at war within hours.'

'Everybody seems to collect in Whitehall, around Downing Street. Crowds and crowds of people. Waiting about.'

I shrugged. 'It's a chance in a thousand. In a million.'

'I suppose so. There are women's hostels, aren't there? Homes for refugees too, I believe. Places like that. She might have gone to one of those.'

I sighed. The possibilities seemed to be stretching out, vast and illimitable. Making for the door, I looked back at Geoffrey. He had taken his glasses off, thus changing his face further. He said, 'I think I shall go into All Saints' at lunch-time. Just for a while.'

There was a time when this would have jarred my nerves.

Now I envied him that he had some place to go and lay his perplexity, the re-opened wound.

I said, 'I have to see Mother first; arrange for her to go out of London. Then I shall try to find Karen.'

He nodded. 'I wonder if I could come and have dinner with you tonight? It would be nice to be with friends.'

'Of course. Telephone Griselda and let her know.'

As I left the office, I still carried a picture of him, sitting at his desk with his glasses off and his revived pain.

§

'A daughter,' my mother said. 'No, I'm not at all surprised.'

'You're *not*?'

'Did you want me to be?' There was a trace, in the little turn of her head, of the younger woman, expecting a compliment.

I sat forward on the sofa. 'Yes, I think so. After all . . .'

'David and Juana . . . it was so plain they were in love with each other. It seemed an unfinished story, somehow. Tell me all about her. Is she pretty?'

I described Karen as best I could. While I talked I felt the small throb of impatience in my head; I wanted to be off, looking, doing something about it.

'Poor child,' my mother said, 'poor child. I never liked Juana very much; she wasn't the kind women cared for; too attractive: I was jealous of her, I suppose. But now . . .' She drew the rug closer about her. 'How futile all one's hates seem in the end.'

'If only I can find her—'

'Yes . . . yes. . . .' She was looking towards the window, only half listening. 'How it brings it all back! Fennelhurst . . . Esmond . . . I can see it so clearly. I can see your father's grave in the churchyard. People were very unkind after he died, you know; they said he was careless with his patients

because of the drink, and that drink killed him in the end.'
She sighed. 'I don't think it was true: It was just that he
might have lived longer if he'd drunk a little less. . . .' She
seemed to become aware of me sitting tensely by her side.
'Find her? . . . Yes, I think you'll find her.'

'How?'

She beat one hand on her knee. 'I don't know. I just feel
you will.'

Too easy. I said, 'The odds are against it, you know.'

'Have you thought that she might have gone to a church?'

'No,' I said. It was becoming harder to control an unreasoning impatience; she was doing her best. 'What kind
of church? Her stepfather was a Jew; a synagogue?' The
possibilities seemed to stretch monstrously far: hostels,
homes for refugees, churches, synagogues, Salvation Army
huts—'Why a church?'

'You say she was brought up in Austria. She might have
been a Roman Catholic: a lot of Austrians are.'

'Yes . . . well?'

'I just thought, if she were, she might have gone to a
priest.'

'Yes.' I sighed. 'I don't know any priests. I suppose I
could knock them up and ask them. . . . Oh, it's no good; it's
hopeless; I've just got a wild idea in my head. We must get
on with what I've come for. To arrange for you to go—'

'Simon, dear.' She was turned to me, one hand on my
arm.

'Yes?'

'I hope you won't be angry, but I don't want to.'

'But—'

'I'm quite clear about it.'

'But you won't be able to get to a shelter quickly—'

'I don't want to get to a shelter.'

'London will be his first target, you know.'

'Oh yes, one hears terrible things.' There came through
her voice not disbelief in what she heard, but an unconcern

with it. 'But I want to stay here, near you. I was thinking last night how much you meant to me; how good you'd been, all these years since your father died.' I grasped her hand, remorseful for my earlier impatience; for an impatience, indeed, that still persisted. 'Will it be a great trouble to you if I stay?'

'No . . . no, of course not. If you change your mind—'

'I shan't. What have I to be afraid of? Death? My faith is quite unshaken. It always has been, except for those few terrible weeks after Esmond was killed. You're not angry?'

'Ah no.' I stood up and bent to kiss her. Now that I was going I felt weighted with things unsaid, with comfort ungiven her. 'I'll come back,' I said. 'I'll tell you any news.'

'Yes, I shall want to know. Turn on the wireless as you go . . . Mr. Chamberlain's making a speech, I believe; I'd better know what he says.'

I made for the door. 'I'll come back,' I said again.

'Of course you will. You always do.'

I turned to go. Only music was coming over the air; no news yet.

From a pub at the corner of the street I telephoned Griselda. She answered quickly, as if she'd been waiting for the call.

No, she'd heard nothing; Karen wasn't there. She added, 'I didn't mean her to go.'

'Yes, I know that. Are you still angry?'

'No . . . shaken; wondering what will happen.' After a little pause she said, 'Needing someone.'

The words came surprisingly into the beery impersonal atmosphere of the pub. I said, 'I'll do my best to find her, then I'll be back. Where's Jeremy?'

'I don't know. He shot off this morning after you left, without saying anything. I suppose he's gone to see that frightful Tony Clare.'

'Silly lad.'

I drank a glass of beer in the pub. No one was talking

about anything but war. They wanted something done quickly; there wasn't much time.

Out in the street again. Where now?

Girls' hostels.

Churches.

Whitehall.

No, it was all absurd.

And yet people did find people; sometimes the miracle happened.

§

By mid-afternoon I was in Whitehall. I had walked up the steps of large forbidding homes and hostels; I had waited in dim offices while women turned the pages of registers, glancing at me distrustfully as if they suspected me of white-slave trafficking; then shook their heads. 'No sir; I'm sorry. No one of that name here; if she should come, yes, I'll ask her to get in touch with you.' Turning away, carrying the weight of frustration, losing hope.

Whitehall was grey and crowded. The people stood waiting there as if under a spell. They shifted, changed, but were the same crowd. I began to push my way through them, looking everywhere. The wide street with its solemn buildings seemed just now a symbol of itself, a place built not only of stones but of time and decision.

I walked on, looking for her, haunted by the memory of the street where I had walked with David at my side; where the crowds had welcomed war with cheers and singing.

(These crowds did not cheer; they waited, and as I passed through them, the little current of their fear touched me.)

Do you remember? I said to the ghost beside me. The fine sun, the hot August day; the time of being young? For you there was nothing else but being young: it may be better so; the shadow hasn't come close. We walked here on the eve of war; do you remember? And now I walk here on the eve of war, without you, not young any more, with all my sins on me. You had no sins on you, for I don't believe a merciful God calls those close moments of love, with death such a short way off, a sin. We came this way, young and whole, knowing nothing of war. We had something good: faith, purpose, hope.

All these died in those years.

And yet there is the girl. Your child, David. Your daughter, twenty years old, young as we were young.

Help me to find her.

On, down the street. Policemen stood, waiting for trouble, but there was no trouble: no one shouted *Down with Chamberlain* or *Stand by the Czechs*, as they had a week ago. They stood, holding bulging bags, carrying children, as if to see a procession go by, but there was no procession; or if there was it was a procession of shadows: of men who had marched away and not returned, leaving now an empty road at whose end the tall Cenotaph wore the drifting skirts of its flags.

I pushed on. I felt light-headed, perhaps with tiredness; perhaps with the pressure of memory.

A dark girl, in grey sweater and black skirt, standing alone at the edge of the crowd, her back towards me. I ran, stumbled, ran again, jogging the arm of a man who swore at me. I was so certain that I put a hand on her arm, and she swung, showing, in mixed anger and surprise, a stranger's face.

'I'm sorry. I mistook you for someone else.'

She stared at me from dark eyes, silent, rubbing her arm as if I'd hurt her.

I walked on.

Then suddenly I was halted.

A woman stood, looking away from me towards a man at her side. They were not part of the crowd; they had paused only for a moment as they walked up Whitehall.

Kate.

I stood still, trapped into unwelcome memory; her face so familiar, so closely known, loosed the whole of it in my head from the beginning at the Town Hall to the last violent meeting. Then I looked from her to the man at her side. He was a little bald with wings of white hair, a heavy jaw and the first of a paunch. She made some remark to him, smiled and touched his arm. They moved on.

I watched them go. Impossible not to be pleased that he was balding, grey and paunchy: to the end the striving vanity battled and occasionally triumphed: you had to take it along with you like a tiresome child.

Now I was in Parliament Square. The project seemed hopeless, part of a cloudy unreason in my head. I crossed the wide road, having about me the great stretch of sky above the bridge, and the towers of clock and Abbey. There drifted with the blowing flags a sense of great occasions. (And even now within the House the Prime Minister spoke: to what end?) The green moat of grass about the Abbey conveyed quietness, respite from strife. Army lorries were passing in the road, but as I turned towards the West Door, a further quiet came towards me, a diminution of discord. The familiar place had a pull, like a place out of childhood. I went in.

I felt at first like a stranger, one who trespassed. Two candles burned on either side of the grave of the Unknown Warrior; the lonely representative of those whom I remembered, lifeless, staining the ravaged earth, at La Bassée, Montauban, Gheluvelt: in the valley of the Somme, in the mire of the Salient. About a hundred or so people were kneeling about the grave. It gleamed darkly from its place in the midst of the stone. I stood in the steep vaulted space, with the small people about me. Glancing light from high-coloured windows defined some of the words on the tomb: *Brought from France. . . . They buried him among the Kings because he had done good toward God and toward his house.*

Poppies stained the sombre stone with colour. The candle flames caught an echo on bent heads. The quiet might have belonged to the old centuries whose kings lay here, and not to this present, nervous with the threat of war.

I stood staring. Brought from France. A whole man? Not savaged and torn? Some soldier whose fatal wound had done him the courtesy—as David's had—of leaving him almost unscarred? As I stood there I felt a strange communion with that body, deep below the healing, merciful ground: I had been beside him, we had looked over the desolation, sharing the vivid and terrible adventure. *They buried him among the Kings*. The tall place of ancient heraldry grew about him; the lovely arches sprang to a great distance above his head. *Brought from France*. Carry the lad that's born to be King . . . The tomb seemed an axis on which time swung, the old war with its million dead, the new one, conceived but not yet born.

I moved away from the tomb towards the Nave, and sat on one of the chairs there, reluctant to leave this place with its healing distances of time. Wars from Crécy and Agincourt had scattered relics here: the silence of dust and crumbling bone gave to the little ego inside one's head with its curtailed vision of body and limbs a sense of impermanence and proportion.

Women with shopping bags climbed to their feet from praying, moved away. I still stayed there. Closer and closer came the ghosts. The stretching armies of the Somme; the encampments before Ypres; the old names; the countless dead. Clean black slab with noble words. Nothing terrible, nothing to distort the dreams of the men and women who knelt there, unless their memories provided it; unless the fields of death rose like a mirage in this ordered place, so that upon the decent unobjectionable stone they superimposed the desolate, death-filled mud.

I moved on the chair. I had a sense of time having passed without record, as if I'd slept. The day itself seemed to have moved out of the flux of time: here was a mild dusk starred by candle flame, a suggestion not so much of evening as of a twilight which would neither lighten nor diminish. No sound but the slither of careful feet: the steps of people in a larger presence, of great things, of a mystery.

She might have gone to a church, my mother had said, but of course though I looked among the men and women kneeling and standing there, she was not among them.

I got up from my chair, went back towards the West Door. I passed the men and women praying there. Praying for peace? The Archbishop of York had said, 'Pray for justice and goodwill, not first for the avoidance of suffering.' I thought, if I prayed, I should pray for Karen's return.

But peace?

I saw Juana; I saw the engulfing evil shadow.

And yet . . . *Brought from France*. The armies of the Somme and Ypres; the graves in their white symmetry, silent armies, over the stretching earth . . .

Confused I turned away, still holding to my one reasonless hope. The tall dimmed spaces of the Abbey laid a benediction on my mind, a kind of promise.

§

Nearing home, I heard the newsboy calling.

The paper was loud with news: *Hitler puts off Mobilization for twenty-four hours ; Premier to fly to Munich tomorrow ; Historic Scenes in the House.*

I turned a page, and read that 'Fashionable restaurants and dressmaking establishments were taking the situation very calmly yesterday'.

I let myself into the house. Griselda was going through the hall carrying a soda siphon. She was turned to the door in hope and inquiry, which changed to disappointment as she saw I was alone.

'Nothing?' she asked.

'Afraid not. Nor with you?'

'No.'

I sighed and tossed down the paper with its noisy headline. 'Have you seen that?'

'I heard it on the news. They say there's hope of peace.'

'For six months, I dare say. Where's Jeremy?'

'I don't know. He's been out all day. With that ghastly Tony person, I suppose. . . . You look as though you need a drink.'

I made a face. 'I've covered quite a lot of ground. To no purpose.' (The glimpse of Kate? Better to say nothing of this.) 'I ended up in Westminster Abbey.'

'Looking for her there?'

'Not exactly . . . I'd been walking for a long time and I was tired . . . I just went in.' I smiled and went towards her; she put the siphon down on the hall table, and I put my arms round her.

I said, 'I'm sorry.'

She held me then and said, 'I've been so frightened.'

'Of war?'

'Of everything. Of a kind of loneliness that's worse even than war.'

For a moment we stood in the hall, absurdly clasped together, as if we'd been parted for a long time. Then she pulled away from me, wiped her cheek with her hand and said, 'Geoffrey's in the drawing-room, drinking whisky. He seems very unlike himself.'

I began to climb the stairs. 'Tell him I'll be down soon.'

'He seems anxious to see you.'

She sounded a little surprised. I smiled and said, 'I'm his father confessor at the moment.'

'He keeps talking about Juana.'

'I'll be down as soon as I can.'

Later we sat at dinner, the three of us: Jeremy had not returned. There was a respite in the steep slide towards war: the world waited upon the next day, waited upon Munich.

Meanwhile Griselda found some wine and we drank well of it, becoming in the end rather sombrely drunk. Jeremy's place remained empty, as it had done before.

'Meeting,' I said, 'how can they have a meeting? There isn't any more to say.'

Geoffrey took his glasses off again, and put a fork at right angles to his plate as if he were pointing a direction somewhere. 'You have to think of the cost, don't you? I'm not saying we should knuckle *under*, of course, but . . .'

I looked at him thoughtfully; he didn't irritate me as much as he usually did.

'I suppose they have interpreters,' said Griselda, a little heavy-eyed, speaking with care. 'I mean all four of them, English, French, Italian and . . . and . . .'

'German,' I reminded her.

'Oh yes, German: all four talking different languages—'

'And *four* languages, mark you,' I said, emptying my glass, 'not five. No Czech spoken here. And all for nothing. Why isn't that boy ever here for meals on time?'

'I still have hope,' Geoffrey was saying, arranging a spoon to make a right angle with the fork. 'I don't believe God will allow another war—'

I was leaning on one elbow, chin on hand, as this seemed more comfortable. 'He's allowed Austria. Why should he stop at us?'

He stared broodingly in front of him. 'That's the problem of evil,' he said at last.

'Isn't it just?'

I saw Griselda look at me, as if she had said, You will be *nice* to him, Simon, won't you?

Geoffrey's forehead was wrinkled with wine and perplexity. 'You can't ask me to explain that now—'

'I don't. But I'm interested.'

'All the theologians from the beginning of time haven't succeeded.'

'But you still pray,' I said.

He put his glasses on again quickly as a man might cover his suddenly remembered nakedness. 'Oh yes.'

'Well, how?'

'I suppose,' he said at last, 'because I'm convinced—don't ask me how—that there is a further dimension to this world, and that once you've seen this and become convinced of it everything else takes on a different shape.' He looked up to see if we were listening, found that we were, and went on. 'Much, I dare say, remains *unexplained*, but not inexplicable. Is there a difference between these two? Yes, I think so, I think so. It's possible to accept that there's a way up the mountain, even though no man's ever climbed it, and no one can see the way it goes.'

'Well, it's possible,' I said, 'but . . .'

'We're all hung round with buts,' said Geoffrey, blinking through his spectacles.

'That's what's so awful,' said Griselda. 'I like to be certain.' She looked suddenly tearful. 'If there's a war I shall pray for Jeremy to be safe, but all the mothers will pray for their sons and some of them will be killed—oh, there mustn't be a war: no, not again.'

'And Karen?' I said, shifting the pepper-pot. 'And Juana?'

'I don't know. I don't know. Why should it be so difficult—a great sea that one drowns in—'

'Well, not quite,' said Geoffrey: 'is that someone in the hall?'

Griselda sat up; I looked towards the door, but it was Jeremy who came in. His eye went quickly over the table with its empty bottles and traces of spilt wine. I supposed he'd been planning this fool trip with Tony Clare, and in wine-bred irritation I said, 'I hope you've had a good day.'

He gave me a bright careful glance as he sat down. 'Not too bad, thanks. Hullo, Uncle Geoffrey. Sorry I'm late.'

'I'm afraid the risotto's rather cold, darling.'

He gave his mother an amiable smile. 'Never mind. I'm most frightfully hungry: can I take all that's left? Oh, thanks.'

I said, 'You've heard the news, I suppose?'

'About the old boy dashing off again? Meeting those terrible thugs? Yes, indeed. Can I have the rest of the salad? Oh, good. Any news of our refugee?'

I looked at him sharply: the words, apparently light, were not quite as casual as they seemed. 'No, none. Why?'

He said with his mouth full, 'I just wondered. After all, she must be somewhere.'

I said, 'I suppose you've discussed it all with Tony Clare.'

His eyebrows went up, and Griselda looked as though she were willing us not to have a row. 'Well, I did as a matter of fact.'

'I hope he found it amusing.'

Jeremy chewed for a bit, then said, 'Well, no; he seemed to be rather bored by the whole thing. He said he found all this persecution stuff boring, and Hitler boring and Jews boring, and in particular refugees boring.'

Now we were all looking at him. He was a little breathless; perhaps enjoying himself. But I no longer felt the urge to close with him; irritation ran out, leaving me silent, receptive. Aware of his audience, he drank some wine and went on.

'And I must confess, I found this a bit much. Well, of course I know what he *means*: everything ghastly that isn't happening to oneself is boring in a way: but there's another way in which it isn't: you can't help seeing that, especially when refugees with terribly good legs come slap into your house from what the newspapers call the troubled heart of Europe. Can I have another piece of bread? I don't think I've ever been so hungry in my life.'

'So what happened?' I asked.

'Oh, well, we had a row. Quite fun in a rather beastly sort of way: you know, head spinning and heart knocking, feeling rather sick, and yet getting a lot of things out of one-self that one didn't know were there. And the funny thing was that I turned into a kind of stuffy parent standing up for Values, and Tony was the rebellious son, cynically laughing the whole thing off. Really *quite* fun, when you think of it.'

His eye met mine with friendly amusement.

'And the world tour?' asked Griselda.

'Oh well, that's off.' He threw it out easily, lifting his glass, but his hand shook a little. 'I made a lot of grand gestures and said that absolutely nothing would induce me to go away with anyone who could talk like that about massacres. Frightfully pompous, of course, and I'm not even sure that it's true: I suppose one can go away with anyone providing they keep you amused and don't smell—but anyway, there it is: I can't go back on it now. I dare say I shall regret it: a world tour's a world tour, and it looks as if the world'll be a fit place for heroes to tour in, for a little longer, anyway . . . but it's done now. Bognor Regis, I expect, instead of the Taj Mahal. Better so, perhaps. I hope everyone's pleased.'

'Very,' I said.

'Oh, good.'

'But quarrelling with him couldn't have taken you all day,' said Griselda. 'What've you been doing?'

He gave a small shake of his shoulders, as if he didn't want to be questioned. 'Oh, mooching around, seeing the sights. Britain on the eve of war. Or not, as the case may be.' He ate a large piece of bread. 'As a matter of fact, I had a shot at looking for our refugee.'

'You didn't!' said Griselda.

'Yes, certainly; why not? Pa was, so I thought I'd have a bash too. I had a bright idea: I found some Homes for Jewish refugees and went there—'

The implication being, I thought, that no such idea had occurred to me. I said nothing.

'Quite hopeless, of course: needle in a haystack would be

child's play by comparison.' His young face brooded. 'Poor kid. Where d'you think she's gone?'

'I don't know. I've tried everywhere I can think of.'

'Nothing to do now but wait?'

'I suppose so.' But there was something shifting at the back of my mind, a formless hope.

§

I had not expected to sleep, yet as I lay down weariness swamped my brain, and I was lost in dreams of large buildings where I searched corridors and great staircases for some place which till a moment ago had been mine. More and more desperate, asking questions, stupefied by the absurdity of not being able to find the place, each new hall and stairway strange to me, not the one I had known before.

From this I woke about four o'clock. Griselda slept. I got out of bed, went on bare feet to the window and leaned out. A moist autumn night, footsteps somewhere and the lonely swish of a car. My heart beating with some force, perhaps from the dream.

Later today the men would meet. The sky was without stars, showing reaches of pale swollen cloud washed through with night. Weather on the downslant towards winter, city weather, dun-coloured, losing leaf and light. Weather for betrayal.

Karen?

I had a pressure in my head, as one has on the edge of remembering a forgotten word. Was she perhaps on her way back to us? Did she lie somewhere, awake as I was, having made up her mind to return? I let the curtain fall and climbed back into bed.

I seemed to be following a logical pattern of thought, interesting, progressive, but in the midst of it I must have slept, for I found suddenly that the room was full of light,

Griselda out of bed; a smell of bacon was drifting upwards, and the day had taken a jump ahead of me.

Impatiently I got out of bed.

There seemed no exact moment of revelation: the idea merely to have been there, for my discovery, all the time.

3

Thursday

The station was crowded, blown through with urgency; it seemed already the outpost to some battle: filled with soldiers, with groups of children wearing labels, overawed, being plucked from danger to the safer and softer counties, out of town.

The train was crowded too: children chattered and swarmed; young soldiers thrust the bulging awkwardness of their packs down the corridor.

Bemused, I sat looking from the window. Sky and roof-tops, the sliding places, the mixture of sadness and adventure: *out and away*. . . . Children in a playground; a woman pinning sheets to a line; autumn fields, ragged and yellowing; nothing anywhere to do with war. (And a train, long ago, travelling south in a growing dusk to Amiens, drawing nearer to the sound of guns.) Something dream-like about the journey: what was I doing here? The slow train lagging, stopping, starting again. Time suspended.

The station. Blowing country air, late roses, chrysanthemums, the road climbing the hill. Strange to walk here; my body seemed a little way ahead of me, as if some part of myself still stayed in town amongst the familiar places, waiting for news.

I began to climb the hill, tasting all the past as if I hadn't been here for over twenty years. Nothing was greatly changed from that time: the fields stretched under the grey autumn sky; the riding line of the Downs was clear and ancient and still. The clock on the church tower gleamed with new gold, but the tower was built of the centuries and had not changed. Back. Back. Griselda coming down towards the Rectory; Juana in the greenish gloom of Louis Meyers's house; David in Yarrow's Field—even now visible, tall lonely grasses under a stone-coloured sky.

Here was our house. Newly painted; a skipping rope and a child's red tricycle in the garden. (Esmond playing 'Get out and get under'; David and myself in the night quiet talking about Juana. . . .) A child ran out into the garden, calling over his shoulder. What was I doing here? I walked on.

The Rectory. An air of shabbiness, different from the Birches' day; from an open window the familiar mechanical voice, woven like a thread through all times and all places now: *Munich, Daladier, Führer*. The church looked quiet, forsaken: I could see the people in the summer of that year, crowding in, all come to the very lip of war; I remembered those mornings when I had gone quietly there, believing all things.

Then I walked on till I came to the cottage. The small garden was filled with confused, dying colour; a neglected autumn garden. An upper window was open and yellow curtains blew out. A cat eeled its way round a corner of the house. The place was old but it was not this, for me, that gave it magic.

Mrs. Carne, the housekeeper, opening the door to me, frowned as she always did. 'Oh,' she said, in what sounded like disappointment, though it never appeared that she had been expecting anything better, 'It's you. Come in.'

She was old, moving with bent shoulders, but with force and purpose.

I stood in the low-ceilinged narrow hall. The faint musty smell of an old person's house: a vase of chrysanthemums, their petals moulting on to the floor. It seemed, nothing else.

I was suddenly dry of questions, my heart beating.

But she was nodding, as if she answered them. 'You've come to look for her—'

'She's here, then?'

'Aye, she's here. She arrived last night in a great state, shivering and crying. She wouldn't let us get in touch with you: I offered to go somewhere and telephone, but she got very upset. I was going to write to you today.'

She was here. The journey made sense after all—

Mrs. Carne pushed open the door to the small sitting-room.

It was shadowy on this grey morning, and first of all I saw the old man, David's father, in his usual winged chair. Despite the slack and scored skin his face had authority still; his hair was entirely white, and the dark glasses which he wore now that his sight had gone were sharp in contrast. Mrs. Carne said, 'It's Mr. Calder. I'll bring the coffee.'

The old man lifted his head towards the noise of my presence. 'Simon? How very intelligent of you to come.' His voice, harsh with age, still carried an echo of its old power. 'Karen! Come here, where are you?'

She came quietly into the room. Her face was colourless, her eyes shadowed; she put one hand on the back of the old man's chair, as if for protection. He said, 'It's very strange, isn't it? You're the one who can tell me—is she like him?'

'Yes. Very like.'

She kept her eyes on me, solemn, hunted, a little afraid. I said, 'You don't know how glad I am to find you. But how on earth did you get here?'

'Mother told me about my grandfather. She knew that he was still alive; she used often to talk of him. When I left you, I went to the station—'

'But I looked for you there!'

'That night? I thought no one would know until the morning.'

'I looked everywhere—'

'I'm sorry.' Her eyes, fixed on me in sudden compassion, were David's eyes. 'I went into the waiting-room, on the continental platform. I remembered it, from when I arrived. I wandered about all the next day, wondering what to do.'

'You heard what Griselda—what my wife said?'

She nodded briefly. 'I came downstairs. I couldn't sleep. I thought one of you might still be up, and then I heard—'

'She didn't mean it. Please, Rector, tell her how people can say things they don't mean when they're unhappy; and Griselda's been very unhappy.'

He gave a small grunt. 'She doesn't need to be told that; she knows it's true.' He put his hand on her arm. 'I shall ramble, I expect. I'm so surprised. So touched. She's dark, she says, not fair: but still like him? Agnes should have seen her. . . . What's this? Oh, yes, coffee. The small hump in the morning. Karen, come and sit here on this stool, then I shall know where you are. Coffee, Simon?'

I took the cup and said to her, 'You'll come back with me? We want you back—we'll look after you, whatever happens—'

'Oh, no!' She seemed to crouch into herself. 'I'd rather stay here.'

A pang like a twist in the heart. I looked at the old man as if he could see me. He drew one hand absently over her head and shoulder. 'No, you must go with him,' he said at last. 'I'm too old. You must come and see me sometimes.'

'We all want you,' I said. 'If you knew—how we've talked, searched for you; even Jeremy, my son.'

She bent her head and said nothing. Through the great pleasure of finding her came the little sting of reality, different from the dream: as I searched for her she had in some way been a projection of myself, the apex of all desire;

222

now that I saw her again she was almost a stranger, with her own will, her own difference.

The old man said, 'You'd have no life with me. You must go with Simon. He and your father were the closest friends: Simon was like one of the family. I proposed his health, I remember, when he came of age—we all had a party a little way along the road, at the doctor's house, where Simon's parents lived.'

She said, 'But it's peaceful here. It seems good. As if evil belonged to towns.'

'Ah.' The old man shifted in his chair; slowly put down his cup. 'Yes, I can understand your thinking that. Perhaps it's true; I don't know. But even if it does, you can't hide away from it here. You have to go and face it—'

'I've faced enough.'

'I'm not being harsh. I'm too old for anyone to stay with except Mrs. Carne, and she's almost as old as I am. I don't wander much in my mind, thank God, but I mumble and snore. I'd rather no one listened.' And as she didn't move, 'Go along. Get ready; you can come and see me again.'

She got slowly to her feet. As he felt her move he nodded, put his hand towards her and patted her arm. 'That's right. That's right. Take the coffee cups out to Mrs. Carne, then go and get ready. You can come again.' He turned towards her as she went out of the room, as if he saw in his mind's eye his son's face, and tried to divine hers.

Then he sighed and turned back to me. 'Do you remember these?' he asked, and fumbled for a small pile of grey books at his feet.

I took them from him. They were warped, stained, the paper yellowing. 'David's sketch-books—'

'I've been showing them to her. You remember them?'

'Of course. Of course.' I was turning the pages. The half-forgotten landscape of war: a soldier resting in weariness by the roadside; the barren slaughtered places of battle given

223

shape and a kindlier purpose in the rough skilful lines. I looked up to find the old man's face concentrated on me.

'Simon—'

'Yes—'

'It's some while since you've been to see me.'

'I know—'

'Last time I got the feeling of confusion, of distress.'

'A man of my age—'

'But today, this seems less.'

'I'm so glad to find her safe. I was afraid.'

'Yes. But you've changed.'

'How can you possibly know?'

He chuckled, an old man's sound, rasping, turning into a cough. 'It always annoys people to be told things about themselves, especially by the old. When you're eighty-five and blind, you perceive a great deal. This is a dispensation of the good Lord: I don't question, merely accept. Perhaps, so near death, one borrows some sight from a different world.'

I looked into the ancient blind face. The shadowed country room was quiet. From the kitchen came sounds of Mrs. Carne washing up, and the voice of a child in the road outside. We seemed far off from Munich, and the men meeting there. I said, 'I've always remembered a sermon you preached, just before the war.'

'So long ago? It must have been surprisingly good.'

'I remembered it, in the Salient, just after David was killed. I'm afraid it meant nothing then.'

'Naturally not.'

'You said, "having love, we are more than conquerors".'

'Did I? Yes, I think I remember. It remains true.'

'In spite of Germany now?'

The white head was turned from me; he seemed to be looking to the future of a world in which he would play no part. 'In spite of all that.'

'Then you agree that we shouldn't fight?'

He said on a sigh, 'No, now I believe it's too late for anything but war.'

'So then? Love men, and destroy them with dive-bombers and machine-guns?'

He sighed again, a harsh sigh, almost of exasperation. 'I have no logic with me. Only that the world is full of pain, yet it is possible to discern through the distortion of suffering, a final shape which is inexorably love.'

'A blind step into the dark,' I said.

At the word 'blind' he smiled. 'Oh, certainly. Now that I'm blind, I feel in a way more in man's natural element. Sight confuses one, I think: it encourages the idea that one should understand things with the same clarity that one can see. In the dark one is less likely to make any such assumption: one gropes forward, having only a certainty of the ground below one, and the little distances between wall and wall.'

I sat there, looking at him. So old, his son more than twenty years dead, he seemed to belong not only to the accepted order of time, with its continual flux and decay, but to some other order where the striving ego, fussing and adding, feverishly working out the mathematics of existence and coming to no answer, was released into a larger vision.

He said, 'So why have you changed?'

From the open window came the sound of the church clock, sounding the hour, as I remembered it. I said at last, 'I suppose in middle life one may come to a point when all the comforts, the things which have made a handrail for you to walk by, seem to fall away and you face your own failure, stand on an edge with nothing to prevent you from dropping into space.'

He nodded slowly. 'Well?'

'That's how it was. Guilt abounding for the past; less and less hope for the future. David's death in the Salient; Prue's in that benighted hospital: the more I tried to grab at things to put them out of my mind, the more they haunted me.'

'Of course.'

'And then Karen came, bringing David back, sleeping in Prue's room. Something miraculously saved out of it all.'

He nodded again. I could hear Mrs. Carne's voice, talking to Karen.

'And since then, I've had . . . oh, I don't know how to describe it. In spite of the world at this moment, in spite of all there is to come, a kind of peace.'

'I could call it a return of faith.'

'Faith is a large thing. I can't believe it arrives overnight.'

'No—no. Not often. But once a man has caught sight of that strange distance it's apt to haunt his mind.'

He lifted his head as Karen came back into the room. She looked obedient, a little sad. She bent down and kissed the old man. He put up a searching hand and patted her cheek.

She said, 'I don't want to leave you.'

'You can come and visit me for short times, as long as I'm here. And if you come down one day and find I'm gone, there's no need to be at all distressed. I have lived a long time in much content, and been spared to welcome you. God has been very good to me. Now, good-bye.'

§

Very strange to walk with her here. We went past Yarrow's Field, we came to the church.

I put a hand on her arm. 'Come along. We've time before the train. Come and see the church.'

She came with me. The place was dusky, smelling of autumn, stone and old books; there was a gleam of coloured light defining emptiness, a shine upon the altar. I said, 'Your grandfather's church. Your father used to come here.'

'My father . . . I've so often wondered about him. He used

226

to seem unreal; I could hardly believe he'd ever lived. But now . . .'

She stood, looking about her. I could see behind her the violence in Vienna; Juana and the man she had married; David, in the trench near Gheluvelt. And yet she stood here, amongst the ancient arches, the mottled uneven stone. I said, 'That last Sunday before the war the pews were crowded. We were all there; families went to church *en masse* in those days: my brother Esmond, who was killed in the war; our parents; David; Griselda, who's my wife now. We were all here, frightened and very carefully dressed.'

She looked about her, as if she were seeing it all.

'And here—come and look at this. Your father's name— the names of the men from the village who were killed in the war. My brother's too. So many for so small a place.'

She put up a hand to touch the square stone plaque on the wall; then looked up to the chancel's vaulted roof. 'It's very old,' she said. 'I like old places.'

'Some of it goes back before the Conquest. These stones here . . . and here. Before the Normans came.'

For the first time since I'd arrived this morning, her face seemed to soften, become reconciled, even happy. 'Can I come here again? I'd like to come back here.'

'Of course.'

Outside the church the grasses were blowing; from the churchyard we could see the blue distance of the Downs, between pine trees. We passed my father's grave: James Hartley Calder Loved husband of . . . The inexorable slide to the grave, the turning of the world, the towering foolscap of eternal shade. The girl and I walked in a small transient patch of light; the subterranean dark has crossed the nadir and begins to climb. And yet . . .

I looked back at the church as we went, offering its tremendous hope, in the face even of war, even of death. Wind blew a frayed skirt of leaves against it, weak sunlight touched one window, as if within the church pale flames

227

grew. I thought one could see a time when the great tide of this coming war would have broken itself, leaving peace again at last, and this place would remain, perhaps little changed, shadowed with new griefs, but enduring.

Now for the city again.

§

It had all come back. Though I couldn't see it clearly, I knew that about me stretched the ploughed evil mud; that I must crouch down in this dark trench for fear of the sniper's bullet. The guns were distant but heavy: familiar, unceasing. I pushed my way through the trench. I had some task to perform, some desperate thing to do. I couldn't see the faces of the men huddled there, but I was aware of them, of many people close to me in fear. I had to go on. 'Is he here?' I asked, but no one answered me, and I went more desperately on. 'Where is he? I have to find him; can't anyone tell me where he is?' The close faceless company were all silent; I was frightened, breathless, clawing my way through. 'David? Are you there?' Yet somehow, struggling through the dark fog of this enterprise was the knowledge that he was long dead; that I was on the other side of grief. . . . Whom did I search for, then? Suddenly the ground was familiar; this was the place that had haunted me for so long, where in the slime of the trench I had come upon the body with bright hair; had seen the dead face and known it for Jeremy's face. Fearfully I put my hands forward, but they found nothing. The guns still beat and the close fearful men still filled the air about me, yet I had a sudden certainty that I was looking in the wrong place; that I should not find the body; that there was no body, only my own fear. . . .

'There's more news coming through.'

Climbing back from sleep. Captain Calder, sir. Message from . . .

'More news, father.'

I opened my eyes. The drawing-room, the fallen dead fire; the voice from the wireless, strange in the small hours: the clock pointing ten to three. Jeremy in pyjamas and dressing-gown sitting opposite me, leaning forward.

I pushed one hand across my face. 'I thought you were—'

'Sh. Listen.'

'. . . have signed an agreement, the text of which was issued twenty minutes ago by the German news agency. . . . The agreements which were reached are laid down in documents which have been immediately transmitted to the Czechoslovakian Government. . . .'

The voice ceased; left a silence just filled with the crackling of wires. I blinked at Jeremy. 'So we've handed over the Czechs.'

'Yes. Bad show, isn't it?'

I nodded. I was not quite clear of my dream; I sat looking at him. His hair was ruffled; he looked young, concerned, perhaps surprised. I said, 'I thought you were asleep.'

'I couldn't get off, somehow. All rather exciting; finding the refugee; news from Europe; all that. Then I heard the wireless, and I came downstairs.'

'There was some news at midnight, then some more about half past two. They said there'd be another announcement soon; I must have dropped off. . . . So that's it.'

'No war,' he said.

'Not yet.'

'How long d'you give it?'

'Six months—nine, perhaps.'

His eyes met mine. 'Oh, well. We've got the refugee back, anyway.' He stood up. 'Better get some sleep, I suppose. Night night.'

I watched him go. *Six months—nine, perhaps.* In the empty room the news of Munich, and the ultimate certainty of war jostled with the vivid past; the ghosts were at my shoulder, the remembered names: Ewart, Gann, Wicks; Cartright,

Harrison; Esmond; David. All of them, crowding close, hearing perhaps once more the distant drum.

Again.

And yet I saw the old man in the quiet room, seeing through the blind glasses time in its true perspective of illusion; grief in its setting of hope.

The city was silent now. Within its multiplied and complex darkness, this house, with Griselda, Jeremy and Karen upstairs, seemed a small companionable haven. A few more hours of silence, and then the clattering day would come up, bringing the altered weather, the transient and threatened time of calm.

Nearer and nearer to the appointed place.